"I can't deny what you've shown me, but I can't just say, okay, sure, this kind of stuff exists, you know?"

"I understand."

"So I'm just somewhere in the middle and I hate it. I'm a cop—I was, but you know what I mean. I like there to be answers."

Dane nodded, sniffing the air. "Slower."

Mitch brought the car down to a steady crawl. Every rock in the road, every bit of uneven pavement, jounced them.

Other smells assailed his nostrils, confusing the hunt. These were new and unmistakable.

It only took a minute before he saw one, crouching at the edge of a rooftop. Watching the taxi creep down the road.

Another stood in the shadowed depths between a warehouse and a trailer used as an office.

A third squatted in the tall grass of an empty lot.

"What?" Mitch asked, noting Dane's sudden tension. "What are you looking at?"

"Vampires," Dane answered. "We aren't alone here after all."

Enter the terrifying world of

30 DAYS OF NIGHT

Novels available from Pocket Books

Rumors of the Undead

Immortal Remains

**Graphic Novels/Comic Books
available from IDW Publishing**

30 Days of Night

Dark Days

Return to Barrow

Bloodsucker Tales

Annual 2004 (featuring
"The Book Club," "The Hand That Feeds,"
"Agent Norris: MIA," "The Trapper")

Annual 2005

"Picking Up the Pieces"
(featured in *IDW's Tales of Terror*)

Dead Space

Spreading the Disease

Eben and Stella

Beyond Barrow

30 DAYS OF NIGHT™

IMMORTAL REMAINS

STEVE NILES & JEFF MARIOTTE

Based on the
IDW Publishing graphic novel series

POCKET STAR BOOKS
New York   London   Toronto   Sydney

Pocket Star Books
A Division of Simon & Schuster, Inc.
1230 Avenue of the Americas
New York, NY 10020

This book is a work of fiction. Names, characters, places, and incidents either are products of the author's imagination or are used fictitiously. Any resemblance to actual events or locales or persons, living or dead, is entirely coincidental.

First Pocket Star Books paperback edition August 2007

POCKET STAR BOOKS and colophon are registered trademarks of Simon & Schuster, Inc.

For information about special discounts for bulk purchases, please contact Simon & Schuster Special Sales at 1-800-456-6798 or business@simonandschuster.com.

Cover design by Richard Yoo
Front and back cover art by Justin Randall

Manufactured in the United States of America

10 9 8 7 6 5 4 3

ISBN-13: 978-0-7434-9652-0
ISBN-10:   0-7434-9652-3

AUTHORS' NOTE

In the *30 Days of Night* mythos, *Immortal Remains* takes
place some time after the events depicted in the novel
Rumors of the Undead and the graphic novella
The Journal of John Ikos.

30 DAYS OF NIGHT

IMMORTAL REMAINS

BEFORE

Her house sinks down to death, and her course leads
to the shades. All who go to her cannot return and
find again the paths of life.

—Proverbs 2:18–19

THE WORLD WILL END, or so the sagas claim, in fire and
water.

Earthquakes will fell every tree except Yggdrasil, the
World Tree. Gods will battle one another, and in the wake
of their combat, flames and steam will blot out the sky.
Without the sun's rays, summer will cease to bring
warmth to the mountains and the glaciers will spread
across the land.

Lilith didn't necessarily believe in the legendary de-
scriptions of *Ragnarok*. She had been undead long enough
to know that every religion made up stories to suit its
needs. The Norsemen were no different. But Lilith lived
on land once occupied by Sturmi Bonestealer, whose sagas
described the cataclysmic clash of the gods that would
wipe the planet clean, leaving but two people, Lif and
Lithrasir, hidden inside Yggdrasil's leafy boughs, so she
felt she owed the ancient bard a fair hearing.

She stretched her lean form languorously on the cold
marble slab, her left hand skating up her torso, enjoying
the smooth, new flesh.

Around her, six young girls—young in comparison to Lilith, as everyone was, they had been twelve and thirteen when they were turned in 1967—sponged fresh blood onto her skin, occasionally squeezing drops into her eyes and mouth. Lilith swallowed what she could and let the rest soak in through her pores.

Nothing restored like blood.

Precious blood.

Life-giving blood.

Her world had not ended on that balmy April night in Los Angeles—far across the Atlantic and the North American continent from her home near Alesland, Norway—at the hands of Stella Olemaun. The world had not ended, but it had been close enough for Lilith.

The enormous explosion had leveled the house Lilith had rented for her mission of vengeance in the States. The pain had been intense, enormous, worse than anything she had experienced since her death, so long ago that she could barely remember it. Her skin had burned away, her organs had withered, her bones had shattered.

She had survived, though, and with the help of her young friends, she was spirited away from California, onto a freighter, and finally brought back to the shadowed forests and icy fjords of her beloved Norway.

The Olemaun woman would pay for her deceit.

Oh yes. A thousand times since that night, Lilith had sworn that *Ragnarok* would rain down on her head.

First Stella's husband, Eben Olemaun, had murdered

Vicente—Lilith's lover, companion, and husband these last several centuries. Then Stella had written a book (a *book*!) about those who had foolishly attacked the town of Barrow, Alaska, where she and Eben had been acting law enforcement. In that book, she had described Vicente's murder as if it was a heroic action. As a final indignity, Lilith had arranged to trade Eben's ashes to Stella for a computer disk containing video evidence of the disastrous Barrow invasion—the only known recorded incident of such an event—and Stella had repaid Lilith's generosity by trying to blow her to pieces.

Lilith closed her eyes, trying to focus on the small hands that rubbed blood across her breasts and stomach, up her legs, over her unsettled brow. Soaked in blood, she was healing quickly. But she needed to relax her mind as well as her body, needed to recuperate mentally, not just physically.

Around the world, she was hailed as Mother Blood. She was the greatest of them, giver of eternal life, matriarch of the race. Without Vicente all these months, her strength was even more important.

Without Vicente, she reigned alone.

But reign she would.

Already, as her organs reconstituted themselves, her skin growing anew and spreading over her body, her hair regaining some of its luster if not its length, she had given a great deal of thought to that. Her children were divided, some of them set on a course—like that assault on Barrow—that could only result in their final extermination. They needed the leadership, the guidance, that only Lilith could provide.

"Missus?"

Lilith realized that the girl had already said the word three times, each one with a rising inflection, even a little quiver in her tone. *Heather,* she thought, without looking. Heather's hands were tiny, delicate, fingers no longer than the distance between Lilith's knuckles. She had black hair, blue eyes, and an angelic face that could charm a priest into offering up his own jugular. "What is it?"

"Missus, someone is—"

Heather's voice cut off abruptly. Lilith pressed her elbows against the slab and tried to rise, but she was still too weak. She opened her eyes but saw little more than the red haze of her feeding, with indistinct shapes moving about like shadows in a dark room. She blinked, trying to clear her vision.

"Missus—!" Then a horrible screeching.

Now Lilith could see a larger shape moving among them. The girl-shapes threw themselves at it, fighting with fang and claw, but the intruder—a male, she could just discern—lashed out, his strength more than equal to theirs.

The sound of flesh tearing, blood splashing wetly against floor and walls and even Lilith's nakedness.

In just moments, he loomed over her, his features becoming more distinct with proximity. Tall, his head—like Vicente's—had been completely shaved. Also like her husband, this one's large ears tapered at the top, almost like wings jutting out from his head. For the briefest of moments she thought it *was* Vicente, back from his final death—

No.

This one didn't carry himself with Vicente's regal grace, but slouched like a common street creature. A foul smell assaulted her senses, as if he had been feeding on rancid flesh.

"I do not know who you are, but you have made a terrible mistake," she croaked. Her damaged throat burned when she spoke, forcing the words out as if pushing them across ground glass.

The intruder laughed.

For some reason, the sudden, ghastly sound actually revived in Lilith a raw emotion not felt in what could very well have been ages. It was fear.

"I would think," he said, leaning closer, "that you would be happier to see your father, dear, sad Lilith."

"You—" she began.

"Shh . . . don't try to talk, daughter . . ." he soothed, caressing her cheek with a large hand. "You are not feeling well. Poor thing."

"I—"

The large hand suddenly clamped over her mouth. "You never knew when to listen and when to speak. This is almost sad."

Now the hand snaked to her throat, his strong fingers pressing against the tender skin there like steel rods. He lifted her up toward him, her back losing contact with the slab.

"Hear me now, daughter. The time has come to change our ways. For too long, we have hidden in the shadows, fearing the mortals. But I ask you, does the lion fear the calf? Does the wolf cower from the lamb? Please don't answer, these are simply rhetorical questions, Lilith. And besides, you are so weak."

That laugh again, like an infant's bones rattling in a demon's skull, utterly without mirth. "So desperately weak. No, do not speak, daughter. There will be time for that." He yanked again, pulling her off the slab altogether. She tried to resist but it was useless, her muscles not yet recovered enough to even close her hand into a fist. "For too long we have been hunted by humans, chased as if we were prey instead of predator. No more. It is time for us to push back."

He closed his fingers more tightly still around her throat, until she thought he would tear through the flesh.

Everything fading again. Going black. Only the cruel, unyielding voice filling her world.

"Yes, yes, I know, it's not your way. Or Vicente's. But you see . . .Vicente is gone. And you, daughter . . . you don't really have anything to say about it. In fact, I would like to think you won't be saying anything at all."

PART ONE

THE HEADSMAN

I

THE WORLD TURNED on its axis, night following day following night. Although Dane preferred the night—naturally—the important thing was that with each turn the world changed . . . and everyone, his kind included, had to change with it.

Once New York, nexus point between Europe and the United States, had been at the forefront of global change. Not anymore. Now, Dane believed, Los Angeles fit that bill rather nicely. The Pacific Rim had overtaken old Europe as the center of modernity. Try as it might, New York would never reclaim that mantle. LA had been a sleepy yet glitzy coastal hamlet once, but no longer. Walking its streets at night, listening to the roar of tens of thousands of cars and the hum of electricity and the rush of blood through billions of veins and capillaries, he felt more alive than . . .

. . . well, than when he had been alive.

Half a block away, a young couple stepped from the lighted doorway of a liquor store onto the dark sidewalk. He was black, she was Asian; the perfect pair to represent contemporary mulitculti Los Angeles. Both were dressed casually, in short sleeves and jeans, appropriate to the late summer night. The man carried a paper bag with the shape of a six-pack impressed upon it from the inside. They started up the block, in Dane's direction, but then the young man spotted Dane and took the woman's hand, guiding her out into the empty street, and across it.

"What?" she whispered, although Dane, of course, could hear every word. "It's not like this is Savannah."

"No, it's like this is LA, and there's freaks here, too."

"You think he . . . ?"

"I don't know. Something about him just doesn't seem quite right," the man said.

Very astute, Dane thought. The two reached the sidewalk opposite and cast furtive glances his way, as if worried that he might charge across the street toward them. He shot them a fierce glare, hoping to justify the guy's actions in his girlfriend's eyes. If they thought he looked like some kind of psycho killer, what could it hurt to let them think they had him pegged?

Dane continued down the street, past the liquor store and a travel agency that someone had smashed in the front window of (plywood covered it, travel posters over the plywood, graffiti and metal band flyers covered the travel posters) and a dry cleaners. A street lamp stood on the corner, the only one on the block that worked. Dane passed through its cone of light and stepped off the curb, paused to let a taxi whoosh by, then crossed to the next block.

Interesting that the woman from the liquor store had mentioned Savannah.

The Georgia port city had come up in his consciousness several times lately—enough that he thought he
might lose his mind. The first time was a few weeks ago,
when he'd read online what would be the first of many
articles about the recent killings in Savannah. Initially, he
didn't think much of it, probably due to the fact that the
police were releasing scant information in hopes of screen-
ing out the potential cranks. But then, as more sordid
facts came out—the savagery, the unusual M.O., the
tremendous loss of blood—and the tabloid frenzy began
inevitably ratcheting up via the twenty-four-hour cable
news cycle, Dane found himself on the verge of being obsessed (again).

Instead of feeding (he had a couple bottles in the
fridge, back at his apartment, but had been on the look-
out for something a little fresher), he decided to return
home. His place was a couple miles away, and once he'd
made his mind up, he covered the distance in a few
minutes.

Inside, Dane set the dead bolt and the door chain,
knowing how ineffective both could be against the right
kind of force, and out of habit clicked on the plasma TV
in his living room.

The apartment was small, this room serving as living
and dining space, separated from a small kitchen area only
by an oak bar. A plain wooden door hid one bedroom. The
rent was cheap and because it was over a boutique that
closed at seven, there were no downstairs neighbors, and
he didn't care much about the way the place looked any-

way. He had safe houses scattered throughout the country and a handful overseas. If he wanted aesthetics, he could go to Carmel-by-the-Sea or Santa Fe or Gstaad, and if he wanted luxury there was always the chateau in the Loire Valley. This place was meant to be convenient, which it was, and to house his communications devices, which it did.

While CNN flickered onto the big screen, he booted up his MacBook. With the TV droning in the background (war and unrest in the Middle East, a widening gap between rich and poor here at home, Britney Spears had publicly embarrassed herself yet again), he went to Google News and entered "Savannah + murders."

The search engine found a surprising number of hits. More than the last time he checked.

He started with the local Savannah papers, the *Morning News* and the *Chronicle,* which had dubbed the killer "the Headsman," then moved on to the big nationals, the *Post,* the New York and Los Angeles *Times,* before moving to the major websites like MSNBC.com. Finally, he hit the blogs. These were heavier on rumor and speculation, but he had already digested the facts—those that were known, anyway—and was curious about how people were fitting those known facts into their own narratives.

After reading those, he muted the TV, still waiting for any news from Savannah to come on, picked up a cell phone, and dialed a number from memory. He didn't know where Merrin was these days—Michigan, last he had heard—but even though it was two in the morning in California, he didn't worry about waking his friend up. His kind didn't need a lot of sleep, and Merrin never minded a call.

"Yeah?" Merrin answered. He sounded distracted, as if Dane had caught him during a meal. Which reminded him. He got up off the sofa and went into the kitchen, tugged open the refrigerator.

"Merrin, it's Dane."

"Dane? What a pleasure, my friend. What a genuine treat. All's well?"

Dane uncapped a cool bottle of blood and took a long hit off it before answering. Warm was better, but cool stored longer. "As well as can be expected," he said.

"Understood, my friend." Merrin had been born in Europe, and had stayed there even after being turned, until his family—of whom he had always been protective—had emigrated to the United States in the late 1800s. In spite of his time in the States, he maintained many of his old-world habits, and Dane always enjoyed talking to him. He and Merrin had spoken many times about the challenges facing them in today's world, and both were mostly in agreement. "What's the nature of the call, then?"

"I've been hearing a lot about this situation in Savannah," Dane said. "What do you know about it?"

"Savannah?" Merrin had a habit of repeating questions, or at least parts of them, while he collected his thoughts. He also had a habit of keeping in touch with an incredible array of others—and even an assortment of humans, who had no idea of his real nature—so one never knew what obscure knowledge he might have picked up along the way. "I assume you're talking about the killer?"

"That's right, Merrin. The Headsman murders."

"You always did have a grisly sensibility, Dane. Why don't you start by telling me what you know, and then I'll fill in any blanks I can?"

"I just know what I've read online." Dane sat back down on the sofa, the open bottle in his left hand. "The released facts are basic. At least a dozen people have been murdered there in the past sixty days. All attacked in their own homes, in particularly brutal home invasions. The break-ins have exhibited no subtlety or grace—just smash inside and kill someone, brutally but somehow with a minimum of spilled blood. The killer finishes by cutting or tearing off the victim's head, hence the nickname. In many of the cases, any other residents of the invaded home have simply disappeared. Some people are theorizing some kind of half-wild creature is doing it, a werewolf or Bigfoot or something. Others speculate that authorities will find a mass grave containing the disappeared. I've even read the theory that it's a political death squad, although no one can quite agree on why anyone would select this particular range of victims."

Dane stopped there.

Merrin picked up the slack. "That seems a relatively

accurate and concise summation of the situation as it has been reported," he said.

Dane couldn't help but grin listening to Merrin's banter. The man loved to affect an upper-crust, outdated way of speaking that reminded Dane, for some odd and inexplicable reason, of *A Streetcar Named Desire*. Dane knew for a fact that the way Merrin spoke was intentional. At least it started out that way. One time, long ago, Dane had heard the almost prissy Merrin go on a vulgarity-laden rant that would have given a nun a stroke. The accent he had back then was distinctly old New York.

"With, as you suggest," Merrin continued, "the addition of some rather poorly informed speculation. Which, sadly, is the most common sort of speculation we get in these United States, at the dawn of this new millennium." Merrin had a tendency to wax philosophical at times—or political, which could be even worse. Get him going on Iraq or health care and you'd better have time to kill. As if he needed insurance coverage. "But quite a bit has been left out of those reports, at least, judging from what I've managed to pick up."

"Such as?" Dane sipped more of the blood. Cold, but it did the trick.

"Such as that the 'minimum of spilled blood' you mention is understating it by a wide margin. A few drops, perhaps. Certainly less than a liter. And I mean in the corpse as well as spread about the residence. Difficult to remove somebody's head without spilling more than that."

"Which can only mean . . ." Distracted, Dane kept one

eye on the TV. He knew CNN cycled through the day's bigger news stories, and by bigger that usually meant sensational and grotesque, something to frighten the masses, so it was only a matter of time before there was an update about the murders.

"Precisely. Of course no one will say anything officially, but—"

"Jesus Christ! Hold on, Merrin." Dane pawed the remote off the Crate & Barrel coffee table and jammed the MUTE button. The sound roared on, blotting out the 50 Cent tune that filtered in from an excessively loud car passing outside. "Do you have CNN on, by any chance?"

"I can," Merrin said.

Dane's TV screen showed an urban apartment in Savannah, Georgia. The front door tilted into the front room, attached only at its bottom hinge. A twisted piece of steel visible in the doorway looked like a security bar that had provided no security at all. As the camera moved through the doorway into the living room, it revealed a scene that could have been the aftermath of a tornado.

". . . another home invasion scene in Savannah. This one, on Victory Drive, was reported by neighbors who heard a sound they described as 'like an explosion.' Police arrived to find a single body, reportedly of a male who lived at the residence. Two other residents, a female and a child, were not found on the premises. One law enforcement source has told this reporter that all indications are that the Headsman has claimed another victim."

"It appears that our mysterious nighttime visitor has struck again," Merrin said.

"No shit." Dane punched MUTE again.

"Such a quaint colloquialism."

Dane smiled. He had said it that way just to tweak Ferrando Merrin's usually old-fashioned sensibilities. He could almost see the old guy, his dark hair perpetually graying, the paper-thin flesh of his pinched cheeks taking on a pinkish tinge. "So no blood. Which means . . ."

"You believe that it's one of us." The way Merrin said it meant that he thought so, too.

"Not very low profile," Dane said.

"Hardly."

Both of them knew there were plenty who didn't care about keeping low profiles. More every day, it seemed.

But this kind of blatant massacre, in a major city? These attacks were guaranteed to attract media attention. It was almost as if they had been designed for that purpose.

If the Headsman was just a serial killer—"just" being intentionally ironic—he was a bad one, hard to stop. But the cops would eventually catch up to him, because he substituted violence for caution.

If, on the other hand—as Dane and Merrin both suspected—the killer was one of them, then the police would never get him. They would never even get close, because they wouldn't be able to wrap their minds around the truth of him—or her, serial killers being almost all male, but the reality coming in both flavors. And without being caught and destroyed, he or she would never stop killing.

Not unless someone intervened.

Dammit.

"Are you there, Dane?"

"Yeah," Dane said. A sudden weariness had overtaken him. "I'm here, Merrin. But I guess not for long."

"You're not . . ."

"Someone has to. Right? I mean, to go public like this . . ."

A pause.

"That's just like you, Dane. Just like you, I'm sad to say."

"That's what they say about leopards, right?"

"Those spots look better on you than on me, my friend. Have a safe journey. And please keep me posted."

"I will, Merrin, don't worry. I'll call you from Savannah."

"I always worry, Dane. It's what I do best. But I know you'll be fine. Just don't take any unnecessary chances— you remember what happened a few years ago, yes? The incident with the Olemaun woman?"

"Yes, I remember." *Thanks for reminding me.*

"Just something to keep in mind. It's my understanding that almost turned into a very messy situation for you."

Dane sighed. "Thank you. I do appreciate your concern. I promise to watch my back."

"Good to hear. I'd like to speak with you again, you know."

Dane hung up the phone. He liked talking to Merrin, usually. He almost always learned something.

Don't take any unnecessary chances, Merrin had said. One thing Dane had never learned—who the hell got to define "unnecessary"?

2

DANE STEPPED OUT OF the terminal at Savannah International Airport and into a muggy Georgia night.

Four days had passed since his conversation with Merrin, but this was the first nonstop he'd been able to book a seat on that flew from LA to Savannah at night. Daytime travel was difficult for his kind. Summer seemed unwilling to relinquish its death grip of heat and humidity on the region.

A couple of taxis idled at the curb, their drivers chatting on the sidewalk nearby. Savannah's airport was sleepy compared to most other international airports he had experienced. Dane hadn't decided whether or not he would rent a car or take a cab into town, and as he stood there contemplating the matter, a mosquito brushed against his neck. Feeling a certain kinship with the tiny pest, he didn't swat it.

Not that it mattered. His blood poisoned mosquitoes almost immediately; it would take a long, thirsty drink, Dane would suffer no effects whatsoever, no itching or swelling, and the insect would fly off for a couple of feet, then drop dead to the pavement. When it took off, he rubbed his neck gently where it had landed.

"They're bad this year," someone said.

Dane looked up. One of the cabbies leaned on the front fender of his car, his hairy arms folded across a barrel chest. Hair curled up out of his open-collared shirt, but his head was nearly bald, as if his body had used up all the energy it could devote to growing hair. He had a pale, blotchy complexion, like someone who had once spent a lot of time on the water but lately had been a daytime sleeper. Piercing blue eyes regarded Dane with undisguised curiosity.

"Yeah," Dane said, realizing the guy meant the mosquitoes. The cabbie was probably in his late sixties. He had the kind of creased, folded face that had seen it all, some of it twice. He was probably five-six or -seven, still muscular and hard for his age.

Dane noticed one more thing. Everything about the guy screamed "cop."

Guess I'm taking a cab.

He had decided to stay at the Hyatt Regency on the Savannah River, and he gave the driver the hotel's name. The man nodded and climbed in behind the wheel. Dane only had a small carry-on bag, which he tucked beside him on the dented yellow-and-green Crown Victoria's big backseat. An oldies station played on the cab's radio, Chuck Berry singing about Johnny B. Goode, who could play the guitar just like ringin' a bell.

It didn't take Dane long, on the ride into Savannah's historic district, to turn the conversation to local current events.

"He'll slip up soon," the driver said. He didn't have a low country accent, just the faintest Southern twang. If anything, he sounded like he'd moved here from the northeast, maybe New York State. Checking the driver's taxi badge, Dane learned that his name was Mitch LaSalle. "I used to be on the job here," he went on, confirming Dane's hunch. Some guys just couldn't help looking like cops, and Dane had long since learned how to read people. "I know some of the guys working this one. They'll nail him."

"They have anything that hasn't been in the news?" Dane asked. "DNA or anything?"

"That I can tell you about, you mean?" Mitch laughed.

"I'm just an interested tourist," Dane assured him.

"You'll be fine. Whoever this asshole is, he's focusing on residents, not tourists. I wouldn't wander too far from your hotel after dark. Not because of the Headsman. You look like a guy who can take care of himself pretty good, but there's been a lot of gang activity, you know."

"I'm not too worried," Dane said. That was the truth. He might find trouble here, but it wouldn't come from the city's gangbangers.

His kind had always owned the night.

"Why'd you leave the force?" Dane asked. "If you don't mind talking about it."

Mitch barked out a laugh. "Hell, I don't mind talking. That's the one thing I can still do, right? Same old story. Good at the job but bad at politics. Pissed off the wrong people. Chased the wrong cat up the wrong tree, I guess, and when I was told to back away . . . I didn't. So here I am. Cost me my pension and my marriage. Not that I'm bitter," he quickly added with another laugh, which sounded nothing but acrid to Dane.

"Sounds rough," Dane said. "Getting punished for doing the right thing, that stinks."

"Tell me about it, brother."

"Sounds like you were a detective."

Those intense blue eyes met his in the rearview and Mitch was quiet for a few seconds. "You don't look like a cop," Mitch said. "But I've been wrong before, I guess."

"No, I'm not a cop," Dane replied. He caught a glimpse of himself reflected in the window: dark hair, lean face, jaw and chin edged by a narrow goatee and mustache. He could manage not to look like a monster, but making it all the way to human was always a chore. "I've been around them a lot, had a lot of friends who were." A lie, of course. The others didn't tend to socialize with law enforcement types. But paying attention to them? A crucial survival tactic.

"What do you do?"

"I'm an investor," Dane answered. Another truth, as far as it went. He owned stocks under dozens of identities and corporate names. Over the long term—seriously long term, when you were talking about more than a century— the return was enough to keep him flush. "Kind of a day trader, I guess you'd say." He had more important things to do at night.

The smell of the Savannah River wafted in through

Mitch's open window, a complex brew of fish, diesel, and other odors Dane couldn't peg. He had been to Savannah a few times before, but never for very long, and he didn't know his way around beyond the waterfront area. His hotel was next to City Hall, with the old Cotton Exchange on the other side of it. Up the hill from the river were neighborhoods of old brick homes built around cobblestone squares. Having been founded in 1733, Savannah was one of the few cities in the United States that felt old to Dane, whose own roots only went back to the middle of the nineteenth century.

"I guess there's some money to be made in that," Mitch said.

"I do okay."

"So what brings you to Savannah?"

Dane had to make a quick decision, but not an instant one. His mind had begun to churn as soon as he recognized the driver as a cop, and nothing that he'd heard had dissuaded him. Mitch seemed to know the city, knew the local players, and didn't feel like he owed them any loyalty.

Just the kind of guy Dane wanted.

"Listen," Dane said, "I need to tell you something. But I need you to keep it to yourself. Will you do that?"

"I guess it depends on what it is," Mitch said. "I'm no priest and this cab ain't a confessional." A perfectly reasonable response.

More reasonable, really, than Dane's request would be.

"Okay. Here's the thing . . . I don't think the police are going to catch the Headsman," Dane stated. "Because I

don't think they're looking for the right type of . . .
person. But honestly, that's why I'm here."

"Because you know what type of person they should
be looking for?" The eyes in the mirror had changed, soft-
ened. Curiosity to pity in ten seconds flat. Now the guy
thought Dane was a head case.

"I know how that sounds," Dane said. "But it's true.
The guy they want is a guy like me in some very specific
ways."

"You going to tell me what those ways are? Or am I
supposed to guess?"

"Yeah, never mind." With any luck Mitch LaSalle
would forget he'd ever picked Dane up, or write him off
as some kind of joker. "Just drop me at the hotel, that'll
be great."

"Yeah, okay," Mitch said.

He kept scoping Dane in the rearview, as if trying to
read through the illusion of humanity he cast. *The cop in
him,* Dane figured. He had given the guy just enough to
interest him, to let him know there was a mystery about
Dane, and now he wanted to solve it.

As he'd figured from the jump, Mitch was exactly the
kind of guy Dane needed to work the local angles of this
case. An unfamiliar city, an intensive ongoing investigation, these could be major obstacles. Having someone like
Mitch in his corner could help things run much more
smoothly than stumbling around.

But even though he had identified the right guy,
straight off the plane, the cab ride hadn't given Dane

enough time to close the deal. The best he could do now would be to remember Mitch's name and if the need arose, try to get in touch with him.

The cab dropped Dane at the Hyatt's main entrance, where a uniformed bellman snapped his door open before he could get to it. Dane paid Mitch, including a generous tip. The cop-turned-cabbie thanked him and tucked the cash into his shirt pocket.

Mitch was gone by the time Dane made it through the hotel's front door.

From his room, Dane could see lights on the big freighters that carved the river and the cranes at the docks that serviced them. Savannah was a major Atlantic seaport, with constant shipping activity. Somewhere a siren wailed, and far below, on River Street, late drinkers laughed and shouted as they stumbled along the sidewalk.

Dane had a problem, even more immediate than finding out who was so blatantly preying on Savannah's population, and putting a stop to it before this . . . public relations nightmare spiraled even more out of control. Hunger had started to gnaw at him, and airport security regulations were such that he could no longer travel with precious blood.

Which left him with only one option. He needed to go on the prowl.

Taking innocent life bothered Dane. Of course, he had done it, hundreds of times, if not thousands, over the years. To survive, he needed to feed. He wanted to survive. The math wasn't difficult.

At the same time, he recognized the irony that he had come to Savannah to stop the killings, and it looked as if he would do some killing of his own. When it came to moral superiority, he believed he had the upper hand—for Dane, it would be done only for survival, and he would be discreet about it as well as very choosy. More than the killings themselves, what Dane hated about whoever stalked Savannah was that the murders drew attention—to anyone willing to really see—to the true existence of his kind.

But they had to remain a secret. At all costs.

That was survival, too—for a species, not an individual. The only way they had lasted this long was by making the mortal world believe they were a legend, a story told at night to scare the gullible, or the stuff of popular fiction. Winding up in the twenty-four-hour cable news cycle didn't mesh with that goal.

Clearly the Headsman had a different agenda in mind. Dane's occasional quiet killing—targeted, when possible, at people whom the world could stand to lose anyway—was of a vastly different sort than that.

On his way out the door, he turned off the light in his room, ready to get started. Somewhere on the streets of Savannah, destiny awaited for some lowlife bloodsucker.

3

EVEN A WEEK LATER, Mitch LaSalle couldn't get the memory of that strange guy he had picked up at the airport out of his head.

The problem wasn't just that the guy had started out seeming reasonable and then turned into a wack job with that insane theory of how he and the killer were so much alike.

That was most of it, but certainly not the worst part. No sir.

The real thing that had shaken Mitch so much that he broke out in a cold sweat—having to wrap his hands around the wheel painfully tight so the fare couldn't see them trembling—was when he had glanced into the mirror and thought (not thought, but *knew,* just fucking *knew*) that he had seen the man *change,* physically, his skin taking on color and life, the shape of his mouth and jaw altering, even his eyes doing . . . something that Mitch couldn't put a name to. As if a switch had turned off and a lightbulb faded out instead of just going dark.

Now, the memory flared up in his consciousness at inopportune times.

It came back when he had awakened at eleven in the

morning, after having been asleep since eight, and needed to get back to sleep but couldn't.

It came back a couple of days ago when he had been going at it hot and heavy with a young thing (when you were his age, midforties counted as young, he had learned) but then, distracted by the mental image of the guy's transformation, had lost the mood, the wood, and the broad. "It happens to everyone sooner or later," she had said, pulling up her control-front panty hose in the bedroom of his second-floor apartment on Congress Street. "Why I never got married. There's always another guy who don't have that problem at the moment." She arranged herself back into her bra, then pulled on her Oak Ridge Boys T-shirt with the cutoff sleeves and smoothed down the skirt she hadn't bothered to remove. "You get yourself a prescription, Mitch, you know how to find me."

It came back right now, sitting here in a no-name crab joint on Skidaway, almost to the boundary of the grandly named community of Thunderbolt (of which he had often joked that driving through it took about as long as a lightning strike), with Denny Mulroy and Willard Creech—Savannah homicide detectives assigned to the task force investigating the Headsman murders.

"We got zippo," Creech was saying. "Squat. Jack shit. Nada, nothin', no mo'. It's a sad, sad state of affairs, is what it is." Willard Creech looked like a goddamned skeleton that someone had wrapped flour bags around and called it skin. When he smiled, which was far too often, the effect was ghastly, and not just because he had awful teeth. Mulroy often theorized that his partner had been assigned to homicide because corpses didn't care what an investigator looked like, while live crime victims might have felt they were being violated yet again.

Denny Mulroy, by contrast, was a fifty-five-gallon drum of a man, an inch shorter than Mitch and a hundred pounds heavier. He couldn't have passed a departmental physical, but during his years working vice, he had protected the son of the police commissioner from arrest for picking up hookers down on Montgomery Street not once but seven times, so his future was assured as long as he drew breath, and maybe after. Denny had skin the color of a coffee bean, dark roast, and a tight cap of hair that had turned mostly white during his time on the homicide squad. Mitch had always been fascinated by Denny's palms, which were as pink as fresh salmon and stood out like signal flags against the near-black backs.

The two cops made one of the oddest pairings Mitch had ever encountered during his years on the job, first in Michigan and then, through a bizarre sequence of events he didn't quite believe himself when asked to describe it, in Savannah. But they both had brilliant investigative minds, and together they seemed to be able to solve any crime put before them. If the Feds had a dozen teams like them, Mitch believed, Osama bin Laden would have been doing hard time in Angola or the Q by September thirteenth.

"How can someone who bashes through doors and drains vics of their blood not leave any physical evidence behind?" Mitch asked. "Doesn't sound like subtlety is his strong point."

"Subtle as a mallet to the skull," Creech said.

"Problem is the motherfucker's a ghost," Mulroy said. "A noisy ghost, but what the hell, makin' noise don't matter much if there ain't nobody left alive to hear it."

"This Headsman guy hasn't left any witnesses at all?"

"A handful," Mulroy replied. "Just none who can help us in any way. One woman said she heard somethin' that sounded like a gunshot. Turned out there wasn't no guns fired in this invasion, or any of 'em that we've seen. What she probably heard was this guy kickin' in the front door. Now what use is her testimony goin' to be to us? Better to have no witnesses than ones the defense can use to confuse a jury."

"If we ever get a suspect," Creech added.

"I met a guy the other day," Mitch heard himself say, "actually a fare I picked up at the airport. Probably just another nut job, but he seemed absolutely convinced that you guys were all chasing up the wrong tree."

"He's probably right," Creech said. "I keep telling Mulroy we got to take a closer look at those nuns from Our Lady of the Sacred Heart."

"There's a kindergarten teacher I got my eye on, too," Mulroy said. "She's about five feet tall, ninety-five pounds soakin' wet. Your man's right, we can't afford to just look at big strong guys when we're tryin' to find someone who

can knock down a barred door and carry off multiple individuals."

"That's why I got those sisters in mind," Creech said.
"One of 'em by herself maybe couldn't do it, but the
whole group of 'em? What do you call a group of nuns,
a herd? A pack?"

"Maybe a flock," Mitch offered, battling to keep a
straight face.

"Or a gaggle," Mulroy said. He might have been dis-
cussing suicide statistics or his fifteen-year-old daughter's
pregnancy, for all the mirth displayed. The trio had been
doing this for years, on the job and off, and for as long as
he had known them Mitch had always been the one who
cracked first.

Mulroy's cell phone broke through the reverie. He answered and listened, his dark face turning a kind of ash
gray. A moment later he closed the phone and dropped it
back into his jacket pocket. "He's hit again," he said, his
voice soft. "Headsman's still on the premises. Gwinnett
and Forest. We got to go. *Now.* C'mon."

"That's less than a mile away," Mitch said.

Mulroy's gaze met his, but distantly, as if he were looking at a stranger for the first time. "That's right. We got
to go."

"Go," Mitch said. "I'll settle up here." Mulroy and
Creech made it out the front door before the words were
even out of his mouth. If there was a chance of catching
this guy in the act . . .

Mitch flagged down the waitress (in her early twenties,

tired but still trying to be pleasant, the kind of girl who always made him wonder, if Karin, his daughter, had survived being run down by a drunk driver, would she be like this girl? Friends with her, maybe even roommates?) and gave her two twenties. He hadn't seen the tab yet but it had to be less than that.

Mitch went out to the cab, which he had left parked down the block. Mulroy and Creech were long gone.

He thought about going down to the riverfront, or maybe the airport, looking for a fare. But he was so close, and if they caught the Headsman, goddammit if he didn't want to see it. He headed toward the intersection of Gwinnett and Forest.

Utter chaos awaited his arrival.

Squad cars and ambulances were parked at every angle, light bars strobing. More of them screamed toward the scene, sirens splitting the darkness. A uni was trying to string yellow CRIME SCENE tape around trees and a hastily thrown-together striped sawhorse, but his hands trembled so much he couldn't manage to hang on to the spool. Others stood around gaping at a brick row house with lights burning inside and the front door hanging off its hinges.

Mitch parked the cab as close as he could and walked in the rest of the way. He spotted Paula Owens, a familiar face. He had, in fact, tried to have an affair with her while he was on the force and she was still in uniform, but she had felt that if people found out she had slept with a white colleague it would have hurt her chances of advancement. As it turned out, it wasn't just paranoia; she had probably been right. Backed by her colleagues in the African-American law enforcement community, she had made detective in record time. Being associated with the disgraced Mitch LaSalle could have killed that career arc.

"Paula," he called out. "Mulroy and Creech were headed this way. You seen 'em?"

She turned away from the brick house and he saw the tears in her eyes, spilling down her cheeks. She swallowed, biting her lower lip, not responding.

He started past her, but she grabbed his arm with both hands. "You can't go in there, Mitch," she said, her voice catching in her throat. "You don't have a shield anymore."

"Those men are my friends," Mitch protested.

"That's why you don't want to see them."

Two hours later, Mitch was parked in front of the Hyatt.

As the numbness threatened to overwhelm him, he paid Gaston, the night bellman, forty bucks not to hail him for any reason. Mitch was running out of twenties and hadn't had a fare since before dinner.

At the moment, he really didn't give two shits. He'd sit here in the dark Crown Vic for as long as necessary. Mitch didn't know any other way to find the man he wanted to talk to.

He had described the guy to Gaston, who was pretty

sure the man hadn't checked out yet, but he couldn't be positive.

So Mitch sat and waited.

He watched the hotel's front door, yawned, fought back sleep, despite the gnawing tension in his gut. Every now and then he got out of the cab and walked around it to keep his circulation going.

When the guy walked past him, Mitch almost missed it.

Maybe he blinked without realizing it. Maybe he had been seeing, in his mind's eye, the scene one of the uniforms had described to him, his voice breathless, excited.

Described the unimaginable carnage.

The uniform had gone inside the house after Mulroy and Creech—after their screams had pierced the night. Both men were on the floor, he said, looking as if they had gone through the door and encountered a threshing machine.

Their flesh had been torn to ribbons; arterial blood was so thick on the walls and ceiling that it ran like paint.

"What about the perp?" Mitch had asked, freaking out. "Where is he?!"

"Nowhere," the uni had said. "Gone. The detectives went inside, they screamed, me and Al fucking followed right after them, and they was dead and there was people inside dead, too, but whoever did it was like smoke in the wind."

The uni then looked as if he was going to vomit on the front lawn again.

Maybe Mitch's brain had been looking at all that,

painting the scene by the numbers, because he had not, in fact, gone inside, but he felt like he could see every detail: the blood spatter that almost masked the little flecks of crab Mulroy had got on his necktie, the way Creech's head had rolled to a stop in a corner of the foyer almost underneath the legs of an antique French table on which the (former) residents had kept their mail and keys and loose change in a blue ceramic bowl.

Whatever had distracted Mitch, he didn't know, but he was looking at the hotel's doorway and suddenly the guy was there, pulling open the hotel's front door with that big steel handle and stepping inside, and Mitch had to run to catch him before the elevator sucked the man upstairs and out of sight again.

And when he did, when he burst into the lobby and skidded across the marble floor and caught himself, the guy had looked at him with a little smile on his lips, but not in his eyes—oh Christ they looked like a shark's eyes, dead and black. And the guy said, "Mitch LaSalle, right? I was wondering when I'd see you again." And Mitch wasn't sure he had ever been quite so afraid in his life.

4

PEOPLE WHO FREQUENT antique shops, bookstores, gay bars, or strip clubs know how to find those places when they go to a strange city.

Dane knew how to find a strange city's vampire population.

Not that they were of any help, in this case. Savannah's vampires were an odd mix of a few very old ones—two had been members of Savannah's original upper crust, and a handful had actually been part of a pirate crew that had been turned while their ship had been in port here—and very young ones, still brash and full of their own newfound strength.

One of the old ones explained that what should have been the largest number, those turned in the intervening centuries, had mostly moved on to larger urban centers, particularly Atlanta, but also down into Florida and up into Virginia and the mid-Atlantic states, where the pickings were better and the chances of drawing undue attention were lessened.

Some of them shared Dane's opinion that Savannah's serial killer must be a vampire. Who else, they had concluded, could have smashed his way into some of those homes? Who else would have bothered draining the blood from those they killed and taking away the others?

Dane also realized the risk involved in putting himself out there—after all, it didn't take much for a vampire like that Paul Norris to put two and two together about the LA incident, the bloody and painful end results still fresh in Dane's mind. Now *there* was a memory for you.

Sitting in the darkened parlor of a grand old Savannah home, talking with an assemblage of the gathered, Dane decided he believed them when they collectively said they had considered the question long and hard but had no idea who might have been carrying out the attacks.

"We all, like, know each other," China was saying. China was a little Goth-looking girl, pale faced, with black hair cut straight across and a silver stud in her nose, apparently frozen at seventeen. Being turned had probably been a dream come true. Many vampires, like Dane, preferred to stick to one name, often—although not always—one of their original, human names. China, Dane guessed, had made up her own name—her skin was fittingly as white as bone, with only a few veins of blue tracing underneath. "Fuck, any of us had been the Headsman, we'd know."

"Couldn't there be an outsider in your midst?" Dane had asked.

"I don't see how," another one had answered. This was Adler, one of the old ones. He had been living in this house since the early 1800s. That kind of consistency seemed foolish, even suicidal. But when Dane continued inquiring, he was told, "This is Savannah. People don't like to pry." Adler's house smelled like sandalwood—he kept incense burning almost constantly, it seemed, to mask the sour-sweet odor common to gatherings of the undead.

Dane had met with them, separately and in groups of various sizes, for the last several nights. None of them had been able to shed any light, and he had grown increasingly annoyed with them. These were his kind, but so many of them held ridiculous, outmoded beliefs—that they were the superior species, humans were nothing more than meat that should be raised as livestock, the blood of virgins was somehow fresher and more delicious than any other. Dane didn't bother to ask how they confirmed anyone's virginity, or where they found adult virgins in the modern age. Vampires, like everyone else, had their old wives' tales—sometimes the best you could do was just nod your head and smile.

Tonight he had stopped to feed on a drug dealer he found near an all-ages nightclub, then headed back to the Hyatt. With no wheels, he either used public transportation or he simply ran, clinging to the shadows and letting his undead muscles propel him along. Like a trained ninja, Dane couldn't genuinely turn invisible, but he could seem to disappear because most people didn't know how to watch for him. He slowed long enough to open the door at the hotel, and that must have been when the cab driver saw him, because suddenly the man hurtled, breathless, his pale skin blotched with red, toward Dane as he waited for an elevator.

The reason for his sudden appearance couldn't have been more obvious. Dane invited him up.

There was a momentary silence between them as the elevator hummed in its ascent, Mitch staring at Dane.

"Something's happened," Dane finally remarked, eyebrows raised. "He struck again, didn't he?"

Mitch nodded. His Adam's apple twitched in his throat. Dane didn't like the way Mitch examined him, letting his gaze run from Dane's feet to his head and back again.

"You think that I . . ." Dane started.

Mitch shook his head. Finally, he found his voice. "No, I can see . . . you wouldn't have had time to change. You'd be covered in blood if you had . . ."

The elevator stopped, opened. Dane led the way to his room, swiping the lock with the key card. They didn't speak in the hallway. When they were in his room with the door closed, Dane went into the bathroom and drew a glass of water, then came out and handed it to Mitch. The man sat on the edge of one of the chairs and sipped it, clutching the glass in both hands.

"What happened?" Dane asked him.

Mitch swallowed some of the water, already starting to look more like himself. "Two friends of mine," he said. "Cops, detectives on the task force looking for this bastard. They got a call, responded. He had broken into a home, and the neighbors said he was still inside."

He stopped. Dane didn't want to push too hard. The

cops were friends of his, so Mitch was probably still in shock to a certain extent.

But the scent would grow cold quickly. Dane didn't want to be insensitive, but he didn't want to waste time, either. "And he was still inside, and he killed your friends. Then what? Did anyone else see him?"

"They had the place surrounded, or close to it. I guess units were still responding. Fucking snafu, you know?"

"I'm familiar with the syndrome."

"So the suspect escaped. Meanwhile my buddies haven't been brought out yet because the crime scene unit has to take pictures and measurements of all the pieces where they landed before they can scoop 'em up and pour 'em into body bags."

Mitch stopped again.

"I'm sorry for your friends," Dane said, dispensing his best bedside manner, attempting to bring Mitch around again. "So. Now you want to get this guy." He crossed to the window, pulled back the sheer curtain and gazed out at the ships as if there might be answers written on their hulls. "And you figured maybe I really did know what I was talking about the other night."

Mitch peered into his water glass. "I'm sorry about that."

"You couldn't have known. And at the time, I couldn't really explain."

He directed those piercing blue eyes at Dane again. The hurt in them was palpable. "Explain what? What the fuck is going on here? I don't even know your name, and you expect me to trust you with . . . with whatever this is."

"*You* came to *me.* I'm Dane, by the way."

"Just Dane?"

"That's good enough. I could give you a Social Security number, but it'd be fake. They didn't have those when I was born."

"You're not that old."

"I'm older than I look," Dane said, smiling ruefully. "A lot older." This was always the hard part. Trying to convince someone who didn't want to believe, especially someone who had suffered a loss.

Ideally it was a seduction, a step at a time, with lots of flirting and foreplay before the serious action started. But that took time Dane didn't have. "Look, Mitch. You're going to go through a bunch of stages of denial here. You're going to think I'm full of it, that I'm scamming you somehow. I get all that. But what I'm going to tell you is the truth, and the sooner you can wrap your head around it, the quicker we can get after the guy who killed your friends."

Mitch's head bobbed. Maybe he thought Dane was going to tell him that he was a spy or a contract killer. Mitch would be quickly disabused of those notions, although he might not be any happier learning what he would.

Dane would be happier, though. Keeping his fangs retracted and his flesh looking healthy—by human standards—by warming his skin was wearisome. The longer he held it the worse it got, and of course every time he passed through the hotel lobby, he had to put up the illusion. He could have stayed with the vampire community in town, but then Mitch LaSalle (or whatever human ally Dane had ended up taking on, since he'd been pretty sure he would need one) wouldn't have been able to find him.

"Okay. . . . I'm a vampire, Mitch," Dane said. "Yes, I know. Just keep quiet for a minute or two; don't bother telling me vampires aren't real, because I've heard it all before." He let his fangs extend, stopped forcing blood to the surface of his skin. As it cooled, his flesh paled. The fangs, each more than an inch long, sharp as miniature daggers, altered the appearance of his jaw line and filled in gaps between his somewhat sharper teeth left when he retracted them—gaps that had spawned many jokes about hillbillies and poor dental hygiene.

As Dane's skin went white, Mitch's did too. The cab driver's bright blue eyes widened and his mouth opened and shut like a loose-hinged mailbox on a blustery day. A strangled little cry emerged from his throat.

"I know, this is a big shock for you," Dane went on. The longer teeth and altered jaw changed his voice a little, giving it an echoing rumble that it didn't have in his human disguise. To him it sounded natural, the human voice fraudulent. "I wouldn't say that everything you've heard about vampires is true, but certainly some of it is. I also wouldn't tell you about us if I had any choice. You know the old joke, then I'd have to kill you? Ordinarily . . . well, that's the way it would be."

Mitch didn't respond for a moment. His outward appearance almost led Dane to believe he was suffering from a massive coronary that would settle the issue right then and there.

"Holy . . . This . . . this can't be happening."

"I don't really care what you think," Dane said. "This isn't a movie, Mitch. This is real. As real as it gets, and I'm sure it's going to get even more unpleasant. I need you, and you need me if you want to find the guy who killed your friends. After that, if you can't live with all of this, believe me, we can come to an arrangement. I was only hoping I could trust you."

He counted on Mitch's years as a cop tempering the shock. Cops saw things every week that most people never did. They learned things—about people, about how they could treat each other—that made them believe in evil, in monsters, albeit of the human variety. Cab drivers saw a lot, too, at least if one could believe HBO. So while your average civilian would certainly have a hard time with this information, Dane hoped that Mitch was digesting it more easily.

To his credit, Mitch appeared to swallow back his fear . . . at least on the outside. Color returned to his face. "You . . . you can trust me," he said. "I want that bastard."

"That 'bastard' is a vampire, too," Dane said. "That's why I told you law enforcement would never find him. Because they think they're looking for a man, and they're not. That's why you need me. I don't know this city, and

I don't have the right connections here, and the local vampire community—yes, there is one—claims not to know who the Headsman is. That's why I need you."

As silence descended over the room, Dane opted to play his remaining hand. "Understand that I'm taking as much of a risk with you knowing about me. My kind and I don't always see eye to eye on such things. It's been . . . unpleasant sometimes, let's say."

Mitch said nothing, but looked like he wanted to throw up.

"Okay then . . ." Mitch finally said quietly. "Where do we start?"

"Can you get us into the place where your friends were killed?"

Mitch checked the cheap wristwatch on his left arm. "If the crime scene guys are done . . . yeah, maybe."

"Good. Then let's start there. You're driving."

"Sure, whatever, I'm driving," Mitch said. He still looked pretty shell-shocked as he stood to go. "I gotta be dreaming all this. . . . You even got a license?"

5

ON THE RIDE OVER, Mitch asked a few more questions. He didn't like all the answers he got—getting past the idea that Dane was some kind of legendary monster who killed to live would not be a cakewalk—but at least he seemed willing to let those things go. For now.

No, Dane did not, in fact, have a driver's license, unless you counted the fake one. Motor vehicles offices tended to be open during daylight, and even the ones with night hours wanted more forms of ID than he was prepared to show.

Yes, he did kill people for blood when he had to, but he tried to focus his attentions on people who offered little to society. Of course, he made that determination himself, serving as judge, jury, and executioner, often with only a few moments of consideration.

Yes, sunlight could kill him, or beheading. He had no particular problem with garlic or crosses. Silver bullets were for werewolves. No, they didn't exist, either.

Throughout his line of questioning, Mitch's reaction to Dane's revelation remained surprisingly low-key. Maybe he was still in shock from the deaths of his friends, keeping his emotions buried. That was fine—it would give Mitch more time to process the information before he got agitated about it and make him less likely to come at Dane with a wooden stake or do something equally stupid.

They reached the crime scene about an hour after Mitch had shown up in the hotel lobby.

Yellow police tape fluttered in a gentle breeze off the river. The press had left, and it was too late for casual onlookers. A uniformed officer sat on the house's stoop, the lightbulb over the door shining down on him. He swatted at insects Dane couldn't see until they had crossed the street. Then the uni stopped swatting and stood up.

"Hey, you have to stay on the other side of that tape!" he barked.

"Pat, it's me," Mitch said. "Mitch LaSalle."

"Mitch . . . ? Sorry, I didn't recognize y'all there in the dark," the officer said. "Who's this?"

"Friend," Mitch said. Not much more than a grunt. The uniformed cop nodded as if it meant something. Dane didn't know Mitch well enough yet—maybe it did.

Most humans, in Dane's experience, were small-minded, petty, greedy. They lied when they could, cheated when possible, stole even when they didn't need to. Some, of course, were worse than others, and it was from this category that he chose to feed as often as possible. And vampires? They were just as bad. Worse, in some ways, since murder slotted more easily into their list of personal failings. But, as with humans, there were decent ones . . . terrible ones . . . and the full range in between. If this cop could put confidence in Mitch's monosyllabic claim that Dane was a friend—never mind the lie—that said something for Mitch.

"Mind if we go in for a second?" Mitch asked. "Something I need to see in there."

"I can't let y'all do that, Mitch," the cop said. He tapped on a clipboard hanging from the doorknob by a string. "Everyone's got to sign in. Law enforcement only."

"I understand that, Pat," Mitch said. "I know how it works. We just . . . Denny and Willard died in there, you know? I just wanted to see where, thought it might help me put my mind at rest about it."

"That's the thing, my friend. Two cops died in there. We got to be really careful about preservin' the scene, right?"

"Of course, I know. We wouldn't do anything to threaten the integrity of the scene. I want a solid conviction more than you'll ever know."

Pat shook his head—turning Mitch down obviously gave him no personal pleasure at all.

Dane shouldered past Mitch, impatient.

Mitch tried to grab his arm. "Hey, don't—"

Dane shook him off and leaned close to Pat's face. He locked eyes with the young cop, not bothering to hide his true nature. Not that the cop would remember any of this in a few minutes. "We're going in there," Dane said, his voice low, so soft that someone standing a few feet away wouldn't have heard more than a vague rumble. "We won't be long, we won't touch anything, and after we leave, you'll forget we were ever here."

Pat stepped back as if Dane had pushed him. His

mouth slacked open and his eyes had taken on a glazed expression.

Dane turned back to Mitch. "The part about vampires and hypnosis? Also true, sometimes—if the subject is particularly susceptible. This one is."

"So he's . . . ?"

"He won't give us any trouble." Dane passed him and opened the door. Mitch followed.

The place smelled like a butcher shop. To Dane, it was like a candy store.

Hunger filled him like water flooding into a shallow. He gave an involuntary snarl and glanced at Mitch. He could smell Mitch's blood, hear it rush through his veins. A thick green vein throbbed in his neck.

Dane could tear into that in the space of a single heart-beat, could fill his mouth with the precious stuff.

No one could stop him. No one would know.

Mitch caught him staring, looked back anxiously. Dane swallowed the hunger, barely suppressing it. It was just the blood . . . all the blood in here. He couldn't help his response. But he could control his own actions, and he would make every effort to do so—he'd come a long way since first being turned.

"This isn't like the other scenes," Dane finally said. They stood in a tiled foyer, dark wainscoting on walls that were plastered and painted a soft green above. Blood had stained everything, as if there had been a water balloon fight in the foyer, only the balloons were filled with blood. "There was hardly any blood at those, according to the reports."

"Two cops didn't walk in on the perp while he was still at the scene at those," Mitch reminded him. "All this blood is probably from . . . Mulroy and Creech."

"Yeah," Dane said, hoarse. His throat was dry.

Mitch's face was screwed into an expression of extreme distaste. As much as the place smelled like fine dining to Dane, Mitch was revolted at being here. "You need to see anything else?"

"Maybe."

"Have we seen anything yet?"

"Enough." Dane sniffed the air. "It isn't really about seeing, it's about smelling."

"What's that mean?"

Dane couldn't explain fully. One had to be a vampire—and it helped to have been turned by someone willing to take the time to really teach—to understand how each person's blood had its own individual tang. Even more complex was how he could pick up each one in a scene like this, as if the scents were strings on the floor and he could just grasp one in his fingers and follow it.

"It's the smells," he said, hoping that would be enough. "The Headsman injured one of his victims—a woman—but didn't kill her. She's bleeding. He took her. We're going to follow."

Mitch ran the palm of his hand across his forehead, wiping sweat away from his eyes. "Follow . . . ?"

"You drive," Dane said. "I smell."

"How . . . ?"

"Never mind how. I can. Surely this isn't the most un-believable thing you've heard tonight."

"Maybe it's just one unbelievable thing after another piling up like so much bullshit."

"If you want to just give me the keys . . ."

"No. I'm in this now. Doesn't mean I like it."

"Understood," Dane said. "I'm not that fond of it either. Can we get going? The longer we wait . . ."

"Yeah, I know. The farther away he gets."

"I was going to say the harder it is to separate the smell of her blood from all the other smells of the city, but whatever."

Outside, Pat didn't even seem to notice them leaving. Dane assured Mitch again that the cop wouldn't remember a thing, but he would do his job and protect the scene from anyone else.

As Mitch drove Savannah's dark streets, Dane kept his window open, sniffing the air like a dog on a scent.

Not far off the mark.

The woman (young, he decided, no older than twenty-five) had something unusual about her scent that he couldn't identify, but it made her easier to track.

The Headsman had driven a roundabout route, almost as if trying to throw off any pursuit. From the crime scene they went south down Skidaway, then made a right on Derenne Avenue, just to the Harry Truman Parkway where they cut north again. Traffic on the parkway, even at this hour, wouldn't let Mitch drive as slow as Dane wanted him to. Dane worried that he'd lose the scent at high speed, but the odd quality of the woman's smell kept him locked on. They missed a turn at Anderson Street but Dane realized it immediately, so they left the parkway at Henry and backtracked the block. West again, this time to Montgomery, to Louisville, to West Lathrop.

"Slow down," Dane said. They cruised through a warehouse district, not far from the river. The big buildings—windows shot out or shattered with rocks, bare bulbs over the doors or floodlights mounted high on plain walls and protected by steel cages—were mostly deserted. Tall chainlink fences with grass growing up around them surrounded parking lots of gravel or cracked, weed-strewn tarmac.

"You still got it?" Mitch asked.

"It's fresh," Dane said. "She's either been here recently or she's still here."

"Right here?"

"No. Close by, keep going. But slow."

They hadn't seen another car in motion for several minutes. A few truck cabs without trailers had parked beside the fences, as had a couple of dark cars that might have been abandoned or might have contained people who had brought hookers or secret lovers here for a few moments of privacy, but nothing moved, no signs of life presented themselves. "Should I turn the lights off?" Mitch asked.

"I doubt it'll make any difference," Dane said. "If he sees us, he'll see us, lights or no. We can see pretty well in the dark."

"I hate this," Mitch said. "I really hate this."

"What?"

"You. All this. Maybe . . . I can't deny what you've shown me, but I can't just say, okay, sure, this kind of stuff exists, you know?"

"I understand."

"So I'm just somewhere in the middle and I hate it. I'm a cop—I was, but you know what I mean. I like there to be answers."

Dane nodded, sniffing the air. "Slower."

Mitch brought the car down to a steady crawl. Every rock in the road, every bit of uneven pavement, jounced them.

Other smells assailed his nostrils, confusing the hunt. These were new and unmistakable.

It only took a minute before he saw one, crouching at the edge of a rooftop. Watching the taxi creep down the road.

Another stood in the shadowed depths between a warehouse and a trailer used as an office.

A third squatted in the tall grass of an empty lot.

"What?" Mitch asked, noting Dane's sudden tension. "What are you looking at?"

"Vampires," Dane answered. "We aren't alone here after all."

6

"ARE YOU SERIOUS?"

"You're doubting me? I've seen three so far," Dane said. "Where you can see three, you have to assume there are nine. Maybe more. The undead are very good at staying hidden. The fact that I've seen three probably means they *want* me to see them. Maybe they don't know yet what I am, and they're hoping to scare us away."

"I get the feeling you don't scare easy."

"No, I don't. Doesn't mean I go looking for trouble."

"I thought that was exactly why we came here."

"We did. I'm just saying."

"They going to attack us or something?" Mitch sounded anxious about the prospect, but not afraid. Maybe he still hadn't recovered from earlier, although as the hours wore on that seemed less likely. Dane thought the truth was probably overwhelming, more than he bargained for, rather than getting used to the facts Dane had thrown at him. As the shock wore off, the new reality Mitch had to face took hold.

"I don't know," Dane said. "Maybe."

Mitch shifted forward in the seat, reaching behind himself. From beneath his untucked gray T-shirt he drew a 9mm Smith & Wesson, which he set down on his lap.

"If you have to use that," Dane stated, "aim for their heads. If you can destroy the brain, you can stop the vampire. Anything else will just piss him off." He held up his left hand, flexed the fingers. "This hand was blown off by explosives a couple years ago. I got a transplant. Works pretty good now. We tend to be fast healers."

"A transplant?"

"The donor didn't need it anymore."

Mitch didn't respond, and Dane didn't want to continue on the subject. Instead, he pointed to a warehouse, yellow in the glow of a couple of skewed floodlights. "She's in there."

Mitch pulled his cab into the driveway, stopping only when a locked gate barred the way. "Come on," Dane said. He opened his door. Mitch hesitated, then followed. Dane glimpsed the gun in Mitch's fist.

Dane had taken three steps toward the warehouse when the shadows came alive.

The flap and flutter of clothing sounded like wings in the night. Shoes scraped on the pavement. Dane spread his feet, stabilizing himself, ready.

The first one slammed into him from his right, stinking of sour blood, fangs gnashing near Dane's ear. Dane crashed his elbow into the vampire's chin. The blow sent the other bloodsucker cartwheeling away.

Dane whirled toward Mitch. One was closing on the former cop. Mitch tried to raise his weapon, but Dane saw that the vampire was already too close. Mitch's first shot would miss, and there wouldn't be a second.

Lunging, Dane caught the back of the vampire's collar and yanked. The attacker staggered backward. Dane threw an arm around his neck and twisted.

The vampire looked up at him, eyes wild. "I can finish you," Dane threatened. "Or you can tell me what's going on here."

It responded by spitting blood at Dane's face. Dane closed his eyes but felt it land, hot and wet, on his cheek. Dane twisted more, felt the tendons and small bones in the neck and shoulders giving way.

Mitch's gun went off, three times, echoing down the empty streets. Dane threw the injured vampire to one side and started toward Mitch again, in case he needed to run interference. Before he reached the cab driver, two more of them charged from the darkness, driving Dane to the ground beneath them. Over the rustle of the vampires tearing at him, he heard two more gunshots.

"Mitch!" he shouted. Mitch might have answered, but it was hard to tell with claws snagging Dane's head. He drove his fists out, connecting with hard, muscled bodies. He punched again. Claws bit into Dane's neck—they were trying to tear his head off. He took in momentary flashes: long, dark, greasy hair; a thick, blunt-nosed, full-lipped face. Like him—like most of their kind—they wore black clothing.

Dane wrenched his head from one's grasp, the claws gouging his flesh as he did, and clamped his teeth down on the vampire's hand. It tasted dead, rancid, but the vampire screamed and released Dane. He bumped into the other one, and Dane took advantage of their momentary distraction to grab the second one's legs and topple him onto the first.

Finally free of their restricting forms, he saw that Mitch remained upright, the Smith & Wesson clutched in both hands, a look of openmouthed amazement on his face.

And in the east, the first golden glimmerings of morning lit the sky.

The attacking vampires saw it, too, and scrambled.

Dane let them go and grabbed Mitch's sleeve. "Mitch, we've got to get inside!"

"Why?"

"Sun's coming up!"

"Should we get back to the car?"

"Too late for that," Dane said. "The warehouse."

Dane had another reason for wanting to go inside. The attack had scrambled the scents, distracting him, but now that the others were gone, he smelled her again, stronger than ever.

With Mitch following close behind, Dane led the way through a doorway in the high fence surrounding the property. They left the cab where it was. From the looks of the place, Dane guessed it had been abandoned for some time, so although the Crown Vic blocked the drive, it wouldn't be in anyone's way.

"I saw someone run out of here," Mitch said. "I took a couple of shots at him, but I guess I missed."

"Or you just didn't get the head."

"I guess, yeah."

Around a corner, a doorway stood open, gaping darkly, like an invitation to hell.

"In there?" Mitch said.

"Looks that way." Dane tasted the air.

She was definitely inside.

And someone else had been, very recently. Someone with a powerful presence. Not just an odor, but something more than that. Almost an aura, if an aura could be detected with senses other than sight.

Inside, Dane smelled the river.

The river soaked into everything around here, filling the pores of wood, getting under the paint on metal walls, as if the thickly humid air was just river water in disguise, leaving its mark everywhere. Beneath the river stink was stale urine, mold, rot. The next bad hurricane would probably knock the building down. The concrete floor was slick, glistening with weeds and mushrooms growing up through cracks. A dozen feet in, the faint light of sunset failed to penetrate. Mitch stayed close to Dane.

"I can't see shit in here," Mitch remarked, the barely concealed panic evident in his voice.

"I know. Don't worry, there's nothing to see." Almost literally. The bulk of the vast space had been one empty room, support posts rising up into the blackness of the rafters overhead. Dane saw spiderwebs thick enough to snare rhinos, broken-down shelving units, newspapers and fast-food bags, malt liquor cans, and candy wrappers left behind by squatters who had occupied the place over the last several years, and not much else.

At least they would be safe from the sun's rays. Dane wondered if the vampires outside had found shelter in time. Not that he owed them any sympathy or solidarity. He had been pulling his punches, trying not to kill them until he knew what was going on.

Obviously, they hadn't been operating under the same guidelines.

"What about the woman we've been following?" Mitch asked. "Is she in here?"

"Should be." Dane peered through the darkness. Finally he spotted a staircase made of two-by-fours and plywood hammered together, leading up to a kind of shallow loft. "Up there."

Mitch nodded anxiously. His eyes had adjusted somewhat to the darkness, but he still carried the pistol close to his collarbone, cradled in both hands. A 9mm round wouldn't do much damage to a vampire, Dane knew, but if he could group a few of them in the right spot he might be able to take one out.

Dane thought the immediate threat was over, though. He'd been wrong before, but he didn't smell any undead around anymore, just the trace scents that meant they had been here. Now the overwhelming odor was of the young woman taken from the house, the one with the odd under-scent that Dane couldn't figure out.

He stepped onto the lowest stair, then climbed two more. They creaked under his weight, the half-inch plywood old and warped. Too much weight on the staircase would, he was afraid, collapse it entirely. But Mitch, not willing to let Dane get out of sight, came up right behind him. The staircase complained and shuddered. Dane took two more steps. The wood felt spongy underfoot, but it held.

Struts of steel cable supported the loft area, which was floored with the same half-inch board. When Dane stepped onto it from the staircase, the whole structure moaned and swayed. He gripped the handrail, a two-by-four nailed on top of a series of upright four-bys—not that it would do any good if the whole thing went crashing to the floor.

"Jesus," Mitch said. "This is one wobbly platform."

"Strong enough, I guess," Dane said. He pointed toward what looked like a bundle of rags lying in the middle of the floor. The dust caking the boards around it had been smudged. "*There.* There she is."

"Is she dead?"

Dane could hear a heartbeat and faint breathing. Not in great shape, but alive. "No. She's been better, but they didn't kill her."

"That's a first, then."

"Maybe they wanted her for something else." Dane retracted his fangs, warmed his skin. He thought she was conscious, if only barely, and the last thing he wanted was for her to think he was another of her attackers. When he guessed he could pass for human, he went to her side, knelt on the creaking plywood.

She was young, he'd been right about that. Her skin was a creamy cocoa color, her hair black and soft. When he touched her shoulder her eyes fluttered open, a surprising sea green. She started, as if he had woken her. "Ahh!"

"Shh," he said. "It's okay, we're friends. Are you hurt?"

She made a small noise in the back of her throat and tried to scrabble away from him, but he held her still, afraid that if she was injured, trying to escape would only make it worse. Already a bruise showed on her left cheek, just below her eye, and her neck showed the marks of rough hands. "Honest, we're here to help you. I know you've been through a terrible ordeal."

"How did you . . . who . . . ?"

"Don't try to ask questions. We're here to help you," Dane said, keeping his voice soothing, his touch light. "Just tell me, are you hurt anywhere? Any broken bones?"

Tears filled her eyes and started to run. "He . . . oh my God in heaven, he . . ."

"What is it?" Mitch asked. He leaned toward her. "Oh, Christ."

"What?" Dane asked.

"Dane—she's been raped."

"No."

"Yes. I'm telling you."

Dane realized he knew better than to argue. Mitch had spent years on the police force and had no doubt encountered more victims of sexual assault than Dane or anyone had a right to. While this act by his kind was extremely rare, it wasn't completely unheard of. Since the undead thought of humans as nothing more than food, being sexually attracted to one would be like a human being turned on by a cow.

But rape was less about sexual attraction than about power. And, oh, were vampires all about power.

The Headsman had killed dozens of people and had taken others away for reasons yet to be determined.

Had he violated the others like this as well? Was that part of his pattern . . . or a new, macabre twist?

What the hell is going on here? Dane thought.

7

"WE NEED TO get her to the hospital," Mitch insisted.

"No! No doctors!" the woman cried. Mitch and Dane had moved to the far edge of the loft platform, but didn't try to cut her out of the conversation. "I don't want to see no doctors!"

"You've been injured," Mitch replied. "Pretty badly, from the looks of it."

"She's right, though," Dane said. "If we take her to the hospital, they'll have to do a police report."

"They should anyway," Mitch said. "She was taken from her home by force. They'll be looking for her. We have to let the task force know we found her."

"Mitch . . . I thought you understood by now that we're dealing with something the task force is completely unqualified to handle."

Mitch didn't answer. His lips were clamped together so tight they had disappeared. He held on to the rail with both hands, his gun tucked into his pants again. Finally, gazing into the blackness of the warehouse, he spoke. "We can't take care of her here."

"And we can't leave," Dane pointed out. "Not until dark. At least I can't. If she needs medical attention, we have to provide it."

"You a doctor?"

"I've picked up some knowledge over the years."

"Got any equipment? Even a sterile space?"

"Of course not."

"Then what can you do for her?"

"I don't know. I can start by not getting her killed. The Headsman left her here because he knew we were outside and coming in. He couldn't get away with her. If she goes home or into a hospital—anyplace we can't protect her—he'll come back and finish the job. He'll either kill her or abduct her again."

Mitch didn't seem to like it. Dane didn't either, but he didn't really see a choice. He could let Mitch use his cell to call 911. EMTs and cops would come. He would be forced out into daylight, unless he could find a spot in the rafters to hide.

At any rate, the woman would be taken away, to a hospital where she would be vulnerable to the killer as soon as night fell. Or after examination, if she had no major injuries, she might be released. Would she go back to the house she had been taken from, where presumably any other family members had been killed or similarly abducted? Not likely, since the cops wouldn't have released it yet. Where, then? A friend's place, a hotel? Her world had been turned inside out. She needed safety and security until it could be resettled.

And Mitch's plan offered only more danger.

"Fine," Mitch said. "For now, we do it your way. Unless she has life-threatening injuries—then we call an ambulance and take our chances."

"Agreed." Dane went back to the woman's side. She had curled into a ball, sobbing gently.

"I'm right here," he said softly, wanting to warn her before he touched her arm. "I want to look you over, see what kind of shape you're in. I'm not a doctor, but I know something about medicine. I promise I won't touch you any place you don't want me to, okay? All you have to do is tell me."

"I . . . I'm okay."

"No, you're not okay. You've been traumatized, assaulted. Your home was broken into. Two police officers were killed there, trying to help you. I'm sorry to tell you that whoever else was in there was probably killed, too, or else taken away like you were."

"No one else, just me and Mrs. Waylons," she said. "She's older. I work for her, take care of her. I guess I didn't take such good care after all."

"There was nothing you could have done to help her, believe me," Dane said, glad that she was talking. She had been wearing a cotton nightgown and a terrycloth robe. Both had been ripped, the nightgown shredded, but she had rolled the fabric around herself, covering herself with it.

"Look into my eyes," he said soothingly, hypnotically. "Can I examine you?"

Her face immediately slackened as his penetrating gaze fought to overcome her terror, her voice dropping to a murmur. "He . . . he hurt my face. Choked me, hurt my arm, dragging me around. My hip. I don't think anything's broke."

Dane pulled no punches. "And he sexually assaulted you. Raped you."

She squeezed her eyes together as if she could make the memory go away. Her lower lip quivered and her head gave a barely perceptible nod.

"Did he do that at the house, or here?"

"There. After he killed Mrs. Waylons. He made me watch him kill her, and then he . . . then he did it."

"We've been looking for him," Dane told her. "I'm sorry we didn't find him before he hurt you. But we definitely will find him, I promise you that."

"He the one that's been on TV?"

"Yes, he's the one who's been in the news. The one they're calling the Headsman." Dane pulled the fabric away from her throat, looked at the bruising there. The Headsman had throttled her, rubbed the skin but probably hadn't broken anything. Dane touched her gently. "What's your name? I'm Dane."

"Ananu Reid," she said. "Most folks call me Ana."

"Ananu is beautiful. Excuse me." He drew the torn nightgown away from her breasts, which also showed some bruising, and her ribs. She shifted onto her back, giving him access there. "Tell me more about your name. There must be a story behind that."

"I was a twin," Ananu said. "My mama's people were from Nigeria, and they have a myth, an ancient Fon legend about divine twins. Nyohwe Ananu and Da Zdoji were Earth deities, the twin children of the twin-faced god called Mawu-Lisa. I always liked Ananu, but my brother Zdoji, he went by Joey."

He pressed on her ribs. They seemed intact, although she winced under the pressure. "I can't say I blame him. Where is he?"

"Dead. So are my parents."

"You have green eyes," Dane said. "You're not just African."

"Daddy was a white man. Not as white as you, but you're pretty damn pale. You look like those European royalty dudes, used to powder their faces."

Damn. He must have misjudged his skin temperature, let it slip in the dark of the warehouse and the excitement of finding her alive. He hadn't expected her to be able to see so clearly here, but then again, she had been in the gloom for a long time. "I keep out of the sun pretty much," he said, unconsciously touching his own cheek. "Skin cancer, you know. How did they meet, your parents?"

"In Baltimore, when she was in college. After they got married they moved to Savannah and he opened a shoe store. She did his books and also worked in some office. Like financial stuff."

Dane pulled back the fabric more, leaving her genital

area covered for now. He ran his fingers down her hips, noting which points caused her to wince or moan. "How long since they died?" Anything to keep her mind away from the moment.

"Daddy was shot during a holdup in the summer of '99. Mama almost got remarried three years later, but the car she and her fiancé was in got hit by a truck out near Bluffton, on the way to see some friends of his on Hilton Head."

"I'm very sorry," Dane said. Both for her losses and for what he was about to do.

He gingerly pulled the last scrap of fabric away, exposing her genitalia. She instinctively pressed her thighs together, and he had to hold them, prying them apart. He wanted to make sure she wasn't hemorrhaging. Seeing some bruising but no blood, he heaved a sigh of relief, and broke off the hypnotic contact.

The results were immediate as the horror of Ananu's ordeal came flooding back in her eyes. "God, what if I'm pregnant?" she exclaimed. "I can't get pregnant!"

"When was your last cycle, Ananu?" he asked her, not bothering to point out that what she feared was nearly impossible.

"I'm just about to start." She smiled for the first time since he'd found her, just a flash of teeth, grim and humorless. "PMS and now this, right?"

"Then you should be okay," he said. "If you're worried about it . . ."

"I don't know. It's probably okay."

"You understand I can't check you for . . . other things, though."

"Like what?"

"Well, I can tell you that it's highly unlikely that . . . put it this way, he's not the kind of guy who gets sick."

"Dude *is* sick."

"Mentally, no doubt. But not physically. I can't guarantee it, and you should still see a doctor and get a blood test soon. But I'm pretty sure you'll be fine."

"You know who it is?"

"I know *what* he is. I'll know *who* soon enough. Like I told you, he'll be dealt with, so no one else has to go through what you did."

"Did he . . . did he do this to any of the women in those other houses? Those people he killed?"

"Mitch?" Dane was clueless.

"No. None of the victims showed any signs of sexual assault," Mitch said. "Of course we don't know what he did with the ones he took away."

"And none of those have been found," Dane added. "Until you, Ananu."

"Hooray for me," she said, sounding as if she would have been happier not being found at all.

Dane covered her body again and worked his way down her legs. He poked and prodded, bent her knees, turned her ankles. No evident injuries there. All in all, considering what she had been through and with whom she had tangled, she was in remarkably good condition—physically speaking, of course.

Mental and emotional states were harder to gauge. She seemed tough, able to take things in stride. Maybe having your family members killed one by one did that. But how she would feel a day from now, or a week, or a year? Anybody's guess. She certainly wouldn't come out of this unscathed.

"Is there anyone else you want to contact? Boyfriend, other close friends, anything like that? I don't think it's safe to let the world at large know that you got away, but if there's someone special . . ."

"I spent most of my time with Mrs. Waylons," she said, her eyes downcast. The way she said it sounded lonely. "Not seeing anyone right now. My friends can wait."

"I think that's for the best."

"When do we get out of here?" she asked. "Please."

He examined her arms. More bruises, especially around her left bicep and right wrist, but no broken bones. "Not until dark," he said. "It won't be safe until then."

"What? Dark in this neighborhood is—"

"I know, Ananu. Believe me. But we have other things to worry about than whatever thugs might be roaming around. As soon as it's dark, we'll get you someplace more comfortable." He had an idea about that, although he hadn't brought it up to Mitch yet. "Someplace safer."

"You're the boss," she finally replied. "Least, you act like one."

"Let's just assume I am, for now." He straightened his spine, rose from the floor. "You take it easy for a while.

Sleep if you want to. We're not going anywhere, and you're safe as long as we're with you."

"I wish I knew why I believe you, Dane."

"It's good enough that you do."

"I don't want to die."

"Try not to worry about it."

He left her and returned to Mitch, who sat at the top of the stairs, looking out at the warehouse beyond. Watching the door, Dane quickly realized.

"She okay?"

"No major damage that I can see," Dane said. "If there's any internal bleeding, I can't tell. And of course the assault, that's the worst part. I was able to pull off some minor hypnosis, so she'll play along, at least for the time being."

"Motherfucker has to pay," Mitch said.

"He will. We'll make sure of that."

"You still think you can find him?"

"I've got his scent now," Dane said. "I've seen some of his stooges. I'll find him."

"Good. I want to be there when you do."

"Maybe. It depends."

"On what?"

"On what you think of this. Ananu needs someplace to lay low, somewhere safe and protected. Do you think she could go to your place?"

Mitch's head swiveled toward him. "My place? It's not much."

"She doesn't need luxury, she needs security."

"I don't know."

"If you're not comfortable with it, Mitch, that's okay. We'll figure something out. I just thought that it would be a good option. The killer doesn't know who you are. Nothing personal, but after last night he'll be looking for me, not you. I'd be around as much as I can, when I'm not out looking for him, and we can lay in some heavy artillery, just in case."

"How heavy are we talking?"

"Shotgun's a lot more effective against vampires than a nine millimeter," Dane said. "You can blow the head clean off with that, or liquefy the brain. Either one does the trick."

"As long as we're not shopping for a howitzer or something."

"I wouldn't turn one down, but a shotgun should do."

They sat in silence. Behind them, Ananu's breathing slowed, settling into an even rhythm. She had fallen asleep after all.

As the hours passed, Mitch napped a little and woke up hungry. Ananu probably did, too, although she didn't say anything about it. Dane had been famished ever since being in that bloody foyer.

He controlled the hunger, the urge. He was used to that. When he did feed, he would drink deep. Until then, he refused to attack those who depended on him, and there undoubtedly wasn't anyone else around to pick from.

Finally, the light streaming through the door faded. The block of white they could see outside went gray, then black.

"Can we go now?" Mitch asked. "Looks dark out."

"I'm sure as hell ready," Ananu said. She sat upright, back against the wall. She had tied the ribbons of her nightgown into something that kept most of her covered, and by belting the robe with a strip torn from its hem she successfully hid the rest. Dane thought she was a beautiful young woman, although he would rather have seen her body under better circumstances.

"Sure," Dane said. "I think it's fine now. Ananu, I can carry you."

She pressed her hands against the wall, forcing herself to her feet. "I can walk," she said. "I did earlier when I had to pee." She had gone to the farthest, darkest corner of the platform for that.

"I'll hold your hand on the steps," Mitch said. "Just in case."

"That's a good idea," Dane said. He went down first, hurrying so that his weight would be off the staircase before they stepped on. He waited near the bottom for them, then preceded them to the door. "It's not far to the car," he told Ananu. "Just out and around the corner."

"Okay, whatever. I'm fine. I could use a pizza or something. Maybe a nice big T-bone. But I'm fine walking."

Dane went to the corner first, looking around to make sure the way was clear. When he didn't see any of their attackers from last night lurking around, he beckoned them on.

They reached the corner, Mitch a half step in the lead.

"Crap," Mitch said.

"What?"

"On my windshield. I got a ticket. I guess we're lucky it didn't get towed."

Dane allowed himself a smile. If that was the worst that happened . . .

He had just taken another step when a ray of light stabbed him. He felt it, painful, slicing into him like a blade. A full spectrum beam then, with the same UV balance as daylight. 50,000 lux, he guessed, or thereabouts. Dane leaped away from it, toward the car.

Thunder split the silence and a hail of bullets chewed the pavement, tore into the side of the warehouse, and blew out the windows of Mitch's cab.

8

FBI SPECIAL AGENT Dan Bradstreet watched the assault through night-vision goggles from a rooftop across the street. Snipers lay on their bellies on both sides of him, sighting on their targets and firing away.

On the street below, another team had emerged from a trailer with Colt Commandos, blasting seven hundred rounds per minute at the targets. Lead sprayed around the target vehicle and shell casings clattered wildly to the ground like metallic rain. Dan could just hear them over the roar of the weapons fire.

Finally, a team inside the building he stood on top of trained high-intensity TRU-UV beams at the targets through open windows. These weren't something available on the open market, but had been designed and built especially for Operation Red-Blooded by a little shop outside Cleveland. The op was the shop's only client, and millions in black-bag money had made their way to it over the past few years. The TRU-UV lights approximated the direct rays of noon sunlight and had proved fatal to vampires in both testing and field operations.

Dan hadn't had much time to put this particular op

together, but he had gotten pretty good about pulling things together on the fly. Bloodsuckers didn't tend to advertise when they'd be out and about, after all. And although he could find and eliminate a nest nearly every night, if he wanted to, that wasn't the current mission. Tonight was considerably more complex.

Sometimes it was about quieting those who might talk about vampires, who might stir up the masses. Fear was a potent political weapon, after all, and had to be used carefully. The wrong person raising a vampire alarm at the wrong time could take the teeth (he smiled at the mental pun) out of an announcement saved for when it would do the most good.

Let people worry about terrorists for now, his immediate supervisor had told him once. *If that fades, then we can play the undead card. Until then we keep it quiet, and we try to keep the bloodsucker population under control.*

This particular situation had been brewing for some time. As long as Savannah's citizens thought a human serial killer stalked them, a legitimate purpose was served. It kept them off guard, a little nervous. People kept their doors locked and didn't go out as much at night. Why this would be remained a mystery, since the killer had always attacked people in their own homes, and locks had proven no deterrent whatsoever. Dan didn't waste too much effort trying to understand why people acted the way they did, though—he did what he was told, and saved the psychology for trying to figure out how to use what he observed against them.

Because working against people—as they would perceive it—was really working for them. That's what the
government did. It worked for people even when they
would really rather it didn't.

Dan had guessed early on that the Savannah serial killer
was vampire, not human. His superiors had since reached
the same conclusion. Hence he and an Operation Red-
Blooded strike team were dispatched to Savannah to take
care of things if the news threatened to become public.

From the looks of things, they had already reached
that stage.

A vamp and two "nons" (Operation Red-Blooded par-
lance for non-vampire) had walked out of that warehouse
together, one night after significant undead activity had
been observed in the neighborhood. Action was demanded. Dan had given the order.

He couldn't tell yet if any of the targets had been hit,
but he didn't think so. He hadn't seen anyone go down, although it was possible that one or more had been wounded
but escaped around the corner, beyond his field of view.

He grabbed the radio on his belt, clicked the button.
"Get some weapons and two of those portable TRU-UVs
around the other side and cover that door," he ordered.
"If they're already back inside, move in slow and easy. I
don't want them walking out of there."

"Roger that," came the response. In just seconds, he saw
agents on the move. Like Dan, they wore blue windbreakers with FBI emblazoned across their backs. With
his neat brown hair and his college linebacker's build,

Dan looked like J. Edgar Hoover's wet dream of an agent, and no one who saw him would doubt that's what he was. Local law enforcement had been alerted to tonight's raid, and well warned to stay clear.

If he had been asked, however, the Bureau's current Director would not have known what Operation Red-Blooded was. It had been developed far above his pay grade, as an interagency task force dedicated to the one specific issue. Dan didn't take orders from the Director. Under certain circumstances, though, it was possible that the Director would take orders from Dan. Alternatively, he would very seriously regret not having done so.

Dan could almost taste the single beer he would allow himself tonight, after this op was over. Thanks to over-whelmingly superior firepower and the element of surprise, that cold one was now very soon in coming.

When the first lance of UV light speared him, Dane threw himself to the ground behind the car, counting on that to block the rays. He hoped. At the same time he shouted out to warn Mitch. "Back inside!"

He glanced back and didn't see Mitch or Ananu clear the corner. That was good. Unless it meant they had already been cut down by crossfire from another direction.

Glass sprayed over him from the car's windows. The light beams danced around, looking for their target. Dane felt his flesh smoldering where he had already been stabbed.

Whoever had attacked had come well prepared.

Dane waited until the lights had moved off his immediate area and scrambled back toward the corner.

Bullets ripped into him, through him, as he ran. They hurt, no doubt about that. But they wouldn't kill him, unless they blew his head off, destroyed his brain, so he pushed though the pain and made the corner.

As he did, he saw Mitch shoving Ananu back into the warehouse. The ex-cop stayed by the door with his Smith & Wesson. Against the din of the automatic weapons fire, it looked almost comical, like a toy. "That's not going to do much good," Dane hissed, rushing up to him.

"I know," Mitch said. "But you told me to leave my howitzer at home."

"I thought I told you that you wouldn't need it at home."

"Same thing." Mitch looked at Dane for a second, as if reconsidering an earlier opinion. "Who the hell's out there? Cops?"

"No such luck."

"Then who? Who's got that kind of firepower?" He paused. "Feds?"

"I honestly don't know," Dane said. "But that's more likely than locals."

"Why would they want to kill us?"

"If we could figure out the answer to that one, we'd probably have the who."

"I got a question," Ananu said from deeper inside the warehouse. "What are we gonna do about it?"

"We'll have to get out of here a different way," Dane said.

"You just happen to have a car parked somewhere handy?" Mitch shot back. "Because my cab sounds like it's being put through a shredder right about now."

"That's a good idea," Dane said.

"Fucking up my car's a good idea?"

"No, calling a cab is."

"You're joking, right? I don't think now's the best time."

"Use your cell phone and call someone. *Anyone.* Give an address three or four blocks from here." He pointed away from where the fire had come from. "That way."

"And how do we get there? If we go out to the street, they'll kill us."

"If we go out through the door."

"You see any other exits?" Mitch asked.

"I'll worry about that. You catch us a ride."

Mitch dragged his mobile phone from his pocket and opened it up. Dane went back toward the door, looking outside from the shadows.

Besides the huge rolling doors at the front of the building, facing onto the street, this was the only way in or out. Since the attackers appeared to be well organized, they probably knew that, too. Because of the layout of the building, with this door around a corner from the street, it wasn't vulnerable to attacks from the street or the buildings on the other side. But a small ground force could come in and make things very unpleasant for anyone trying to hole up in the warehouse.

Dane didn't see their new attackers yet. He expected they wouldn't be long.

He hoped this physical fact would protect them. Because anyone looking at the building would know there was only the one door, they would have focused their attention on the street side. By leaving out the back, Dane believed, they could slip away unseen.

All he had to do was make a new door. What could be easier?

Ananu huddled by herself in the middle of the big empty warehouse, arms wrapped around her chest, clutching her own shoulders. Her green eyes were large, full of fear. With her lips parted, Dane noticed a chipped upper tooth, a triangular wedge knocked out of it, just right of center.

Dane had promised to keep her safe and the first thing he'd done was to walk her right into the middle of a firefight.

He gave Ananu a nod that he hoped was reassuring and went to the back of the building. Its shell was made of thin steel around a skeleton of four-by-fours. The walls, like everything else, were covered in mold and mildew.

This would be noisy, but there was no getting around that.

He closed his hands into fists, opened them, flexed the fingers a couple of times. Then, fingers held rigid, straight out in front of him, he drove them through the steel wall like ten hole punches. Feeling air on the other side, he closed his hands around the wall and pulled down.

It felt like trying to handle fire barehanded. As a human he would have broken his fingers with the first move. But he was stronger now than he had been then. Much stronger. Beads of bloody sweat popped out on his forehead. His shoulders screamed.

He tore the wall, steel bending and curling behind his hands.

A minute later, he set the section he had ripped out down on the concrete floor. It left a gap a little more than two feet wide and five feet high.

"Lady and gentleman," he said. "We have a door. So then . . . do we have a ride?"

9

"DO WE KNOW no one's gonna shoot at us if we go out there?" Mitch asked, looking scared half out of his mind.

"Not until we go out there," Dane replied. "But unless they heard me making the door and figured out that's what it was, they wouldn't have any reason to think we could get out this way."

"I reached a friend who's going to swing by, about six blocks from here. It'll take him about twenty minutes to get here, though," Mitch said.

"That sounds like a helluva long time," Ananu said.

"It might take us that long to cover six blocks," Dane said. "We'll have to stay low, stick to the shadows. I'm guessing that whoever's out there didn't bother to surround us, figuring that we'd have limited escape options. But I don't know that for a fact."

"We should go. Like *now*," Mitch said. "I'm surprised they haven't come through that door already."

"I'm sure it won't be long now. And we'd better be gone when they do, because it's not going to take them much time to find us." Dane glanced at Ananu. Oh hell, she was barefoot. The streets around here were uneven, filled with gravel, shards of glass, and worse. "Can you run?"

"Look, that motherfucker did me wrong and killed Mrs. Waylons. I don't really know who you two are, but he ran away when he knew you were comin', so that's good enough for me. You want me to run, I'll run. Maybe my feet might get cut up some but compared to the shit I've just been through, that's nothing."

"Let's go, then." Dane didn't wait around for an answer, but ducked and turned to squeeze through the doorway he had created. Outside, he stood up, showing himself to the sky.

No one shot at him, no bolts of light scorched his flesh. It was an improvement over his last trip out of the warehouse.

Ananu came out next, followed by Mitch. When Mitch had cleared the door he started to say something, but Dane held a hand up to stop him. He listened.

On the other side of the real door, he heard the scuff of a boot in gravel.

"They're coming," he whispered. *"Go, go, go!"*

Not far away a section of the chain-link fence had rusted out or been cut. Dane ran, leading the others to that and through it onto the street. They had come out a full city block away from the street that had proven so dangerous before. Looking back that way, he couldn't see any of the people who had shot at them.

He knew they weren't that far away, though, and that soon they would find the hole in the wall. When they did, they would sure as hell know where to look.

Dane motioned for Ananu and Mitch to follow and broke into a crouching run.

On the next block he could see another warehouse, unfenced, in deep shadow because the only nearby street lamp was broken and the building had no exterior lighting of its own. Trying for a balance between quiet and speed, they reached it in less than two minutes. So far, Dane hadn't heard any alarm raised.

They skirted the dark building, clinging to the shadows like barnacles. When they reached its end, they saw an alley between two smaller buildings and took that because it got them off the main street.

Now Dane did hear a commotion behind them. Shouts, running feet. Their assailants had discovered the makeshift doorway.

"We need to step it up a notch," Dane said. "They'll be fanning out around the whole area in no time. At least, that's what I'd do."

"Still ten minutes before AJ gets here," Mitch reported.

"Maybe he'll be early."

Ananu stayed quiet. Dane happened to glance down at something glistening on the pavement—*look at this, she's leaving bloody footprints a Cub Scout could have followed*, he thought. "I'm going to carry you, Ana," Dane said. "Not because I don't think you can keep up, but because I don't want to post a neon sign showing where we've been."

She followed his gaze to the prints she'd been making. "Shit," she said. "I didn't think about that."

Dane bent forward, put his shoulder against her stomach and hoisted her in a fireman's carry. Sometimes the strength of the undead came in handy. She gave a little squeal, then settled in, and Dane started to run like hell.

As he did, he could make out just enough to know that their would-be assassins were on the move. The sounds had become more organized. Vehicles. He still had no way to know how many there were, but it sounded like a fair-sized force.

And he still didn't know who they were.

Who would come at them with that kind of firepower and intensity? The assault had been like that of a SWAT team or a military unit. Dane had been asking questions around town, but mostly of the local undead community. Until tracking Ananu and her captor to the warehouse and fighting what he had to assume were the Headsman's personal army of vampire thugs, he hadn't done anything to draw the attention of authorities. He doubted Mitch had either.

Ananu, then? Was she something more than she seemed? Over his shoulder she felt just like a young woman. Light, slender, soft where she should be. Could there be some aspect to her he didn't know about, something that had generated such a powerful response from somebody?

The thing about the world was that you couldn't write off any possibility, all things being equal in paranoia. All it took was being turned into a vampire to convince you that you didn't know everything after all.

Mitch suddenly grabbed Dane's left arm, breaking into his thoughts.

"This is where we're supposed to meet AJ," he said. Mitch pointed to a nearby intersection. Sweat ringed the armpits of his gray T-shirt and he was breathing hard. "Mundy and Mell. I got four more minutes, by my watch."

"Let's stay here in the shadows and hope they're making a careful building-by-building search," Dane said, standing Ananu back on her own feet. "If they're covering ground in a hurry, they'll be here by then."

Ananu sat down and started picking bits of glass and rock out of her bloody feet. Dane had to work to keep his gaze away from her, his hunger under control.

He heard a truck growl through its gears. One of the search vehicles, he guessed. He hoped they didn't have helicopters.

Boots on pavement. Engines grumbling. Dane braced for the sound of gunfire, of shell casings caroming off the street. He half expected spears of light to skewer him at any moment.

"Look!" Mitch called out, thrusting his arm toward the street. "It's AJ!"

A cab, white with black lettering and the words OFF DUTY glowing on its roof light, cruised up the street as if hunting for a fare. Which, in fact, it was.

"Flag him down," Dane said. Mitch stepped carefully into the street, checked both ways, and waved his arms. The cab drew to the side and the driver, a deeply tanned, white-haired guy in a Hawaiian shirt and puka shell choker, rolled down his window. He could have driven right out of a Jimmy Buffett song.

"Mitch? Hey, what the hell are you up to now?"

"Shut up, AJ," Mitch said. "Just be ready to put the pedal down." He opened the back door and waved Ananu and Dane in. While Ananu carefully slid in, Mitch ran around to the passenger side and climbed in front. By the time Dane had closed his door, the vehicle had started to move.

"Fast is good," Mitch remarked. "Faster is better."

"What the hell?" AJ asked again. "You in some kind of a jam?"

"I wasn't in a jam I wouldn't call you to come out someplace like this and pick us up," Mitch replied. "And I wouldn't have called in my marker."

Dane didn't know what marker he was talking about. He cracked his window, peering through the gloom and listening. AJ raced up Mundy. "Shit," he said as he did.

Dane swiveled in the seat, looked behind them. He saw the muzzle flashes, and only then heard the distant *pop-pop-pop* of the automatic weapons. He reached out and pressed Ananu's head to her lap. "Down!" he shouted.

Bullets struck the back of AJ's car as it roared up the street, but he had put too much distance between them. Nothing penetrated the passenger compartment—the rear window remained intact.

AJ made a hard, screeching left onto Hudson and then an immediate right onto Graham, followed by another left, then one more right. In a few minutes he was in a more populous area. He took the on-ramp to the Lynes Parkway about thirty miles per hour faster than the posted limit and slowed only when other traffic surrounded them.

"Nice driving, AJ," Mitch said.

"Not surprised, are you?"

"Well, I *have* seen you fart along like my grandmother on Sunday afternoon."

"Whatever the circumstances warrant," AJ said. "Now will someone tell me what's up?"

"We can't really do that," Dane told him. "Not without possibly endangering your life."

"Hey, buddy, somebody shot at my car, all right?"

"That's true. Whatever your usual fare is, we'll triple it. More. Just don't ask any questions, please, because I don't want to lie to you. But I can't tell you the truth."

AJ thought that over for about five seconds. "Fine, whatever. Deal. Where am I taking y'all?"

Mitch caught Dane's eye. "We can't go to your place," Dane said. "Like I suggested before. Anyone who could mount an operation like that—and make sure the local cops didn't respond—will know who you are and where you live ten minutes after they open up your car."

"Yeah," Mitch said. "That's what I was thinking. I sure

love that apartment, though." He turned to the driver. "AJ, you still got that joint in Pooler?"

"If you're talkin' about my home, then yes."

"You haven't burned that shack to the ground and bought a real house?"

"It's been too wet out," AJ said.

"We need to borrow it."

"For what?"

"Just to lay low for a while," Mitch said.

Dane handed his plastic hotel room card key to Mitch. "You can stay in my room at the Hyatt, AJ," he said. "Order all the room service you want."

"Well. I guess that could maybe work out," AJ said with a small grin.

"Good," Mitch said. "Then take us to your place." He settled back in his seat. Ananu did the same, closing her eyes and resting her hands on her lap, the fright still visible on her face.

Twenty minutes later, AJ pulled into a two-track, grassy driveway beside a little cottage. Crickets trilled a running play-by-play while toads croaked color commentary. Broad-leafed trees pressed in on the cottage's sides like insecure lovers. The front porch was screened and sagging, the paint peeling. The whole thing could have fit into Dane's LA apartment, lot and all. A bare bulb burned over the door, inside the screened porch.

"Home sweet home," Mitch said, climbing out of the cab. He then went to the porch door. It screeched as he opened it. "Hope you don't need a lot of space, Ana."

"I'm not used to much," she said, eyeing the place suspiciously.

"Perfect. Because I don't think I even fit in the bedroom. I'll take the couch in the living room, which if I remember right is also the dining room, library, parlor, and game room."

"You all make yourselves at home," AJ said.

"Thanks, AJ," Ananu said.

AJ went back to the cab's trunk. "I got those items back here, Mitch."

Mitch let the screen door swing shut with a bang, with Ananu on the inside. "Let's have a look."

AJ popped it open and a light flared on inside. Dane watched as AJ pulled out two Mossberg pump-action 12-gauges, handing one to Mitch.

"Shotguns, you said. Not howitzers, right?"

"Howitzers wouldn't hurt, but shotguns are better than that BB gun you pack," Dane said. *Against vampires, anyway. Against whoever that was today, I'll take the howitzer.*

"There're some boxes of ammo in the trunk," AJ said. His teeth glowed when he grinned, almost ultraviolet in his dark face. "Can you get 'em?"

Dane reached in and brought out six boxes of shells, birdshot and buckshot. "Mitch, let's start with the buck," he said. "We can switch to bird if we have to. But if we have to, we're probably in dire straits, and it won't do much good."

"We can get more buckshot," Mitch said.

"I hope we don't need it," Dane said. "But I'd rather have it and not need it than not have it."

"Leave those boxes of bird in the trunk, then," AJ said. "My wife's brother owns the gun shop. He hates returns but he'll do it for me . . . or he'll have a damned unpleasant Thanksgiving this year."

10

DANE THREW ADLER across the back of an antique English love seat. The old vampire slammed into a wheeled wooden cart holding a silver tea service and utensils flew everywhere. A creamer bounced off an oil painting by Winslow Homer, slicing a two-inch gash in the canvas.

Dane felt bad about the Homer. He might have felt equally bad about knocking an old man around, except of course, it would take more than some rough treatment to cause Adler any real pain.

Adler gripped the upended tea cart and braced himself, rising to his feet, the elongated, large-knuckled fingers of his right hand touching the corner of his mouth. He wore a silk smoking jacket and a for-real paisley ascot.

Surprising vampires wasn't easily done, but Dane had accomplished just that—waiting outside Adler's front gate until the undead (who always seemed to congregate in his home) had left, then letting himself in the front door. Not that he would have minded taking on the whole treacherous lot of them, but he had a feeling he could inspire more cooperation one-on-one.

"I must say, this is not the traditional response to my

hospitality," Adler said. His voice rasped like a rusted hinge. The odor of sandalwood was strong, but beneath it Dane could smell the fear Adler attempted to disguise.

"You almost got me killed!" Dane raged. "All of you, telling me you didn't know who the Headsman was. It's not some outsider crashing your turf, it's a local, with his own muscle, and *you know who it is.*"

A day had passed since the attack at the warehouse, during which Mitch had driven AJ's old Dodge pickup to the Savannah police to report his cab stolen, then stopped at Target and a pharmacy to pick up some things for the three of them, including the Plan B pill that Ananu hoped would put an end to any potential pregnancy arising from her assault. Dane had borrowed the truck to come back into Savannah after dark, with the sole purpose of confronting Adler.

"Say that I do," Adler replied, his lilting southern accent, more Carolina than Georgia, stretching out the final vowel. "If I didn't tell you before, did you think that perhaps it was for your own benefit as much as mine?"

"Not for a second. Unless you have a strange idea of what might benefit me."

"Turning around and going back where you came from might be a good place to begin."

"Not an option. Especially now."

"Might I ask what happened?"

"You might," Dane said. "I might even tell you if I knew myself. All I really know is that the Headsman has now killed two Savannah police detectives and raped a young woman."

Adler straightened the cart and began replacing the pieces of the tea service. "All humans. So . . . what concern of ours?"

"Killing police officers is a good way to turn up the heat, for starters. You want this renegade to be the one responsible for letting humans know about our kind, once and for all?"

"I can imagine worse scenarios." He touched the rip in the Homer painting and shook his head sadly.

"And vampire-on-human sexual assault? That's okay with you, too?"

"It's exceedingly rare," Adler admitted. "For good reason. I can't imagine why any of the *nosferatu* would want to commit such an abomination. Sometimes I think it's bad enough that we have to get close to them in order to feed."

Dane wanted to hurl the old bloodsucker against a few more walls. "So you're intentionally covering for him."

"*You* are an unknown in all of this. You say your motives are pure, what's 'best for our kind.' But many disagree with that approach, and although some of us have heard of you, Dane, none of us *know* you. Why ever should we give up our secrets to you?"

"Okay, here's the other part," Dane said. "After we fought the Headsman's muscle, we were attacked. UV lights, automatic weapons, a regular military-style assault force."

"And yet, here you are."

"I am, as you might say, an exceedingly lucky man."

"So it would appear." Adler, having picked up all the fallen silver, set to organizing it with the fervor of an obsessive-compulsive. "However, I agree that what you describe is worrisome in the extreme. UV lights? Armed for us, then?"

"Exactly," Dane said. "There's something going on here and I want to know what it is." He saw Adler cast another worried look at the Homer. "Over the fireplace, the portrait, that's John Singer Sargent, right?"

"You have an educated eye."

"Plenty of spare time. The Homer can be repaired, restored, almost to new. I can make sure the Sargent can't be if you don't tell me what I need to know. Then maybe I'll go to work slashing the upholstery on some of these antique chairs. Georgian, right?"

Adler looked horrified. "You wouldn't."

"It's either that or I tear your head off and leave the rest of you in the yard for sunrise." Dane started toward the Sargent.

"Wait!" Adler said. "Sit . . . I'll tell you what I know."

Dane stopped, picked one of the antique chairs, and parked himself in it. Adler came out from behind the love seat and sat down on it, crossing his legs. He clasped his hands together on his lap, prim as a schoolmarm.

"I'm waiting," Dane said.

"I'm trying to decide how to begin," Adler replied. "It isn't something any of us talk about much. It would be like living in Sicily, I suppose, and being asked questions about the *capo di tutti capi.*"

"So now you're telling me we live under mob rule."

"It was a simile, Dane, that's all. No, we are under no one's rule. But yes, I'd be lying if I said we weren't a little . . . *afraid* of him. More than we are of you, or at least until you came in here like a barbarian and began threatening works of surpassing beauty."

"I'm as in favor of beauty as the next person. But I'm also in favor of keeping my skin."

"As are we all." Adler paused, looking at his own hands. Dane gave him a minute to collect his thoughts, but he was ready to get up and go after the artwork if Adler stalled any more than that.

"He is powerful," Adler finally said. "He is frightening, as well. I do believe that he's quite mad. And he doesn't care what any of us have to say." Adler now had a faraway look and was silent again for a moment before continuing. "He wants to do . . . what he wants to do. I'm certain that your arguments would fall on deaf ears—he's the kind of fellow who would love nothing more than all-out war with the humans. He's convinced that our kind would win, and then we could raise humans like farmers do cows. Dinner on the hoof. Only without the hooves."

"Who is he? What's his name?"

Adler glanced away again, and when he spoke, it was too soft for Dane to hear.

"What?"

"Bork. Dela," Adler said, louder but with a tremor in his voice.

"Bork Dela."

Dane knew the name. His reputation preceded him. What he hadn't known was that Bork Dela was still among the undead—it had been years, it seemed, since he'd been reported anywhere.

Yet here he was, in Savannah. Apparently waging a one-man campaign to change the rules of engagement with the human world.

"You're sure about that? You're sure it's really him?"

"Absolutely," Adler said.

Now it was Dane's turn to be quiet. An antique clock ticktocked relentlessly in the background.

"From your silence," Adler said, "I take it you're aware of his reputation."

"I'm plenty aware, yes. I just didn't know he was in the United States."

"He prefers it that way. Half the *nosferatu* believe he's dead. The other half are afraid to wonder."

"It sounds like he's making some moves now. What's he been up to in the interim?"

"He was one of Vicente's bodyguards for a long while," Adler said. "Of course, he didn't go to Barrow with the exalted one, or I'm sure Vicente would still be with us."

Dane knew that Vicente had died in Barrow, killed by Stella Olemaun's husband Eben after the sheriff had turned himself in order to defend his town. That much was now common vampire lore, but what few knew—what Dane only knew because Stella had told him—was that Dane's own maker, Marlow, had been killed by Vicente. Most of the undead believed that Eben Olemaun had killed them both.

For all the hell Marlow had put Dane through, all the trouble and pain, Dane had loved him regardless.

Vicente had killed Marlow, so Dane didn't worship Vicente's memory the way most vampires did. Vicente had been the closest the undead world had to a regent, but he was short-tempered and bloodthirsty, and Dane believed they were just as well off without him.

"And now Bork Dela's here, threatening to expose us all," Dane said. "And you thought you'd just go ahead and let him."

"Dane, there's a deep philosophical divide between our kind. We don't all think that would be the tragedy you do."

"I don't see you joining him on his home invasions. Or do you? Maybe you take his sloppy seconds."

Adler waved a hand in front of his nose as if to ward off an unpleasant stench. "Hardly. I have no love for Bork Dela. Like I said, he's completely mad. But neither do I want to make an enemy of him. However, it appears that you do, in which case, I would advise you to get your affairs in order."

Dane rose from the chair, glad he wouldn't have to destroy it after all. "I'll take my chances," he said. "What does Dela have to do with the military assault I told you about?"

"I have no idea at all," Adler said. "I would guess nothing. It's certainly not his style, and it hasn't happened to anyone else."

"Has anyone else crossed him?"

"A few unfortunates. Bork dealt with them personally. He's not the type to send subordinates to do his killing."

"But he travels with guards."

"Yes, when he doesn't want to be interrupted at his business. It's not the same. They're undead as well. They don't use weapons like UV lights."

Dane had thought that was a strange choice for vampires anyway—most of them wouldn't want to be on the same continent with such weapons. "Okay," he said. "I can buy that. Where can I find Dela?"

Adler pursed his lips. "Surely you can't expect me to tell you that," he said after a long moment.

"Surely you'd like to keep the Sargent intact."

"Very well," Adler said, sighing. "Once a barbarian, always one, I suppose. There's an island, called Braddock Key on the maps that bother to show it. It's out past Harvey Island and Raccoon Key. It's uninhabited, officially, although there's an antebellum mansion out there from the days when it was believed that with enough slaves one could make any place inhabitable. That's where he stays."

"Braddock Key."

"I tell you this only because I know you'll never survive an attempt to find him there. You're a tough one,

Dane. You've demonstrated that. But *he* is Bork Dela, and he's not all alone."

"What makes you think I am?"

"Unless I've completely misread you, I don't think you're the sort to involve others in a suicide mission."

"If I find out you've warned him," Dane said, knowing that he would need at least a day to arrange the trip out there, "you'll wish *you* had committed suicide a long time ago. Are we clear about that?"

"Perfectly clear," Adler said. "Have no worries on that score. I am not at all interested in telling Bork Dela that I gave him up to you. I still think you're on a fool's errand, young Dane. But I wouldn't want to bet my life on it."

II

"YOU OKAY in there, Ana?"

She didn't answer for a second. Ananu had been in AJ's bathroom, vomiting for the past several minutes. The place was small enough that there was no avoiding the sound of her retching. He was starting to feel a little sick from listening to her.

"I'm okay," she croaked at last. The toilet flushed, then Mitch heard running water. More long seconds passed before the bathroom door swung open. Ana stood there in the white undershirt and cotton boxers he had found for her in AJ's dresser. During the day Mitch had bought her some jeans and a couple of T-shirts, underwear and socks, and even some Day-Glo orange sneakers that reminded him of traffic cones but that he thought she would like. He had forgotten about nightclothes, though. Ana was less than half his age, younger even than Karin would have been if she had lived, and he felt strange about watching the way her breasts jiggled beneath the undershirt, her nipples poking tents in the fabric where there had never been tents before.

Especially since she was ill and had gotten a few flecks of vomit on the right sleeve. Her face looked greenish, which might have been from the fluorescent light fixture mounted over the sink in the bathroom. But that was behind her; most of the light falling on her now was from an incandescent bulb in the hall.

"You don't look okay."

"Well, I'm puking my guts out. How you think I should look, like Beyoncé?"

Mitch rubbed a hand through his short hair. "I don't know who that is. . . . She's a singer, right?"

Ana wiped her mouth with the back of her hand and looked at him like he had grown arms sticking out of his head. "Right."

"If she wasn't one of the Ronettes I probably haven't heard of her," Mitch said. "Musically I got stuck in the fifties and never quite made it past 1967. Any story you can't tell with three chords and some sweet harmonies isn't worth telling. Back that up with a wall of sound and you got an epic novel, way I see it."

"I guess that's why you got all that vinyl and no CDs."

While Mitch had been shopping, Dane had told Ana about Mitch's apartment on Congress Street, including the Wall o' Vinyl in his living room he had described to Dane. If whoever had attacked them at the warehouse messed with his record collection, he would be forced to kick some serious ass. "I try to live a simple life."

"Simpleminded, more like."

"Look, do I need to call you a doctor or anything?"

"I don't know, okay? I'm sick. I think maybe it's that Plan B you got me doing its thing. Least that's what I'm hoping because I don't want to have the flu on top of everything else."

"Let's hope you don't, because there's not enough room in this house for both of us and your germs, too."

What passed for a hallway was no bigger than his apartment's walk-in closet. Besides the bathroom and the bedroom Ana used, a third door hid a linen closet. An open doorway led into the living and dining area, with a small kitchen on the far side of that. From the kitchen, a door opened into the backyard, which was so overgrown it looked like jungle. Having been here before, Mitch hadn't expected luxury, but he hoped the girl wasn't too disappointed with the accommodations.

Ana took a half step forward, then her eyes fluttered and she started to pitch toward him, catching herself on the doorjamb just as Mitch put his hands out to break her fall. She blinked twice and gave him a lopsided grin. "I guess I better get back in bed."

"You want some water or anything?"

"A glass of water would be good, thanks," she said. She swiveled and headed into the bedroom. Mitch went to the kitchen, drew a tall glass of water. When he got back to the bedroom with it, Ana was in bed, breathing steadily. Sound asleep. Mitch put the water on the nightstand crowded in beside the bed and returned to his own place on the couch.

He lay on the couch with a sheet pulled up to his chest, wishing AJ wasn't such a cheap bastard that he wouldn't spring for central air. How much could it cost to cool a shoebox like this? He had known humid summer days in Detroit, but nothing like this. The low country seemed its own special kind of hell. He wished for a moment that he could've just gone back to Detroit after his first summer here, but that mistake on the job there had sent him south for his health. He couldn't go back.

Now a mistake on the job here had cost him almost everything else he had left in life.

His chest itched from the heat and humidity and the couch had a spring sticking in his kidney and people had tried to kill him. *Every time you think you've hit rock bottom . . .*

Somewhere the high-pitched whine of a mosquito sounded, but he couldn't locate the little bastard. He figured he'd have to wait until it landed on him, then he could swat it, hopefully before it bit him.

Is that what Dane's like? he wondered. Moving from one victim to the next, drinking blood, never tasting fresh seafood or pasta or Kung Pao chicken? Mosquitoes, with rare exceptions, didn't kill their victims. Mitch guessed Dane was more like a shark, a relentless death machine that very few survived.

Still . . . despite what Dane was, as fantastic and terrifying a person, Mitch had never felt threatened by him for one second. He had come to truly believe that Dane was a vampire—reluctantly, but finally he hadn't seen any other possible explanation for the things Dane showed and told him. *What did they call that? Occam's razor. Yeah, that's it.* The simplest explanation was always the right one, no matter how crazy it seemed.

He thought that Ana was safe under Dane's protection, as well. Safe as she'd be anywhere. Mitch had both Mossbergs loaded, one standing next to the couch and the other by the front door, ready to grab at the slightest hint of trouble. He would do what he could, but somehow he thought if things got really bad, he would want Dane at his side.

The guy might be a monster, but sometimes you need a monster around.

He heard the mosquito again, swatted at empty air, and silently prayed for Dane to get back as soon as he could.

Bork Dela.

Nothing Dane had ever heard about him made him want to take the vampire on.

Dela was, as far as he could tell, absolutely bloodthirsty, even for the undead. He didn't kill just to live, he *thrived* on it, making a hobby of death.

He liked to see how long he could stretch it out, the stories said. Or how painful he could make it. Some said he would put off his own feeding if it meant he could watch a human suffer that much longer.

Vampires had enough bad press without specimens like him around.

The first time Dane remembered becoming aware of Bork Dela had been during the Second World War. Dela had been a man then, not a vampire. A Romanian, he had somehow nonetheless gained Hitler's trust and had become one of the mad dictator's closest advisers.

The rumor was that Bork Dela had been the one who introduced the Führer to the world of the occult, to which Hitler had taken immediately. Hitler had devoted considerable resources, most notably his SS, to pursuing supernatural knowledge. Bork Dela had also continued working in that direction, somehow coming to the attention—probably through his own investigation—of the vampire community. Once turned, Bork Dela had gone right back to work at Hitler's side, disappearing after the Nazi leader's suicide.

Another rumor was that Hitler hadn't been a suicide at all, but that Dela, recognizing the reality of the situation, had killed his own patron and fed on his blood. From everything Dane had heard about Dela, he had no trouble believing it. Bork Dela could have had the blood of every insane megalomaniac in history running in his veins.

Dane obviously didn't object to the idea that something needed to be done about the Dela situation here in Savannah. It could only be good for their species as a whole. But Dela was tough, almost impossible to kill.

If it had to be Bork Dela, then so be it, and damn the consequences. Dane had faced difficult challenges before and had always come out okay.

If one considered remaining a virtually immortal bloodsucker to be okay.

Some nights, Dane had his doubts. So far, he had always managed to put them aside and keep going.

Driving AJ's truck back to Pooler along country roads so dark, the stars blotted out by cloud cover, he might have been the only sentient being for a hundred miles. The dark had always been the natural refuge of his kind, a country the human world could visit but never really know.

The last time Dane had stood in the sun had been in the spring of 1859.

The slavery issue was drawing to a head, but New York was largely in the abolition camp. That day had been one of those first warm sunny days that came after you started to think winter would never end, then suddenly you were peeling off your coat outside before you even realized that you weren't freezing anymore.

He had been walking home from work—he was a carpenter by trade, a journeyman, building cabinets for a fine new house in Harlem—and had come across what looked at first like a parade blocking Broadway. Holding his coat over his shoulder, he stopped to see what the commotion was, and realized from the signs and slogans that it was a pro-slavery demonstration. There must have been three hundred people. He wove through the crowd, anxious to see what sorts of New Yorkers believed it was a good idea to buy and sell fellow human beings simply because they had been born with dark skin and had come from Africa instead of Europe. He couldn't understand that, had been convinced that it was the sole province of ignorant Southerners, and that in such a sophisticated place as New York City it could not possibly gain a foothold.

And yet, there they were, three hundred New Yorkers marching down Broadway on a late spring afternoon with the sun slanting between the buildings at them. Dane had to take a second look when he realized that he recognized some of the marchers.

Herman Koslowski, the master carpenter to whom he had been apprenticed, the big Pole who had taught him how to find the heart of a piece of wood, how to shape it and sculpt it and join it to its fellows in order to make anything from the smallest box to the biggest mansion.

Deila Carmony, who had lived in the house next door to his parents since he'd been ten. Now thirty-two, Dane had his own place but he still saw Deila Carmony nearly once a week.

Dane shook his head in astonishment. People he had called friends, marching in support of slavery. He felt like someone had punched him in the gut with a fist weighted down with pennies. Maybe if he talked to them, to Herman and Deila (her hair white, her face lined and small, as if it had collapsed over these last few years), then he could explain to them why they were wrong. Maybe there was just something they didn't understand.

But they had already passed him by. He started after them. The crowd of people watching had grown thicker—most of them opposed to slavery, catcalling, hurling profanities at the marchers—and he couldn't work his way through as easily as he had before. By the time he reached the front rank of spectators, the parade had moved on. Dane started following it, wanting to catch up to his friends.

It didn't occur to him that to the onlookers, he might appear to be just another of the pro-slavery contingent, a little on the slow side but still dedicated enough to march down Broadway.

After three blocks, that false impression was made abundantly clear.

A big man with fists the size of hams broke from the crowd as Dane passed. He muttered something Dane didn't understand in a thick Irish accent, and when Dane didn't react appropriately, one of those massive fists caught Dane on the cheekbone, just beneath the eye. Dane's head snapped back, flashes of colored light, like fireworks, exploding in his vision. The guy followed up with a left to Dane's other cheek, and Dane's feet flopped out from beneath him, his knees turning to noodles. By the time he hit the ground, the man had moved back into the crowd. A couple of other people, braver now that the big Irishman had put him down, came out of the crowd, kicking him. One woman, older even than Deila Carmony, spat a thick gob of phlegm in his face and called him a word he didn't think old women knew.

As quickly as he could, Dane got to his feet and ran the other way, back up Broadway, away from the marchers. When he got to a place where the people hadn't seen him, he struck into the crowd, then through it and onto a side street. The sun had finished setting, the spring sky purple and blue—like, he guessed, his eye would be soon.

As gas lamps were lit, he wandered the streets, running through the events of the last forty minutes or so, wondering where he had gone wrong.

How could this happen to him, on the streets of his own city? How could his friends make such a mistake, and how could perfect strangers simply believe he had made the same one and lash out like they had? Were there any sane people left in the world?

He had been walking with his head down, hands jammed into his coat pockets, more intent on the questions raging in his head than on where he was going. At about the point that he realized he didn't know where he was, he noticed a man walking by himself on the other side of a narrow road.

"Excuse me, sir," Dane said. "I seem to have wandered onto unfamiliar territory. Can you direct me toward Broadway?"

The man stopped and gazed across the road at Dane.

He was a singularly unpleasant looking fellow, at least as far as Dane could determine. A slouch hat shadowed some of his face, but the light that did reach him, from the gas lamps overhead, revealed a stout man with heavy jowls, narrow lips, a slightly bulbous nose. His flesh was as pale as the thin crescent of moon that floated low in the night sky. His eyes—what Dane could see of them—appeared black and lifeless.

"Broadway, hmm?" he said after regarding Dane for several seconds. "Yes, yes, I suppose I could."

The stranger started across the road. Dane could hear him perfectly well from where he was. Some primal aspect of Dane rather preferred the man at a distance, and the closer he came, the more Dane wanted him to stay away.

One didn't chase an elder off, though, especially when the other had offered to help. The man stopped a foot or so from Dane, pursing his lips as though thinking over a matter of some complexity. "Broadway, you said."

"That's right," Dane answered, beginning to think he'd made a bad mistake asking this particular man for assistance. A strange odor wafted over him, like meat left unsalted for too long. "But I'm sure I can find it, if—"

"Nonsense," the man interrupted. "It's just . . ." He raised his left hand to point down the road, and his right as if to draw Dane nearer, taking him by the shoulder to make sure he had the correct angle of view to see something.

Politeness pulled Dane into the fellow's partial embrace. He cringed to feel the man's gnarled, clawlike hand on his shoulder, through his jacket. The spoiled meat aroma grew worse. " . . . just down here," the man continued. "A few blocks this way, and then turn left, and . . ."

Dane felt the man's hot breath on his neck. He was about to twist from the man's grasp with a few well-chosen words when the hand on his shoulder dug in harder, fingers punching through fabric and flesh alike. Dane screamed, tried to wrench away. The man dragged him closer, his other hand catching Dane's throat. Dane lashed out with his fists but his blows had no effect. He might as well have been hitting a tree or a wall.

Then the man used something—a claw, a hidden knife, Dane couldn't see what—to slash Dane's throat. As the world went dark, Dane saw blood fountain from beneath his chin and heard its liquid splash against the cobblestones.

When Dane finally came to, his eyeslids scraped as if someone had plastered them with dry sand.

He had been taken inside someplace—he saw bare stone walls and a hammered tin ceiling. He felt strange, his entire body aching and as weak as a newborn. Before Dane could even try to rise up, the man from the street loomed into his field of view. The hat was gone now and Dane saw the man's bald head, round as a cannonball. He was no more handsome than he had been before.

"Welcome back," the man said. "You'll have a lot of questions, I imagine. I'll do the best I can to answer them and to help you find your way in this new world."

"New world . . . ?" Dane echoed, unable to force any more than that out.

"You'll see, soon enough," the man said. He tried on a smile that came off as a pained grimace. "My name is Marlow. And you, my son . . . shall live forever."

12

"WE NEED A BOAT."

Mitch lurched upright on the couch, snatching up the shotgun standing beside him but knocking its stock into a table, upsetting a water glass. "Shit!" he snapped. "Is that you, Dane?"

"If it wasn't, odds are you'd be dead already."

"Sorry. I guess I drifted off."

"It's been a long few days," Dane said. He closed the front door behind him and sat down on a fake leather chair. "No harm done, I suppose. How's Ananu?"

Mitch shook off the sheet covering him and put the shotgun back down. Swinging around, he set his feet firmly on the ground and then leaned his elbows on his knees, cradling his forehead. "Not good, Dane. She's sick or something. She's been waking up and getting sick, puking all night."

"Maybe the medicine she took."

"That's what she thought," Mitch said. "I don't know." He straightened, catching Dane's eye. "I had a kid once, Dane. She died a long time ago. But I've never forgotten what it was like when Marie was pregnant. During the first trimester, she looked just like Ana, seemed like almost every morning. Kind of green around the gills, you know?"

"So what, you think she was already pregnant? If it was that, she wouldn't be showing symptoms this fast."

"She said she doesn't have a boyfriend or anything."

"She got very upset about it back at the warehouse, saying she couldn't afford to get pregnant, and I had the sense that she wasn't already."

"I could be wrong."

"You could be. Or she might not have known. She's asleep now?"

"Unless I woke her up when you came in." Mitch straightened up the glass that had fallen over, which had been almost empty. "In which case she's sitting there listening to all this, 'cause AJ's place ain't big enough for privacy."

Dane rose, crossed over to the abbreviated hallway and listened outside her room. Her breathing sounded regular and deep. The strange way she smelled—the scent he had tracked across town—had intensified.

He decided not to wake her yet and returned to the chair. "What was that about a boat?" Mitch asked him.

"You know a place called Braddock Key?"

Mitch considered briefly. "Nope."

"How about Raccoon Key? Harvey Island?"

"I think I've heard of them. Then again, I don't really get offshore much."

"I need to get to Braddock Key. I've been told that's where the Headsman is. Do you know anyone who has a boat we can borrow?"

Mitch cracked a smile. "I almost hate to say it."

"Really. AJ has a boat?"

"He's happiest when he's out on the water. That's why he lives in this dump—it's cheap and he puts most of his dough into his boat."

"We're going to owe him a rather large debt."

"He'll bitch a lot, but I think he's kinda liking all this. Driving a cab isn't the most exciting gig on the planet, you know? So even though we haven't really told him what's going on, I think he's getting a kick out of helping us just the same."

"I want to go out there this evening," Dane said. It was already past 3 AM. "We can stay here during the day, get everything organized. But as soon as possible after the sun goes down I need to get out there, before anyone can warn him I'm coming."

"You find out who the Headsman is?"

"Yes, I found out," Dane said. "Why don't you go back to sleep, Mitch? I'll stand watch until morning, then you can cover while I get some rest."

"That sounds good." Mitch bit back a yawn and immediately put his feet up.

Dane sat in the chair while Mitch's breathing settled into a comfortable rhythm. The crickets outside quieted as dawn approached, but their strident racket was replaced by birdcalls. Just as the gray light of morning began to show through the front window, Ananu got up and went into the bathroom. Dane listened for any sign that she was sick, but he just heard her pee and then flush the toilet. The sink ran for a minute. Another minute passed and then the door opened and she came into the living room. Her hair was mashed down from sleep and her eyes were hooded, as if she could use a few more hours, but she gave Dane a wan smile. The chipped tooth in front added charm and vulnerability to her appearance, he thought—without it she might come across as aloof, unapproachable.

"Are you feeling okay?" he asked.

"I don't know. I feel weird. My stomach is really upset. And, I don't know, I'm a little dizzy, lightheaded."

"Like you have the flu?"

"I don't think so. I don't have the muscle aches, or a fever."

Well, that's that then, isn't it? Dane glanced at Mitch, who stirred but remained asleep. He beckoned Ananu toward the kitchen. The counter tiles were yellow and the walls white and a window faced east, so the lightening sky brightened the room before it reached the rest of the house.

"Are you pregnant, Ananu?"

"I don't see how. I mean, before the other night."

"You haven't been with anyone recently?"

"I don't really go out very much," she said. "Mrs. Way-lons, her health hasn't been good. She needs me around most nights. Needed."

"You're certain."

She showed him a tight-lipped smile. "When you don't have much of a life, you keep track of what you do have."

"You're a very bright and attractive young woman, Ananu. I have a hard time believing you don't get out more."

"Sorry to disappoint you," she said. "Mrs. Waylons paid good money. I figured I could set some aside, then after a couple of years maybe go back to school, finish my education, right?"

"That makes sense to me, I guess."

"Glad to hear you approve."

"What I approve of has nothing to do with it. I'm just trying to figure out what the situation is."

"The situation is that you think I'm knocked up and I'm starting to think maybe you're right. I know I've never felt like this before. I just don't get how it could happen."

"There's generally just the one way," Dane said.

He hesitated. There *was* a variation on that way—so rare as to be almost unthinkable.

While Ananu dressed and Mitch roused and started breakfast for the two of them who hadn't fed during the night, Dane sat in the fake leather chair and stared out the front window, the ramifications of what was happening to Ananu sinking in and taking hold.

Like the human world, the vampire world had its own myths and legends. Some of these stories were rooted in fact; others were imagined and spread because they carried some instructive lesson or moral.

Garlic, for instance—vampires were said to be afraid of garlic. The truth was that garlic tended to grow best in sunny, warm climates. By warning against garlic, vampires really meant to avoid the sun.

Another story Dane had heard involved vampires and human pregnancy.

It shouldn't be possible. Vampires were dead, after all, and the dead didn't procreate. Not that way. They propagated their species by turning humans, through feeding and sharing fluids but taking care not to destroy their victims. Basic copulation seemed a throwback, a return to the humanity they were so thrilled to have left behind. And why would a vampire ever choose to fraternize in that way with a lesser being?

Dane had fraternized himself, a time or two. But he didn't necessarily share the opinion that all vampires were superior to all humans. There were jerks and assholes in both camps, and extraordinary individuals, too, if you looked hard enough.

Don't look too hard, Dane, he thought. *Extraordinary individuals like Stella Olemaun, perhaps?*

Better not to think of that now.

Somehow, the old wives' tales survived. Marlow told a couple, and just about every ancient vampire Dane had met seemed to know others. No two were precisely the same, and Dane had never bothered to track them, as an anthropologist might, to some common root. He just assumed they were all a load of crap.

The only common element all the stories shared, besides the basic setup, was the conclusion. In each of the pregnancy stories Dane had heard, however the union happened to take place, the end result was that a baby was born. Knowing that any such infant would be hopelessly tainted with human blood, the baby was beheaded at birth (or, in a few instances, staked out for the rising sun to incinerate).

So, Dane wondered, what would it mean if Bork Dela had impregnated Ananu, but then had his prize snatched away before the pregnancy could come to term?

And even if vampire-human pregnancy was impossible, when Bork Dela was involved, who knew what could happen? Dela had studied the supernatural for decades—he might well have come across arcane and forbidden secrets no one else knew.

Could he really have planted his seed in Ananu? And if so, could it already be manifesting itself? The answer to both questions would seem to be no.

But when the vampire in question was Bork Dela, it didn't pay to be too certain of anything.

Dane would have to keep a careful eye on Ananu, just in case.

Still, for now he had to get to Braddock Key. Bork Dela had outstayed his welcome. And like it or not, for all their sakes, it looked as if it were up to Dane to deal with it.

13

AJ'S BOAT WAS a 1987 Sea Ray Weekender with *Midlife Crisis* painted on the stern. AJ wouldn't loan it to them, no way, but he said he'd pilot them anywhere they needed to go.

He wasn't anxious to stick around Savannah anyway because, he said, a couple of stiff-necked mutts in suits had called for his services, then when he had arrived, all they'd wanted to do was ask him questions about the dents in the rear of his cab and if he had been down near the waterfront the other night. He was pretty sure he'd convinced them that they were barking up the wrong tree, but just the same if he had to spend a couple of days at sea, it wouldn't entirely be a bad thing.

Anyway, he was proud of the vessel, telling Dane and Ananu about its 255-horsepower Mercruiser engine and fiberglass/composite hull, and throwing in other details Dane wouldn't retain for more than a few minutes. Belowdecks were a little galley with a dinette table, a head, and a V-berth with a good-sized bed. Ananu spent most of the journey there, in close proximity to the head, because between her upset stomach and the motion of the waves, she had relapsed badly.

After AJ told them about his interrogation, though, Dane wasn't about to let anyone stay in AJ's house for another night. If they had found his taxi, they could find his house, and he didn't want another run-in with UV lights and automatic weapons. If he actually found Bork Dela it would be no picnic, but Dane hoped he would be easier to deal with than whoever was after them.

They boarded the boat at the Fountain Marina across the street. AJ took the wheel and guided the vessel deftly out of the marina and into the Wilmington River. To their port side they passed Whitemarsh Island, then turned hard to starboard and down the Skidaway River, between Dutch Island and Isle of Hope and Pigeon Island on their starboard side and the huge Wassaw Island on their port. Below Pigeon Island, the Skidaway merged with Moon River, then in quick succession the Burnside, the Vernon, and the Green. This would take them just north of Harvey Island, then Raccoon Key, and finally Braddock Key, according to AJ, who fished these waters whenever he could.

Mitch took control of the radio. Failing to find his favorite oldies station, he settled on classic rock. Dane sat back and felt the back-and-forth motion of the boat and listened to Neil Young singing to an old man, telling him that he was a lot like the old man was. Dane's thoughts inevitably turned to Marlow again.

Marlow was a bastard, no question about that.
He was vicious even when he didn't have to be. He be-

lieved the lowliest vampire to be superior to the human filth in every way, and himself to be superior to every other vampire. Perhaps Vicente and Lilith were the exception to that hierarchy, but there were times when Dane wasn't so sure.

During his lifetime, he had been Roderick Marlow, a small-time criminal, a thug with delusions of grandeur. Once he was turned, the first thing he did was to kill the man who had run the gang he worked for—even though at that point he couldn't advance up the ranks, he still wanted to take revenge on the individual who had held power over him. Marlow made himself an important figure in the world of the undead, following the example set for him by the man he had so detested in life.

As a teacher, Marlow was a complete disaster.

He filled Dane's head with a mixture of fact and fiction, leaving it up to Dane to discern—sometimes with painful consequences—between the two. When Dane asked questions that displeased him, even for reasons Dane could never fathom, Marlow was quick to administer harsh beatings in place of answers.

One of the worst of these came in 1863, during the War Between the States.

Traveling by night, living in the shadows, knowing that to be seen by armed soldiers meant almost certain destruction, they cut a swath south and east across a nation ravaged by combat. Marlow claimed his purpose was to demonstrate to Dane just how horribly people treated one another, as a means of impressing upon him that showing them any mercy was pointless, because the quick death a vampire offered was actually more merciful than allowing the humans to live out their own lives.

They wound up at Vicksburg, Mississippi, days after an extended campaign by General Grant resulted in the Confederate surrender of the city. Vicksburg and its environs had been the site of battle after battle, and the city had been shelled almost to rubble. Now, as summer's heat settled on the region, came the aftermath, the cleanup. Mass burials took place. Church bells, at least in the places where churches still stood, tolled for hours on end.

And across the battlefields, trawling among the dead and dying, were the vampires.

Every battlefield attracted scavengers, Dane had learned. Vultures, wild dogs, rats, and other creatures were naturally drawn to the carcasses of men. Other humans crept from corpse to corpse, stealing currency, boots, and weapons.

But the vampires, desperate for easy pickings, went to the recently dead and the near dead, drinking their fill of blood. Too lazy to even bother hunting, Marlow said. Every war in human history had known them. These vampires, oversated, lolled around the battlefields and the homes of the dead until the rising of the sun made them scramble for cover. To Dane they were as worthless as mosquitoes, not deserving his sympathy or appreciation. If he had to be a vampire, he told Marlow, he at least wanted to do it in a way that demonstrated courage and dignity.

Standing at the edge of the Vicksburg Canal, where dozens of riverboats had been moored to provide shelter for those whose homes had been destroyed in the shelling, Marlow turned on Dane in a sudden rage. He carried a cane in those days—an affectation, as he didn't need it to walk—and with it he beat Dane savagely. Dane fell to the ground and Marlow kept up the assault, lashing out with one vicious strike after another. When he decided he was done, Marlow stopped with no more notice than he had started and reached down to help Dane back to his feet.

"Sometimes I just don't know how to reach you, Dane," he said, a small smile on his face. "You keep acting as if human traits are somehow still worthy of emulation. Courage, dignity, mercy—those words have no meaning for us anymore. They are ideas we left behind with our mortality, and well that we did. You are now of the *nosferatu,* Dane. You hunt. You feed. You kill. Trying to cling to the old ways does you no good. Of course, from time to time, if you see an exceptional specimen, you might choose to turn him or her, as I did you, to continue advancing our species with the best it can offer. But the time is nigh that you gave up trying to cling to a humanity that you are no longer part of."

And from that day forward, Dane had never turned a single human.

He killed only when he had to, in order to survive. He could not bring himself to think of humans as livestock. He could not shake his respect for the accomplishments of humanity: the great books, the philosophies, the scientific achievements, the ideals of freedom and democracy that had remade the social landscape of the planet since his birth in the first quarter of the nineteenth century.

Despite Marlow's beatings, he could never agree that every vampire, even those mosquitoes scavenging the dead, was more worthy than every mortal.

The dispute would lead to greater confrontations, in the years to come.

"Dane."

Dane realized he had been drifting in his past instead of paying attention to the present. Mitch stood before him on AJ's boat. "We're here," he said. "Or close enough, anyway. Braddock Key."

"Let's not get too close," Dane said, refocusing. "If Dela is here, I don't want him to sense Ananu nearby. I can go in on a raft if AJ has one, or swim if I need to."

"I've got a nine-foot Zodiac inflatable with an outboard," AJ said. "It's all inflated and ready for you."

"Perfect," Dane said. He rose from his seat and stretched. He'd been thinking about ancient history when he should have been figuring out just how he would go about facing Bork Dela. He supposed he would have to deal with that question when he got onto the island. "AJ, do you know anything about Braddock Key?"

"It barely qualifies as an island," AJ said. "At high tide almost half of it's underwater. A guy named Clayton Bowdoin built himself a mansion on it once, apparently as part of a plan to create a plantation there. Had slave quarters, docks, the whole bit. But even with the slave labor, he couldn't make a go of it out there. Hard to grow anything when your crops are submerged half the time. He tried bringing in boatloads of soil, hoping to build up the thickness of the key, but that never worked, either. Finally he killed himself, or so they say. Other people claim the slaves rebelled and murdered him in his bed. The house still stands, but it's haunted. That's the rumor anyway. People tend to keep away from it, though, so maybe there's something to it."

"You think the docks are still there?"

"They were last I checked, but man, that was probably seven, eight years ago. And 'still there' don't necessarily mean functional, right?"

"I just wondered if I'd be able to tie up the boat there."

"Yeah, probably. There'll be pilings at least. You might get a little wet between there and the house."

"That's not a problem."

AJ had cut the boat's lights and chugged on toward Braddock Key by the light of moon and stars. When he declared that they had come as close as they dared, Dane looked but could only see the island as a smudge of black against the dark water and starry night sky.

He went down to the berth to say good-bye to Ananu. She was awake, still not feeling well, and he left her more convinced than ever about her situation. On deck, AJ had unlashed the Zodiac from its place on the bow and tossed it into the waves. Dane promised to send some kind of signal when it was safe for Mitch and AJ to come ashore, or to get himself back to shore on the Zodiac if necessary.

When he was on the open sea with the motor humming, one hand on the till, Dane was able to relax and stop pretending to be a human. Mitch knew his real nature, but he hadn't yet revealed it to Ananu or AJ. Keeping up the illusion was draining, to say the least.

Fortunately he wouldn't need it with Bork Dela.

But what *would* he need? That was still a mystery. As the little boat skimmed the tops of the waves and the island hove into view, tall palms cutting silhouettes against the stars, the stab of fear hit him again, and he knew he would find out soon enough.

14

AJ'S DESCRIPTION of the docks proved accurate. Even after so many years and the wet, humid conditions, a few planks of rotted wood jutted out from the shore. They didn't come close to reaching the pilings, some of which rose from the water a dozen feet or more from the rushes indicating land's edge. Detached pilings swayed in the gentle waves like blades of grass being pushed by an intermittent breeze.

Dane had cut the engine as soon as the island's outline became clear to him, and rowed in the rest of the way. The current pushed him toward the pilings, and he switched from rowing to using the oar to keep himself from being dashed into the ancient wood. He worked his way to the only sturdy-looking one near shore and tied the Zodiac there, stowing the oar carefully.

Climbing from the boat, he waded a few feet through cool knee-high water. At the shoreline, saw grass spiked out toward the water, knife edges slashing at him as he shoved through them. The growth here was jungle thick and he pushed through vines, tangled kudzu, and more as he made his way inland, looking for any hint of the house AJ had told him about. The fetid, rich smells of fertile soil and abundant growth quickly overwhelmed the acrid, salty tang of the sea.

He stumbled upon a path beaten down by foot traffic over long years, with tall grasses lining it on either side. Working his way up it, away from the shore and toward where he hoped the house would be, he soon heard voices speaking in hushed tones. He couldn't make out the words, just the murmur of speech underneath the splash of waves and the wind rustling through the foliage. He stepped off the vestigial trail he had found and squatted behind some heavy brush.

A minute later their odor wafted to him.

Vampires. Looking for him? Probably—Bork Dela didn't strike Dane as someone who left security to chance.

Dane waited. When they came into view, he knew he had seen them before. One heavyset, thick faced, the other lean with long, greasy dark hair. These were the ones he had fought outside the warehouse where he and Mitch had found Ananu. He hadn't known who they served then, or what the warehouse concealed. If he had, he wouldn't have let them walk away.

But Dane knew better now.

When the two had reached the place where Dane hid—the thick-faced one sniffing the air, catching Dane's scent—he struck. "There he is!" the heavy one shouted as Dane lunged.

Dane reached for that one's face even as he turned toward his companion. The fingers of Dane's right hand dug into the flesh behind the vampire's jaw. In midstride,

Dane shifted his weight, aiming for the skinny one. The heavy vampire, reflexively trying to pull away, threw his weight in the opposite direction. Dane tugged the vampire's skin as he reached for the long-haired bloodsucker, and the heavy one gave a howl of agony.

Dane slammed his forehead into the thin one's chin, sending him reeling back. At the same moment, Dane turned to see the heavy one stumbling toward him, the left half of his face hanging in shreds, blood spilling onto his thick chest, muscle and bone gleaming in the moonlight.

Blinded by pain and blood, he swung a meaty arm at Dane but missed. Dane easily sidestepped his assault and closed on the other vampire. The long-haired one had recovered from Dane's surprise attack and charged at Dane with fangs bared. Dane met his charge, grabbing two fistfuls of greasy locks. Stepping back to use the other's momentum, he spun the vampire and yanked him off the path, slamming his head into a nearby tree.

Spanish moss draped a low-hanging branch. Still holding his hair with one hand, Dane reached up and snapped off the branch, close to the trunk, leaving about six inches remaining on the tree. The skinny vampire snarled and clawed at Dane's throat, but Dane kept him off balance by tugging on his hair. Finally, the vampire reared back, ripping the hair from his own head in order to free himself from Dane's grip. He was too late to save himself, though—Dane doubled his fists together and drove them into his ribs. When he bent forward in pain, Dane grabbed his head in both hands and plowed it into the jagged stub of branch he had left on the tree.

The vampire screamed and Dane freed his head, then repeated the process. He felt the vampire's skull give under his hands as the branch destroyed it from the other side, pushing through to Dane. The fight went out of the long-haired one. Dane left him hanging on the section of branch to focus on his stockier companion.

Still mostly blind, this bloodsucker lurched and stumbled toward Dane, arms flailing before him. As he hunted for his prey, a ghastly roar issued from his ruined mouth. He sucked a flap of loose skin in at the end of it and spat it out and roared again, a wordless, senseless sound of agonized frustration.

Dane almost felt sorry for him. He waved at the vampire's good eye and the bloodsucker saw him and swung his whole body around as if a pole ran up through him and he couldn't swivel at the waist or neck. Dane watched him take an unsteady step, two, and then he took the vampire's head in his hands, the fingers of his right sinking into the muscle, scraping bone, and he twisted.

The heavy vampire dropped to his knees, keening an unintelligible wail, like a mourner from ancient Babylon. Dane went around behind the guy and kept twisting, twisting, and the bloodsucker waved his arms helplessly. Liquid bubbled from his mouth and from a hole that had opened in his neck, hot and foul smelling, and then the bones in his neck snapped and muscle tore and the vampire went silent. Dane released him. The thick body flopped forward like a felled tree, the rank liquid streaming from both ends, only a few strings of skin and gristle holding the head to the body.

Dane wiped his hands off on some broad leaves, eager to cleanse himself of the foul gore.

If Dela doesn't know I'm here by now . . .

Fifteen minutes later, Dane saw the white house looming ahead of him, spectral in the silver moonlight.

Empty window frames gaped like eyeless sockets. Columns—Doric? Ionic? Dane couldn't remember— fronted the structure, but two had fallen over the years, tumbling forward and breaking into smaller cylindrical shapes, giving the whole thing the air of an ancient Greek ruin. Fittingly, a trio of bats flitted in front of the full moon.

Maybe it's not haunted, Dane thought. *On the other hand, it definitely looks that way from here.*

He approached it slowly, carefully. On the way up the path, Dane had encountered two more vampire sentries, quickly dispatched with a stout length of wood that he used as a club to smash their heads in. He fully expected more guards or other security measures here at the house.

Whether or not Bork Dela even used the house remained an open question.

Most vampires, in Dane's experience, appreciated creature comforts when they could get them. A roof and four walls to keep out the elements, furniture. And if Dela had, in fact, been kidnapping people for some reason, he would need someplace to hold them. The warehouse where they'd found Ananu might have been a commonly used transit point, but Dane had seen no evidence that it was a final destination.

Four steps, the middle two rotted through and caved in, led up to a wooden front door. The paint on the door had weathered mostly away, leaving just the ghost of the original white. Rust had tried to claim the hardware, but bending close, Dane could see indications of recent wear on the knob.

He stood back on sagging porch boards and took another moment to study his situation.

He smelled the air, catching whiffs of vampire activity, but if this doorway was commonly used, that would stay in the air, even seeping into the wood. He heard only the wind in the trees and, distantly now, the rumble of the surf.

Approaching the doorknob again, he stood to one side and reached over, giving it a twist. If anything came through the door, the exterior wall would protect him.

He hoped.

The knob turned easily in his hand.

He gave the door a gentle push and it swung open silently, on hinges that obviously saw plenty of use.

He waited a second, tasting the air that came through the doorway. It was a little mustier than that outside, but not much—hardly surprising since the windows had no glass in them.

When nothing happened, Dane risked peering inside.

The floor looked much as one would expect it to. It had been constructed of hardwood, which had weathered and rotted out in some spots. Leaves had blown in. Moss and even some weeds grew up through the holes, and one section of wall, near a staircase, had mushrooms growing through it, forming little fungal shelves.

In spite of the ease with which the door had opened, the house didn't look inhabited from here.

Bracing himself for anything, makeshift club at the ready, Dane stepped through the door.

The place had been a regular Southern mansion once, it seemed. Wallpaper had long since frayed and rotted away, but he could make out remnants of it on some walls. Furniture remained in place, most of it broken, eaten by termites, or simply too old to have survived. Dane passed from room to room, finding more of the same. Dining room, kitchen, pantry, parlor—none showed any signs of recent use. A spiderweb blocked the doorway to the parlor; the spider crouched near its center, almost as big across as Dane's hand. Holes had been gnawed at the baseboards, rodent droppings everywhere.

He returned to the foyer and looked up the staircase. It rose to a landing halfway up, then turned and continued out of sight. The faint moonlight through the open door and windows didn't illuminate anything above the landing.

Some of the stairs appeared rotten, but others seemed whole. Dane realized that one could climb the solid ones, stepping over the decayed ones without too much difficulty. He started up to the first good stair, putting his foot down close to the wall to minimize creaking. As he did, he heard a soft rustle from overhead. He froze, club raised.

The sound didn't repeat. A rat possibly, or the ghost of Clayton Bowdoin stirring. Even a branch blowing against the outside wall.

Or someone setting a trap.

No way to find out from here. Dane continued up the stairs.

When he reached the landing, he carefully tested the boards ahead of him. The first one he tried creaked loudly, so he stepped past that and tried the next.

He had just placed his toe on it when a voice called out, distant and plaintive. "Help, mister!" It sounded like a child's voice, but it had a weird, ethereal quality. "Help us!"

Us? Dane froze, listening for more.

Then another voice, this one louder, more intense. "Dane! Help!"

Ananu? He had left her on the boat—and the boat well offshore—specifically to keep her out of Dela's hands. How had he captured her again? Did he have Mitch and AJ, too?

"Ananu!" he shouted. "Where are you?"

"Dane!" she called again. She sounded somehow more distant this time. "Help me!" He couldn't tell if she had heard him at all.

He wanted to dash up the stairs and find her. But he

knew the steps couldn't all be trusted, and it wouldn't do either of them any good if he fell through or snapped a leg on the way.

Above the landing, moving into darkness—through which he and other vampires could see perfectly well—the air smelled fresher. Again, this made sense—the upstairs windows were broken, too, which would have created some cross ventilation, but more growth would have taken place below, closer to the ground and the tides.

Dane kept going, still hugging the wall, sniffing for Ananu.

As he neared the top he could see a long hallway, lined with doors. Some were open, moonlight filtering through windows into the hall. The rustling noise hadn't recurred. The house seemed empty—maybe not haunted, but not occupied either.

The first door on the left of the stairs was closed. Dane listened, then hearing nothing, he opened it.

Immediately inside was another door. This one was steel, like the door to a meat locker. Dane leaned his club against the doorjamb, worked the latches and swung it open.

The smell of blood rushed into his face. Fresh, rich, human blood—lots of it. Sudden hunger knotted Dane's stomach.

Inside, he saw that it was a meat locker, or something like one, which had been hidden in this old house. The floor must have been reinforced to support the steel room, almost the size of the original room it occupied.

The locker was vacant. Blood congealed in pools on the floor. Leather straps had been mounted on the walls, just at the right height to restrain people seated on the floor. Slots high in the back wall indicated a vent that allowed air circulation from outside. The unique aroma of Ananu was not present, and Dane hadn't heard her since the landing. He hadn't heard the kid again, either.

Apparently this was the place where the captives were held. Or one of them—for all he knew there were several rooms like this secreted on the property, or elsewhere on the island.

At a sound in the hallway, Dane whirled.

"You must be Dane."

The tall figure had a scar in the center of his forehead where a bullet had struck him, and his lower lip had been slashed through once. Still, he cut an imposing figure. Short blond hair was slicked back on his head. A black silk shirt, open to midchest, showed a muscular torso and broad shoulders. His eyes were a pale gray and without any warmth at all.

"I am Bork Dela. I've been expecting you."

15

"THE HEADSMAN, in the flesh," Dane replied. "I've been looking for you." Dane wasn't about to let on the surprise he felt about Dela already knowing who he was.

"You certainly didn't show up here by accident. I myself try to stay off the beaten path."

"You succeed admirably," Dane said. Since the voices hadn't recurred, he was convinced now that they had been a trick of Dela's, meant to freak him out. He didn't even want to give the vampire the satisfaction of knowing he had reached Dane. "But you've been making a nuisance of yourself in town. Created quite a stir with all of us."

"Is that why you've come to Savannah, Dane?"

"I'm astonished that you've heard of me."

"I make it a point to stay current. I understand the low country is pretty far from your usual stomping grounds."

"*You* were drawing unnecessary attention to us, to our kind."

No reaction. Dela merely stood in front of Dane, apparently unarmed. Dane knew he should do everything in his power to kill him right now. But something about the vampire's approach made him want to continue the conversation, to find out why Dela had been so blatant, so out there.

"So. Here I am," Dela said, as if reading Dane's mind. When Dane didn't respond, he continued. "I take it you . . . *disapprove* of my activities?"

"Of course," Dane said. "Not only were you killing indiscriminately and kidnapping for no apparent purpose, but you could have exposed us all."

At that, Dela laughed. His accent sounded only vaguely Continental, as if he had been living in the United States for decades. "Those philosophies you cling to, Dane. So outmoded. *Hiding* from humans? *Indiscriminate* killing? *Kidnapping*?" He shook his head. "Dane, you sound as if you believe them to be our equals. Like they're deserving of any consideration whatsoever. Do you know what they are to me? Containers. The same as a bottle or can is to a human. They hold the blood, confine it, keep it fresh and hot. Other than that, they are utterly worthless."

"I'm afraid I can't agree with that. We were human once. We haven't left it all behind."

"We were apes once, too. Does that mean we cling to our ape-ness? Do we celebrate ape culture? Or do we move on, embrace the way we've improved over our earlier, primitive selves?"

"That is not at all the same."

"Isn't it? Or is it just that you want to keep deluding yourself into thinking that they're different?"

"I'm not the one who's deluded."

Dela grinned, wicked teeth bared. "By the way, I believe you have something of mine. I've been wondering where you put her."

"You mean, Ananu?"

"She had a name? How adorable."

"They all have names, Bork."

"Maybe. That doesn't mean we have to use them."

Dane felt the anger now simmering inside him, heading toward a boil, dispelling whatever fear he once felt. In his surprise, he had almost forgotten why he had come. "*I* use them."

"*Pfft*, no matter. We've already determined that you are nothing but a fool. Look at where you are standing, Dane. At what's behind you. That room is just *one* of my storage facilities. Things are going on all around you that you can't even hope to comprehend, as long as you remain mired in the past."

"Murder and kidnapping are hardly revolutionary."

"Like I said, you'll never understand. Big things, too grand for you to see with your blinders on. Why, you probably still think the attack on Barrow was a mistake."

"It was."

Dela barked a laugh. "See? Barrow was *nothing*. Compared to what's going on up north today? A street scuffle, nothing more."

Dane wondered if Dela had meant to say that, but he couldn't think of any subtle way to wring more information from him. "So what's going on? Why don't you tell me?"

"If you hadn't blinded yourself, you could have already seen. If you didn't side with idiots you might even have been invited. Paradise on earth, for those who are worthy of it. You do have a reputation, Dane, I'll give you that much. I've heard you're a tough one. But I've also heard you're a sympathizer. Bottom line: *no one trusts you*."

Dane's anger flared, reaching the critical stage. "Ananu trusts me. You raped her, got her pregnant? You'd have killed her if I hadn't come along."

"Perhaps," Dela said. "Or perhaps I'd have shipped her out, like the rest. I do feel bad, honestly. The same way I'd have felt, back in the old days, about kicking a puppy."

Enough. Dane let the rage take him over.

Instead of answering, Dane charged, his right hand clawing at the other vampire's face, his left scooping up the end of the club he had left by the door.

Slamming into Dela, his momentum carried them both out into the hall and across it, where Dela's back hit the wall. Dela snarled and caught Dane's face in his hands. Dane wrenched it away. He jabbed the club into Dela's ribs.

Dela grunted in pain, doubling over the weapon. Pressing his advantage, Dane raised it high and swung down, an arc that should have plowed through Dela's skull.

But Dela wasn't there any longer. He had moved faster than Dane's eye could follow. Somehow Dela had gotten behind him. Sharp claws dug at Dane's throat, strong fingers squeezing the veins and muscles of his neck. Dane tried to swing the club behind him, but it was too awkward from this angle.

Instead, he dropped it and lurched backward, driving Dela into the doorjamb. The fingers on his neck loosened and Dane did it again, breaking Dela's grip.

Once again, Dela moved too fast to see. The vampire must have picked up some occult tricks over the years. Either he truly moved with preternatural speed, or he was able to temporarily cloud Dane's vision. The result was the same. He struck Dane a glancing blow on the cheek with a fist that felt like stone, then he vanished again, appearing on Dane's other side, hitting him in the temple. Sparks filled Dane's eyes.

Dela struck again, vanished, struck.

None of the blows were, by themselves, enough to do serious damage. But one after another after another, they started to wear Dane down. Dizziness overtook him. He stumbled, ran into a wall. Dela kept up the attack, and Dane knew he was bleeding from at least a dozen wounds. The fresh blood pooled in the meat locker offered salvation, but he couldn't get to it.

He pictured Ananu, rolled into a pathetic ball on the floor of the warehouse, whimpering with terror when he approached her.

The image renewed him, at least for the moment. It wouldn't last long.

Sensing another attack from behind, Dane ducked beneath Dela's blow and snatched the club from the floor. As he rose, he spun around, swinging the club in a wide circle with himself at its center. The branch struck something solid, and Dela cried out in pain.

Dane jabbed the club at the same spot and hit Dela again. He kept it up. Dela couldn't dodge away as long as the blows came fast enough. Finally, Dane had pinned Dela against the corridor wall with the branch held under his throat, pressing in.

"You . . . don't think you can change anything, do you . . . ? You're . . . pathetic, Dane."

"Me? I'm not the one assaulting women that I believe aren't even on my evolutionary level. You disgust me, Dela." He gave another shove with the branch, then tossed it aside. He needed to use his hands, needed to feel Dela, not part of a tree.

Dela raised a hand to ward him off and Dane grabbed it, fury engulfing him at the cold touch of the vampire's flesh. "Humanity wouldn't have you!" he shouted.

Dela tried to yank his hand away, but Dane caught him at the shoulder as well. He hurled Dela to the ground, still holding shoulder and wrist. The vampire glared up at him with sudden terror blossoming in his gray eyes. The sight turned Dane's stomach. He pressed his foot against Dela's neck, pushing him away, pulling on the shoulder and wrist at the same time. Dela clawed uselessly at Dane's boot.

Dela screamed as the tissue tore. His shirt, already ripped in the battle, turned red at armpit and shoulder. Dane kept up the pressure. He wanted to literally tear Dela in half with his bare hands.

He couldn't quite accomplish that, but when he felt Dela's arm loose in its socket he knew he could come close. He gave another, harder shove with his foot and tugged on the arm with every ounce of strength he could muster.

The arm tore from the socket with a wet, ripping sound. Blood jetted against the wall. Dela's shriek rattled doors, his feet kicking the floorboards.

Dane threw the arm to the ground. Spitting like a wild beast, Dela charged him, lopsided, blood spraying.

Dane dropped him with a stiff arm to the throat. Dela fell onto his back, and Dane grabbed his right ankle.

"I don't understand *why* you would do the things you've done," Dane said. Dela frantically clutched at a broken floorboard as Dane gave his leg a furious twist, wrenching it from the hip. "Tell me why!"

Dela shrieked again. Blood soaked through Dela's black pants, pattering on the floor like a sudden cloudburst. "Why?" Dane shouted again, giving a final yank on the leg.

It came off in his hands, held close to Dela only by his blood-saturated pants. Dane released it. Dela writhed in pain, slamming his one remaining hand, kicking his left foot. He ranted but Dane couldn't understand his words.

Still in fury's horrific embrace, Dane straddled Dela. *"You still haven't told me WHY!"* he shrieked. Dela snapped his fangs but Dane easily avoided them. He bent forward, reached down, grabbing Dela's head in both hands and planting a booted foot squarely on the vampire's chest, pinning him to the floor. "You don't deserve to have *ever* been human!"

Straightening with one quick smooth motion, throwing his hands toward the ceiling, Dane heaved Dela's head from his shoulders.

The scream died in Dela's throat only as his neck split, vertebrae snapping, muscles separating. Beneath Dane's foot, the body jerked a few times, then went still.

In his hands, the head snapped and bit, eyes glaring into Dane's with utter hatred.

Breathing heavily, nearly spent, Dane started to toss the head aside, then decided against it. He twined his fingers through Dela's hair and walked through the house, locating each meat locker–style room and checking to make sure Ananu wasn't there. Empty.

Still carrying the head—now lifeless, eyes glazed— Dane made his way outside and back down the path to the pier where he had left AJ's Zodiac boat.

He debated for a moment. Would Ananu want to see the head of her tormentor, or not? Probably not. Eventually, he swung the head in a circle a few times like a hammer thrower, then released.

The head sailed out over the Stygian water, vanishing in the night. Dane never even heard the splash.

Steering the little boat out to sea, using his free hand to release a flare gun from its watertight box, Dane's arms started to shake. He felt a certain grim satisfaction at Dela's destruction, but he was troubled by the depth of his own murderous rage.

Maybe Bork Dela, Marlow, and their kind were right after all.

Maybe when he became a vampire, Dane left the last vestiges of his humanity behind. Had he just been fooling himself for all these years? Was he the monster they all said he should be—the monster he should embrace? Dane had been so sure of himself up until now, of his position, a moral gray area, but suddenly he felt confused.

He headed away from the island, away from the relative stability of land into trackless water. Into the dark. Into the black uncertainty of eternal night.

The flare he fired arced high into the air, but its light couldn't seem to reach into his soul at all.

16

THE FIRST DAYS after being killed had been excruciating for Dane.

Every muscle in his body ached. He could barely stand up. His guts were twisted in knots. He felt like an addict going cold turkey, although he couldn't quite fathom from what.

Marlow dropped in from time to time, and when he left the little room where he kept Dane, he locked the door behind him. With each visit, he shared a little more information about what he had done to Dane, what Dane was becoming. Dane didn't know it at the time, but Marlow had turned many people, almost always men, largely because he hoped to create a kind of street gang like the one he had once been a lowly member of.

On the third day, he came to visit Dane bearing a paper bag. The two talked—Dane demanding answers, Marlow responding with vague generalizations. The whole time, the bag twitched in his hands. Finally Dane, hunched over on the bed he had been provided, arms wrapped around his belly, asked what was in it.

"Oh, yes, my apologies," Marlow said. "This is for you." He handed over the bag.

Dane took it, unfolded the top where Marlow had been crushing it, and looked inside.

The bag contained insects in wide variety, some content to lie on the bottom, others climbing the sides, one beetle spreading wings and flying toward the light as soon as Dane opened it. Crickets, cockroaches, ants, some spiders, and another beetle with an iridescent green carapace. Others he couldn't identify.

His stomach clenched. He thought he might be sick. "Why . . . ?" he began.

Marlow simply looked at him, smiling.

Dane looked in again. His stomach lurched. A cricket jumped against the side of the bag. Dane watched it. Its legs were powerful, its body thick and sturdy.

Dane reached inside, pinched the cricket between two fingers, and drew it out.

Marlow watched him.

Holding the cricket close to his face, Dane smelled it. He had never smelled a cricket before, or any insect, for that matter. It smelled a little like freshly cut grass, but with a hint of a meaty undertone.

Barely realizing what he was doing, he put the cricket's head in his mouth, then pushed it in a little farther. The cricket wiggled in his fingers, trying to escape. Dane bit down. Cricket blood washed over his tongue.

Delicious.

He finished the cricket and reached in again, scooping out a small handful of insects. Without even looking, he popped them into his mouth and chewed.

He couldn't remember such a heavenly meal.

"It's a phase," Marlow said. "It will pass soon, and you'll move on to more interesting feedings."

Dane didn't answer. That beetle was somewhere in the room, and he wanted it.

His first kill, under Marlow's close supervision, had been a young woman with hair the color of corn silk.

They found her walking by herself on a quiet street, after dark, carrying a basket of flowers. "It's like she's looking for you," Marlow whispered in Dane's ear. "Or hoping you're looking for her."

"She is quite lovely," Dane said.

"I suppose," Marlow answered curtly. He seemed to have very little interest in women, for any purpose. "You know what you need to do."

Dane hesitated. Hunger gnawed at him, but Marlow had made it clear that the bugs would no longer suffice.

He needed blood, fresh blood.

Without it Dane would weaken, wither, experience incredible pain. Eventually he might die, but that wasn't certain. He might also live for a thousand years, racked by hunger, before he did.

Finally, Marlow shoved Dane's shoulders, forcing him out of the alley. The startled woman raised a white-gloved hand to her mouth.

Dane knew he had to act quickly now. He tried to smile reassuringly. "Good evening, madam," he said as he approached her.

She backed away a step and he lunged, catching her as she tried to run. He clapped a hand over her mouth to muffle her screams, and threw his other arm around her waist. She writhed and kicked, but he dragged her into the darkness of the alley. As Marlow had shown him, he used her hair, knotted around his fist, to yank her head back and expose the curve of her throat.

Her eyes pleaded for mercy. He offered none.

When he had feasted—the blood so rich and satisfying, the finest meal he had ever had—Marlow made him sever her head and leave the body in the alley. Otherwise, he warned, she would become undead, and she would be Dane's responsibility. Since Dane still didn't know his own way around his new world, he couldn't take on another.

Well fed, he slept for hours the next day. But those eyes, wide and desperate, haunted him that day and every one to follow.

On the night that Marlow told him they would be leaving New York—Marlow had taken it in his head that he wanted to spend some time in the Balkans, the legendary home of the *nosferatu*—Dane went out to hunt by himself. Instead of feeding, however, he went to three different streets and stood in the dark, outside three homes.

The first was the home of his parents. He watched the windows, catching occasional glimpses of his mother moving from room to room in desultory fashion. He had stopped here from time to time since Marlow had turned him, and she had always seemed the same, as if losing a son (and worse, losing him with no word, no answers to the questions that must have tormented her) had stolen away her energy, her life, as surely as if he had drained her blood himself. His father passed by the parlor window once and stopped, staring outside, like he sensed Dane's presence. But Dane stayed in the shadows, confident in his invisibility to them.

His next stop was outside the house of Vanessa Steward, a young lady he had courted. He had not been able to bring himself to look upon her since that fateful night, but decided he couldn't leave the country without a final glimpse. Vanessa was slender but strong, with skin like fine porcelain, a firm jaw, eyes that flared like a torch shielded by panes of pure emerald, and hair that cascaded around her face and down her back in copper ringlets. Her curtains were drawn when he got there, and he waited as long as he dared. Once all the lights inside had been extinguished, he gave up in the sad certainty that she would not show herself until morning.

Finally, he went to the house where his brother lived with his wife and two children. Dane had adored visiting them, enjoyed the role of beloved uncle, and his heart broke over his two nephews as much as it did for his own parents, mourning the lives they would now never share. As at Vanessa's house, though, the windows were dark.

By the time he got back to Marlow's lair, the sky was turning gray in the east. The night had been a waste, Dane decided, filling him with sorrow but offering nothing to ease his suffering. He didn't know then, but learned in bitterness later on, that he would always feel those losses.

Nothing he could ever experience as a vampire could even hope to replace the loved ones he knew when he was once alive.

Despite the beatings and abuse, the misinformation and outright lies, the fact that Marlow only explained what he wanted to and that his motivations were frequently obscure, self-interest his only driving goal, Dane found himself growing close to him over the years they spent together.

Usually others were around, too—the group Marlow had gathered—but sometimes everyone went their own separate ways. Other times it was just Dane and Marlow, or Dane and one of the others.

One evening he, Marlow, and five others were in Washington, DC, for a reason Dane couldn't remember. They had been observing a candlelight vigil against the Vietnam War (yet another opportunity for the mosquitoes to gorge themselves, Dane silently mused). This was in 1965; the antiwar movement wouldn't reach its zenith for years yet, and the vigil was small and sparsely attended, mostly by unkempt souls in black turtlenecks and blue jeans, the women in tights and skirts.

After the vigil they walked around the neighborhood. Flowering trees were in bloom, the night scented with spring.

"Reminds me of the night we met," Marlow remarked to Dane. "Do you remember? You had been watching a protest that night as well."

"I remember," Dane said.

"They never learn," Marlow had said. "War is one of the only constants their race knows."

"That doesn't mean it's a good idea," Dane replied. "I don't understand what we're doing in Vietnam, either."

Marlow's reaction when Dane identified himself with Americans, or with any other group of humans, was swift and brutal. He backhanded Dane. "Idiot!" he seethed. "They're killing each other, that's all we need to know. It's a good thing. Never forget that."

Some of the others echoed Marlow's sentiments. Dane rubbed his jaw as Marlow turned his back to him, looking up at the steeple of the cathedral they were passing, where the vigil had begun. "Do you suppose becoming a vampire is just God's punishment for my sins?"

Marlow stopped dead, and the rest of the group glared at Dane in stunned disbelief. "What did you say?"

Dane didn't bother to repeat himself. Vampires could hear the blood flowing in someone's veins from a block away—Marlow had heard him just fine.

Marlow didn't carry a cane anymore, but he threw two punches before Dane could react. "God? Did you say *God*?"

"Yes," Dane said, putting his fists up to block. Because Marlow had made him, Dane defended himself against attacks, but he didn't fight back.

"Come here." Grabbing Dane by the ear and twisting it hard, Marlow led Dane up the steps and through the cathedral's front door. With a glance and a wave of his hand, Marlow let the others know to wait outside.

Inside the cathedral, quiet reigned. A few candles flickered. One old woman knelt in a pew, praying silently. At the sight of Marlow and Dane, she gasped, crossed herself, and ran away.

Dane cringed from all the crosses. Marlow had told him that crucifixes had no effect on vampires—but on another occasion, he had told Dane that to touch one meant instant, painful destruction by fire. Dane hadn't wanted to test it.

"Do you see God in here?" Marlow asked, raging, dragging Dane up the main aisle toward the altar. "Do you hear God? Do you smell him, Dane?"

"I smell candles," Dane said. "That's all."

"Exactly. That's all there is. Idiot," Marlow said. "God is dead, Dane. If he ever lived at all, he died long ago. If he was alive, he wouldn't let us walk here, would he?"

"I don't . . . know. . . ." Dane's ear felt like Marlow had driven a hot poker into it. Marlow didn't let up the pressure.

"How many people around the world die of hunger every day, Dane? How many babies never reach their first birthday because of preventable diseases? What is it about the world that makes you think there's a God who gives a shit about any of it, much less about *you*?"

As if to illustrate the point, Marlow used Dane's ear as a handle to hurl Dane the rest of the way down the aisle. Dane tumbled and rolled and finally came to rest at the base of the altar, his face jammed against the feet of a statue of Jesus.

Dane jerked his head away, afraid of what the contact might mean.

But his skin wasn't burned. He reached out, cautiously, and touched the statue. Nothing. Cool marble.

Marlow had told him that would be the case—but then again, he had also told him the opposite. As with most things, the only way to know for sure what was true and what wasn't would be to test it for himself.

Dane looked down the aisle at Marlow, who approached slowly, casually. Still holding on to the statue, he rose to his feet to meet his maker. "I guess I know now," he said. "All the garbage you've told me about keeping away from crosses and religious icons . . ."

Marlow just kept coming. Dane released the statue, not liking the determined set of Marlow's face. He held up a hand as Marlow neared, but Marlow batted it away and bent toward Dane, his breath hot and putrid. Dane tried to put his hand up again but Marlow struck too fast, like a snake, and suddenly his fangs had clamped onto Dane's neck.

For a moment, Dane didn't know what to do. The bite was agonizing—he had never heard of a vampire biting a vampire, didn't know what the result of such a thing might be. Marlow held it for a few moments, then released Dane, shoving him away with a look of pure contempt. "You've turned almost human, Dane," he said. "Maybe now you'll remember what you really are."

Dane clapped his right hand over the wound, but not before blood had spurted onto the white marble Jesus. "What the hell . . . ?"

"Something had to be done," Marlow said. "You were making me sick."

Dane wiped his blood off the statue. As he did, a strange feeling passed through him. He had never believed in miracles, and didn't think this was one—there was, no doubt, a perfectly reasonable scientific explanation for the sensation, which he could only compare to holding on to a live electrical wire. But instead of throwing him to the ground or paralyzing him, it infused him with new energy.

Dane felt stronger, suddenly, than ever before. Vampires were plenty strong, and he could hardly remember how weak he'd been in his human days. This, though . . . this was different. A new level of strength, a difference he could feel without even testing.

There is one way you can test it.

He looked at Marlow, who watched him with a curious expression, as if he could tell something was going on but didn't know what. He was maybe a little afraid of Dane. Not without reason.

Dane could tell without checking that the blood had stopped flowing from his neck. He was pretty sure the wound had already closed.

"Dane . . ." Marlow said.

Dane didn't let him finish. He lunged forward, grabbed Marlow by the lapels, and hoisted him off the ground. "Dane! Son!" Marlow shrieked.

Dane spun around like a carnival ride, whirling his maker at shoulder height. Terror blazed in Marlow's eyes, and a sudden feeling of satisfaction, of limitless power, coursed through Dane. He wheeled Marlow ever faster, then released him.

Marlow took off as if he had the power of flight.

He sailed above the pews, on an upward trajectory. Instead of plowing into a wall, he crashed through a huge, ornate stained-glass window and kept on going, vanishing from Dane's sight. Colored glass tinkled to the ground, shattered debris raining down after it.

Finally, other people in the cathedral knew about the intruders. Dane heard voices raised in alarm, coming his way. He hurried toward the door, not wanting to have to explain the damage done.

Outside, Marlow was unhurt. He had just been helped to his feet by the five other vampires.

Seeing Dane emerge, Marlow thrust an arm in his direction. As one, the others turned and fixed Dane with angry gazes. Marlow said something to them, and they released his arms and started toward Dane.

By throwing Marlow through the window, he had broken with the group. He had turned traitor, and this would not be taken lightly.

But the energy still buzzed around in him as if he

had swallowed a rattlesnake. He raced to meet them.

Just before they clashed, he heard Marlow shout, "Destroy him!" Dane didn't mind—it told him just what the stakes were. This wasn't about merely punishing his infraction.

He responded in kind. When the battle was joined, it was for keeps.

Years later, Dane heard that one of the priests who had watched the struggle from the cathedral's doorway had been turned himself. That priest had described the battle to every vampire he met, and the story eventually filtered back to Dane.

The onlooker described the combat as "epic."

Alone, obviously filled with some kind of mystic fire, Dane had torn into the five others like the very spirit of vengeance. His opponents had been powerful, but Dane had been beyond that, tearing through the others like a threshing machine through a wheat field.

Marlow witnessed the entire affair, making no moves to interfere. When it was all over—when Dane stood, weary but unbowed, among the remains of the others—Marlow met his gaze and gave him a look that was almost like pride, as if Dane had met all his expectations.

And then Dane simply walked away, leaving Marlow with what was left of his entourage.

Dane had been born again—ironically, inside a church. The bite hadn't had the effect Marlow had hoped for, but it hadn't been pointless. Somehow, it had imbued him with new strength, maybe double what he'd had before. He was faster, with sharper reflexes and more acute senses. He eventually even stumbled upon the possibility that, with a lot of practice and not a little effort, he could dabble with hypnosis, temporarily retract his fangs and warm his skin to appear human. Marlow always said that science was for humans, that vampires were meant to be feared, not understood, so Dane didn't even know how to begin to figure out what exactly had happened.

In the end, the *how* didn't matter. It *had* happened.

And even better, his new power didn't fade with time, as he feared it might.

Dane's reputation among vampires grew.

Like a gunfighter out of the Old West, and because of his notoriety, challengers came out of the woodwork after him—some friends and followers of Marlow, others simply vampires looking to boost their own reputations by taking on Dane. He wound up hiding, trying to let the stories burn themselves out. He found other vampires who felt the way he did about things, who appreciated the necessity of keeping low profiles, of staying in the dark and letting humans continue to believe the *nosferatu* were myth.

Ferrando Merrin, who stood beside Ananu's bed, was one of these.

Since they still didn't know who had attacked them outside the warehouse, they couldn't go back to AJ's house or Mitch's apartment. Dane had called Merrin, who had pulled some strings and rounded up a safe house in the country between Savannah and Statesboro, on the Ogeechee River. The place was much bigger than AJ's tiny cottage had been. Merrin agreed to stay with Ananu and had arranged new identities, in Florida, for Mitch and AJ.

Dane and Merrin had been telling Ananu stories all week, trying to convince her that vampires were real and that Dane was one, and that neither fact meant that she was in any danger from Dane, Merrin, or—now that he had been dispatched—Bork Dela.

Which didn't mean she was out of the woods. Somehow Plan B had failed to stop the pregnancy, and both Dane and Merrin increasingly believed that no traditional abortion method could stop it either. The unborn fetus was Dela's final curse on the world, and its birth could not be prevented.

Not only that, but Ananu's pregnancy advanced at a remarkable rate. Her stomach looked to Dane—and Mitch, who had been through it—like a fourth- or fifth-month stomach, after only a week. The whole business worried Dane, although having Merrin around tempered those concerns a little.

The birth of a child created by vampire and human could be a miraculous event—or an apocalyptic one. Dane didn't know. Neither did anyone else, because no one they knew had witnessed it.

Dane didn't know if he'd get the opportunity himself, because something else Dela had said—about something going on "up north" that would make the attack on Bar-

row look like small potatoes—demanded his attention as
well.

He had taken Dela out, which Dane believed made it
his responsibility to follow up on whatever the killer had
been talking about. The inevitable argument ensued between Dane and Merrin about the logic behind this, but
in the end, what could Merrin do? Prevent Dane from
leaving, take his car keys away like he was some errant
teenager?

The worry lines on Merrin's face seemed to grow
deeper as the days passed.

Over the last week, Dane had worked to settle Ananu
comfortably into the safe house, getting her accustomed
to Merrin, helping Mitch and AJ adjust to the dangerous
new reality they faced.

Dane itched to make his next move, however. He just
had to find out what Dela had meant, if it all had something to do with all the people he had stolen from their
homes in Savannah.

"Up north" was impossibly vague. Dane only knew one
place he could begin his search, though, and where else?

Barrow.

Could he actually ever go back there? God, there were
so many reasons never to step foot in that frozen shithole
again. Barrow wasn't the same place it was before the
first attack. These days it was tough, gritty, ready for anything, and from what he'd heard, vampires were killed off
on a pretty regular basis up there. Any vampires stupid
enough to try to enter town, at least.

Of course. He was letting his own mind play games with him. He actually *wanted* a reason to go back to Barrow.

Not for any noble cause as he would like to think, but because deep in his heart . . .

Stella.

But what if she wasn't there?

And what if "up north" meant some other place?

Dane didn't trust his instincts on this one and he had no one he wanted to discuss it with—certainly not with Merrin again.

To retell the entire story, to truly understand what happened? Dane had no desire to relive everything—his wild scheme to use Eben's ashes as a lure to kill both Stella and her sheriff husband once and for all for murdering his former master . . . not to mention the added bonus of shutting down Stella's very public crusade of dragging the entire vampire community kicking and screaming into the sunlight, literally, and worse, figuratively.

Even that seemed so strange now. The driving force behind the desire to avenge Marlow was always unspoken, but Dane supposed he was like so many abused children and spouses. Somewhere within the pain was also a twisted allegiance to the abuser. Dane, with all of his undead experience, was no different.

And to admit that he'd had an albeit brief affair, a sexual liaison with a human woman? Not many vampires he knew would be very understanding about that.

But he couldn't get around it. *I need information . . . and allies. If she's still in Barrow, then maybe.* Eben Olemaun was another matter altogether. Was he truly back from the dead as whispered . . . had Stella managed to prove a vampire myth as truth? And if so, did Eben know about what happened between Dane and Stella?

Things were already plenty complicated, but Dane had a feeling that it was only just the beginning.

Dane's self-inflicted mind games played over and over in his head, and with each turn, he knew he had already made the decision. He would return to that forsaken little town and find either the answers he sought or a whole new batch of trouble. History was repeating itself once again, it seemed.

And history, painful experience had taught him, also had a bad habit of sneaking around and biting people on the ass.

PART TWO

BARROW

17

THE INUPIAT had originally called Barrow *Ukpiagvik,* which meant "place where owls are hunted," and as far as Dane was concerned, any owls around could have it back.

Barrow was once a bustling little burg of just under four thousand people, most of whom were either trying to catch flights out before the sun went down to stay or were preparing for the long, cold winter. Most of those who had stayed wished they hadn't, if they had a chance to wish anything at all.

The last time Dane was here, in 2003, had almost cost him everything.

This time, getting to Barrow had been no easy task. Dane had taken a night flight from Macon to Denver, where he spent the day in a hotel room with the drapes drawn tight. From Denver he repeated the process, passing a day in Seattle. The next night took him to Anchorage, and the one after that to Fairbanks.

From there, he had to travel over land, since he didn't trust flying into Barrow's closely watched airport. The sun hadn't set between May and early August. It moved across the sky, dropping low on the horizon but never disappearing completely. Even now, in late September, the nights were not as long as Dane would have preferred, although they were getting longer all the time. In late November, the sun would set until January. Perfect for his kind . . . which was how the whole trouble started in the first place.

At a bar in Fairbanks—an old Quonset hut that had been decorated, if one used the term loosely, with pelts and antlers and spat tobacco—he found an Eskimo who owned a cargo van with no windows. For the right price—right to Abner, the fiftyish, dour-faced Eskimo— Abner would let Dane ride in the back of the van, with a curtain between the cargo area and the windshield. Before they left town, they visited a yard sale and bought a pile of furniture to make the load look authentic, in case they were stopped. They took the pipeline road as far as they could, through the Brooks Range, Dane driving at night. Finally, they had to cut west on dirt roads, dodging oil and lumber trucks.

Melting permafrost had turned some of the roads, which should have been hard packed, into soupy bogs. Twice, the van got stuck. The first time, an oil tanker came along and towed them out of the muck, but the second time they had to wait until the darkest hour of the day when Dane could get out of the van and help dig. As they waited, Abner pointed out polar bears and Arctic foxes crossing the bluish, slushy snow, curious about the immobile vehicle.

Fifty miles shy of Barrow, they stopped until two in the

morning before continuing the rest of the way into town. Abner explained that during the long days, people slept when they were tired and did their daytime business when they felt like it. Shops might be open regular business hours, but they might not. Many people tried to sleep during the "nighttime," so it would be easiest to try to get into town then. Dane had told him that a skin condition required him to stay out of direct sunlight, and he had retracted his fangs and warmed his skin. But he couldn't tell if Abner believed him or simply humored him. Since a skin condition wouldn't explain why he wanted to be careful about entering Barrow, he suspected the latter.

As long as Abner didn't betray him, he didn't really care. It would be while going into Barrow that Dane would be most in danger, and he hoped the bonus he had promised Abner at the end of the trip was sufficient to buy the man's loyalty.

It was almost four-thirty when they pulled up to the town's main entrance. Even from the back of the van, Dane could see the guard towers scratching at low clouds and the miles of razor wire still surrounding the town.

When Abner slowed for the gate, Dane saw armed guards and more razor wire. He had crossed international boundaries with less security. Abner slowed the van to a crawl, then stopped and cranked his window down. Dane feigned sleep on a couch in the back.

"Welcome to Barrow," a voice said from outside. "You moving in?"

"Just bringing some stuff for a friend," Abner said.

"Uh-huh." A pause. "Mind if I take a look in back?"

"Knock yourself out."

Dane braced himself. The rear doors of the van swung open and he raised up on his elbows on the couch, acting as if he had just woken up. Only some of it was an act— he blinked against the thin sunlight, drawing back from it in mild pain. He just hoped the guard didn't make him get out. Cool air blew in through the open door.

"Hi," he said, feigning a yawn.

"Sorry to wake you," the guard said. He was the size of a refrigerator, with a thick red beard and a stocking cap, and his plaid flannel shirt was open over a Felix the Cat T-shirt. He carried a small flashlight. Another guy stood behind him with a shotgun in his hands. "We gotta check everyone who comes to town."

"Check?"

"Yeah, it'll only take a sec." The guy raised a flashlight. "Can you open your mouth?"

Dane shrugged as if the request made no sense, but did as he was asked, confident that his fangs were fully re-tracted, and that some low-level hypnosis, for good meas-ure, was also in effect. The guard shone the light into Dane's mouth, then whistled. "Shee," he said. "We got a good dentist here, Doc Finnegan. You oughta give her a call while you're here, dude."

"I'll be sure to do that," Dane said.

The guard shut the doors and pounded twice on the van's exterior. "Good to go!" he shouted.

"Thanks," Abner said, putting it into gear. He drove a

few blocks into downtown Barrow and stopped. Dane opened the back, got out.

Most of the buildings had been rebuilt, but some were still fire-blackened husks. Blue plastic tarps protected some still under construction. He had seen a lot of those blue tarps since flying into Anchorage, as if they were doled out to Alaska residents along with their oil royalties.

"This good?" Abner asked.

A gold neon sign a few blocks up signaled the TOP OF THE WORLD HOTEL. A smaller one flickered VACANCY. Dane dug his backpack out of the pile of furniture in the van and shut the rear doors. "This'll do," he said. He fished out his wallet and peeled off the five hundred bucks he had promised Abner as a bonus. "Thanks, Abner. Now forget you ever saw me."

Abner grinned. "Forget what?" He got back into the van without looking back at Dane, started it, and drove away.

Dane headed to the hotel to check in. He couldn't help feeling a strong sense of unease.

He was a vampire. In Barrow, of all places.

Talk about being in the belly of the beast. . . .

18

Having managed to fly beneath the radar and actually enter town was a feat in itself.

Now, Dane thought, *how the hell do I locate Stella Olemaun?*

It wasn't the kind of thing you could just ask a passerby, and his acute senses were more or less useless in Alaska's climate. The freezing cold made it impossible for him to sniff much outside a ten-yard radius.

The town had numerous ways in and out but every single one was monitored by guards, armed with either firearms, a UV light, or both. Walking by the checkpoints made Dane nervous. He'd recently felt those UV rays and was not eager to try it again. But being seen was part of his plan. He wanted to let the guards spot him as often as possible, so when he decided to wander outside the town proper he wouldn't be noticed—or at the very least, be less conspicuous.

Dane had a lot of respect for the citizens of Barrow. They had faced a terrible threat and survived not once but twice. God knows how many times places like it had been hit by vampires over the centuries. The Arctic Circle had a long secret history, all the way around the top of the world, of undead invasions during the winter months of darkness.

What the vampires did in 2001 was but one in a long series of unreported attacks.

That's what irritated Dane so much about that incident—the arrogance of the undead, of Marlow, in thinking they were the first. Far from it. Attacks in Alaska went back hundreds of years. Possibly out of all of the occurrences, Marlow led the stupidest of them all, because now a few more humans believed in the undead and that major error was the first step on the road toward vampire extinction.

But right now, as Dane walked toward the outermost ridge of Barrow's far west side, he was more concerned about his own survival. The humans who manned the checkpoint there eyed him with an unnerving glare and shined a flashlight on him.

"You," one of them said. "What are you doing out here?" He was a large man with a voice like gravel.

Dane thought about running. He could disappear before they knew what hit them, but then he would only alert them to the fact that "one of them" had gotten into town. Instead, Dane stopped and looked around, feigning confusion.

"I seem to have lost my way," Dane said. "I'm staying at the Top of the World Hotel . . . am I heading in the right direction?"

The burly man looked at his companion—both of them so bundled in outer garments that there wasn't much difference between them besides size and shape, and smiled knowingly.

"You're about as far from the right direction as you can get, bud," the slightly smaller of the two said as he pointed back the way Dane had come. "You want to be all the way *that* way."

Dane did his best to play the befuddled tourist and looked around. "Huh. How about that . . ."

Both guards eased up. Not in any way a normal human could see. Dane noticed their muscles relaxing ever so slightly beneath the bulk of their layered clothes, and their hands slackened.

Dane decided to test the waters a bit. "So, what's out this way then?" he said, pointing beyond them.

The larger man lost interest in the exchange and started banging his gloved hands together to create some body heat. The smaller sentry shrugged and answered, "Nothing but a lot of frozen . . . nothing."

"Nothing?" Dane repeated as though he didn't understand.

"Got some hills and the ocean not too far off, but I'll eat my hat if you can find a tree within fifteen miles thataway," he said.

Dane nodded, running his mind over a few facts about the previous attacks. Most of the vampires came in from the east and south. Could that possibly be where Stella was holed up? She certainly wasn't in town. Maybe she and Eben (if he was still around) found someplace out on the frozen tundra to hide out.

Dane thanked the checkpoint guards and headed back the way he'd come. After a hundred yards or so, he quickly looked about to make sure nobody was watching, then sprinted and jumped the fence with a graceful, almost diverlike, spin of his body, landing outside Barrow's fenced parameter.

He stared out into the dark horizon, took one last glance back at town, then ran as fast as he could into the darkness.

Dane traveled in the nothingness for a while before he stopped and looked back. Barrow was still somewhat visible, with his heightened night vision.

Suddenly, there it was—a presence around him, moving in a circle. When he tried to get a fix on who or what it was, he couldn't.

Then the presence divided and became two, continuing to circle.

Dane prepared for a fight. He was sure it was his own kind. Only they could get so close without detection. If it was Stella and Eben.

Surely they couldn't have advanced in skill this quickly? Not that it would have been unprecedented. Some people were just born to be undead.

The wind picked up and ice shards slammed against Dane's face and eyes as he tried to make out the shapes moving toward him. They were human shaped, but he couldn't make out much more than that, so he raised his hands, waiting for the attack to come.

Then, one of the shapes stopped.

"Dane?"

In an instant, Dane relaxed and an uncontrollable grin spread on his face.

It was *her*.

"Stella?"

The slender form, the way she stood with her weight thrown onto her left leg, hip cocked, the way she filled her snug jeans, the short, spiky red hair. She wore a heavy yellow cable-knit sweater, tight at the waist.

It was Stella Olemaun.

Then she stepped through the haze of the storm and Dane saw her face, saw the recognition dawning in her blue gray eyes, saw her lips parting, her mouth falling open, and he felt like a mule had kicked him in the gut with both feet.

"Dane? Oh my God. . . . What the hell are you doing here?"

He shrugged, trying to appear casual. Probably not succeeding very well. "It's a long story."

He had always expected to find her around these parts—word had spread a while back throughout the vampire community that she and her husband Eben had returned, both as full-fledged vampires themselves, and almost single-handedly saved the town from a repeat attack.

Until now, Dane never had the opportunity to explore if she was even up here, before that asshole Paul Norris nearly blew his head off. And ironically, that was over Stella as well.

Yet here she was, the one and only Stella Olemaun, out in the open wilderness of Alaska.

He hadn't expected what seeing her would do to him.

It had been a century and a half since he had felt anything like love, before he met Stella. He'd had to let her go. It hadn't been easy, but dammit he thought he was coping. Now . . . now all that coping flew out the window. He wanted to scoop her into his arms, carry her back to the hotel.

"Well, I always love a good story," she finally replied.

Why wouldn't she come up to him, though, why was she holding back? Then he saw she ticked her head toward the other shape who had been a couple of paces behind her, circling him—one had stopped and come to her side when Dane had said her name.

A sturdy guy with broad, sloping shoulders, he had short dark hair and a long, scarred face.

He fixed Dane with a steady, penetrating stare.

"Dane, huh?" the man remarked. "Eben. Eben Olemaun."

The husband. The man Dane had given her up for, even though—at the time—Eben had been nothing more than a box of ashes. In an incredible display of courage, Eben had turned himself in order to fight Vicente and save what was left of Barrow during that first assault, back in 2001. Although it certainly didn't start out that way (an understatement), Dane had eventually helped Stella get Eben's ashes back from Lilith and had told her how she might be able to use those ashes to restore Eben back to life.

By the time he had done so, he felt that he'd never made a bigger mistake. Without those ashes, and the hope they offered, Stella might have stayed with him. Maybe. After all, he was the one who made Stella think differently about vampires, at a time when all she was interested in was carrying out all sorts of creative new ways to expose and destroy them.

It could never have been, though. And so Dane vowed to forget about Stella. For his own sanity.

Until now, of course.

Eben started down the snowy sloping surface toward Dane, extending a hand. His damaged face broke into a grin. Dane put a hand out in anticipation.

"Stella has told me all about you," Eben said as he neared. "And I mean *everything*."

When he reached Dane, Eben balled his outstretched hand into a fist, drew it back, and swung it in a fierce uppercut that collided with Dane's chin. Dane's head snapped back. He almost lost his footing, but recovered just in time to see Eben following up with a left hook.

Dane threw up a defensive arm. Eben's fist plowed into it like a cannonball. The force of the blow knocked Dane into the snow.

My God, is he strong.

"You wanted to kill me?" Eben snarled. "In front of

her? Get up, now's your big chance. . . . I said *get up*!"

Dane didn't want this. It wasn't the reason he came here. "Listen, Eben," he said, getting balanced and braced for another attack. "Eben, wait!"

"Get. Up." The words had barely cleared Eben's mouth when he threw himself into Dane. The two men staggered farther into the open wilderness, then Dane's ankle wrenched beneath him and he went down, Eben on top of him, pummeling him with fast, powerful blows.

Dane swung back, landing a couple of good shots—punches that would have killed a human. Maybe even some vampires.

But not Eben. The more he fought, the angrier he got. The angrier he got, the stronger he became.

As he tried to absorb the punishment raining down on his body, Dane had an epiphany of what was going on with Eben. Of course, he had to have it in human form, even before being turned, although it wouldn't manifest until after. Or so the stories went—as with most things vampiric, nothing like a scientific study had ever been done.

In life, according to everything Dane had heard, Eben had been a fighter. The same trait remained with him after life—legend had it that it was to make him a more powerful and fearsome combatant when fueled by rage.

Just my luck I'm the one he's pissed at.

Years ago, Dane's second bite from Marlow had increased his strength to nearly unheard-of levels, but Eben was now pounding him like he was Mike Tyson and Dane was a speed bag.

But Eben had been dead—completely dead, burned to ashes—for a year and a half before his resurrection. Maybe that had somehow enhanced his abilities?

Gathering every ounce of power he could, Dane threw Eben off him and managed to gain his feet, brushing the snow off himself as he did. Bruised and bloody, he knew he'd be hurting tomorrow.

"Eben . . . *Eben*!" Stella advanced on the two of them. "Knock it off, Eben. You too, Dane. You're both acting like a couple of kids."

"Okay with me," Dane said, wiping blood away from his lips. "Truce?"

Eben eyed him savagely. "Fuck off," he said. He turned to Stella. "He probably came here looking for you, anyway."

"He knows that's not possible," Stella said.

"Whatever." Eben turned back to Dane with a wicked smile, long teeth bared. "Sorry pal. We don't like bloodsuckers around here."

What? Talk about the pot calling the kettle black. And, Eben had not only come back as a vampire, but he had obviously fed on Stella, turned her—the ultimate act of selfishness, Dane believed. Dane hadn't turned Vanessa Steward all those years ago, after all, even though he hadn't wanted to leave her behind.

Then again, Stella knew what she was getting with Eben. *She* chose to bring him back. She accepted all possible risks in full when she did. Dane wondered what kind of a strain *that* put on a relationship.

Dane would have loved to find out how Stella was handling the irony of being turned, after all the damage she caused the vampire community as a human.

"We're kind of a special case in Barrow," Stella said. "Grandfathered in, you might say."

"I've heard the rumors," Dane said. "Believe me, after last time, I wouldn't have come back here if I thought there was any way around it."

"Then why did you come?" Eben asked. "And how long till you leave?"

"I don't know the answer to that one," Dane replied. "I came because of Bork Dela—"

"Who?" Eben asked, barely concealed contempt in his voice.

"A . . . very nasty fellow murdering and abducting people down in Savannah. Making a big spectacle out of it. The media had even given him one of those serial killer names they love to hand out. The Headsman. I guessed it was a vampire; his actions threatened to expose us all. . . . And when I poked into it I found him. He said there was something in the works 'up north' that would make the first attack on Barrow look pretty tame."

"What? Did he say what it was?" Stella asked.

"I couldn't get any more out of him," Dane said. "So I figured I had to come here, to make sure he wasn't talking about yet another attack."

"They've already tried that," Eben said. "I don't think they'll be in a hurry to do it again."

"I know, believe me," Dane said, remembering. "But this was the only starting point I could think of."

A thoughtful expression had settled on Stella's face. Looking at her, Dane was taken all over again by her brittle beauty, by the grace with which she carried herself. "Thanks for the warning," she said. "We'll stay alert."

"Which means you can go," Eben said.

Dane shook his head. "Not yet. I don't know if it's Barrow or something else. I don't have much to go on, but I don't think I can leave until I can dig around some. I can't just let this go."

"If you find anything, Dane, let us know," said Stella.

"I will. You do the same?"

"Don't push it," Eben said. "You're lucky I'm not staking you down somewhere right now. Sun'll be up in about forty minutes."

How noble. Eben had not only spared him, but had given him fair warning about the sunrise.

Eben didn't like the fact that Dane was in Barrow, he had made that plenty clear—and "didn't like" was probably putting it far too mildly. Didn't he understand that Dane shared his agenda? Since Stella had told him everything, as he had put it, she had no doubt also told him that Dane was now on the outs with most vampires.

Dane didn't want the race extinguished. Neither, he hoped, did the now vampiric Stella and Eben.

Dane was obsessive over his desire to have vampires knock off the rampant murder, and he wanted nothing more than a universal change in how they viewed humanity. He would fight for these ideals. Was that what Stella and Eben were about, too? Were they on the same side, perhaps? If such a thing were possible?

Stella reached out and shook his hand. He'd have preferred a hug, but that would probably have set Eben off again. Eben didn't offer a hand and neither did Dane, but both men nodded tersely to each other as they parted.

Dane hurried back to town and his hotel at top speed, barely making it in time to pass the daylight hours.

In his room, he brought his hand to his nose, catching just the faintest whiff of Stella. He could still remember the taste of her, his first view of her nude body, the way she moved when he was inside her.

And now she was undead. As long as she had been human and he vampire, there had been no real future.

Now—if it was what she wanted—they could have forever. Literally forever. He realized that he had never wanted anything quite so much. And he could never ask for it. Not while she had Eben.

He sat in his darkened room, staring at the wall, wishing.

19

AFTER THE SUN SET, Dane went out again. This time he wandered the streets. Getting the lay of the land, as it were. He located the plasma center he'd found listed in the hotel's phone directory. Two armed guards stood outside its door.

So it looked like feeding would be a problem, once he used up the supply he'd acquired in Fairbanks. He couldn't risk killing, not here of all places. And apparently he couldn't surreptitiously snag a bottle or two of Type O from the blood bank. He'd have to get out into the wilderness, he guessed, catch some wildlife. He could live for a while on animal blood, but he'd be weakened, nauseous. A piss-poor substitute, but better than starving.

Dane estimated the nighttime temperature to be in the mid-30s. He wore a red nylon parka over a sweater—more than he needed, but he desperately wanted to fit in, and by pulling the parka's hood up against the stiff wind that blew through town he was also helping to disguise himself.

He saw a few people out and about, many of them armed with shotguns or at least semiautomatic pistols. A blue neon bear drew his attention to a place called the

Polar Bar, which blazed with light from inside. He tried to swallow his anxiety about wading into the thick of the local population and pushed through a heavy wooden door.

Country music twanged from a jukebox. People—mostly white men, although not exclusively—hunkered in booths with sodas or coffee and hot meals on the tables in front of them. A cheerful guy in a stained white apron dried dishes behind a bar, and when Dane entered he raised an empty glass toward him. "Welcome," he said. "Sit anywhere you want."

"Thanks," Dane said. He hoped his growing nervousness wasn't noticeable. He found a table near the window. The inside was paneled with knotty pine and tiled with black and white linoleum squares, but the pine was almost completely obscured by photographs and seemingly random objects—a white kid's tennis shoe, a French horn, a rifle with the barrel bent at a ninety-degree angle, and much more. Red and green Christmas lights had been strung around the ceiling line sometime in the past decade and then forgotten—now they had faded to barely tinted near white, and almost as many had gone out as remained burning. The bare fluorescent tubes overhead washed down as if to drive away any possible shadows. The lights felt harsh to Dane's eyes, but they wouldn't hurt him like an ill-intentioned UV light.

The guy in the apron dropped a menu on his table. He looked like a partially shaved polar bear himself, burly and with long white Santa Claus hair and beard. "Get you something to drink?"

"Just coffee," Dane said. He'd liked it in his human days, and could stomach it now when he had to. As long as he could down some blood on top of it before too long. Otherwise he found it too acidic and it gave him heartburn. He pushed the menu back toward the bartender/waiter. "That should do me for now, thanks."

"Coffee it is," the guy said. "New in town?"

"Visiting," Dane said. "Always heard about it, so I wanted to see what it was like. Before the sun goes down."

"Good plan," the guy said. He left to get the coffee. When he brought it back, in a thick white china mug, it steamed. Cream and sugar were already on the table, which Dane didn't bother with. Again, a little hemoglobin would've helped, but that wasn't available.

Taking small, slow sips from the cup, Dane looked more closely at the walls. The place was, he gradually realized, a virtual shrine to the memory of the first attack on Barrow. Photos framed in black must have been the deceased. Others he guessed showed survivors. Pictures had been taken of the whole town, in the aftermath, showing the extent of the destruction by fire and explosion. A few pictures depicted survivors in small groups, defiantly holding guns.

On the wall behind him, where there were no windows, the holiday lights had been strung as a kind of frame around the biggest of the photos. With the sun slanting onto them from one side, Stella and Eben Olemaun smiled at him, wearing crisp sheriff's uniforms and holding hands.

"That's Eben Olemaun and his wife, Stella," a man said as Dane stared at the photo. "They used to be the law here. Local heroes, both of them."

Dane turned and regarded the speaker. His head was shaved and he wore a T-shirt, tight over bulging pecs and enormous biceps. He had draped his parka over the back of his chair. A leather choker hung around his neck with what Dane could only guess was, incredibly, a vampire fang dangling from it. A mostly eaten lunch sat on his table. "So I've heard," Dane replied.

"You've heard of them?" The guy sounded surprised.

"Well, she wrote that book, right?"

"*30 Days of Night,*" the guy said. "But I also understand that was supposedly a novel."

"Didn't read like fiction," Dane said. "I mean, a good writer can make fact read like fiction sometimes, but this one—it had the feel of reality to it. Maybe not in all the details, but enough of them. After all, there they are, right? Husband and wife sheriffs. Just like in the book."

The burly guy thrust an open hand toward Dane. "Name's Andy Gray," he said. "Pleased to meet you."

Dane shook the hand. The grip was powerful for a human's. "I'm Dane," he said.

"You want to join me, Dane? I'm relatively new in town myself. If you have any questions or anything . . ."

Dane moved his coffee to Andy Gray's table. "Thanks," he said. He had plenty of questions, few of which he would dare ask. He'd been feeling strangely unsettled, and being here, in the midst of people who would love nothing better than to destroy him, with no real idea of why he had come or how to find out, threw him all the more off balance. "I guess . . . I didn't quite know what to expect when I got here."

"Around here, people get ready for winter," Andy said with a grin. "No, there's hunting. Fishing. Global warming's playing hell with things around here, in some ways—the ice is melting too early in the year, and the local Inupiat people are having a hard time adjusting their fishing season to the constantly shifting conditions. But you can still throw a line in and catch something from time to time, and if you go into the interior more, there's lots of good river fishing. Snowmobiling if you're into that. And of course there's just the natural beauty of the area, the northern lights, wildlife viewing, that kind of thing. Like I said, I'm pretty new here, but I took to it fast."

He stopped talking long enough to down some of his meat loaf and mashed potatoes, washing it all down with a Coke.

"I'm not sure how long I'm staying," Dane admitted. "Hopefully I'll get time to do some of that stuff."

"Well . . . do it before the dark comes," Andy said between chews, wiping his mouth on a napkin. "It's hard to do any of it then. Except viewing the northern lights, I guess."

Dane finished his coffee and put the cup down on the table, then laid a couple of dollars next to it. He sensed there was a lot more to Andy than the guy let on. The fact that he wore a fang like a badge of honor meant something just in itself. "Thanks for the tips," he said. "I appreciate it." He paused. "Guess I should have told you up front, too—I *did* know Stella Olemaun."

Andy Gray's eyes widened in surprise, though he did a good job of keeping it from registering on the rest of his face. "Really. That a fact?"

Dane waved to the bartender on his way out the door, then stopped, halfway out, and held Andy's gaze. "I still do," he said. "I'm at the Top of the World Hotel if you want to talk more later."

Andy gave him a nod, and Dane walked outside. The air was a little colder, but the town's lights kept the darkness at bay.

Andy Gray watched the man who called himself Dane step through the door of the Polar Bar and disappear. *Something about that guy* . . . he couldn't put his finger on it, but there was definitely more to him than met the eye. He fingered Paul Norris's fang resting against his chest. He couldn't be a vampire, no way, not here in the heart of Barrow. Anyway, he didn't look like one—no fangs, normal human skin tones.

But it *was* night. Andy hadn't been able to adjust to a normal sleeping schedule since he had come to Barrow a while back. Fortunately there were plenty of late-night places like this where a guy could get lunch at midnight or 1:00 AM.

And Dane hadn't eaten anything, either. He'd had coffee. Andy picked up the cup, sniffed it. Just coffee. Black.

It had been a couple of years since he'd been a full-on FBI agent, but certain habits were hard to break. Andy was suspicious by nature, and his years of Bureau training had intensified that trait. He finished his lunch, glanced at the watch on his wrist. Time for another Coke before his workout, if he wanted it. He had started a fitness regime since moving to Barrow that far exceeded what little exercising he had done before, in his old life—when Paul Norris had been alive, and so had Andy's wife Monica and their girls, Sara and Lisa.

Andy had not died and been brought back, the way vampires were. But there was an equally strict dividing line between his former life and his new one, and that line was the day he had awakened and found his family murdered while he slumbered, drunk in his own home office.

For a long time he thought the line was when Paul turned into a vampire. Paul had been his closest friend, his partner, and in many ways he loved Paul more than he'd ever loved Monica.

Eventually, though, time had showed him that he was wrong. Paul's change had upset his life, turned it inside out, and shaken all the crap loose. But Andy had retreated into booze and work and research, hiding from his feelings, from real life. It was only when Paul killed Monica and the girls—framing Andy for their murders—that he had thrown off those things and started to remake himself into the person he had become.

When, after months on the run, Andy, along with John Ikos, finally killed Paul in the fields outside Barrow, he knew that he was complete and that he had finally found someplace to call home.

He had started rebuilding himself physically then. When he looked at pictures of himself before—thin and pudgy at the same time, soft and sallow—he barely recognized himself. That wasn't the man who looked back at him from the mirror. The man in the mirror was strong, filled with energy and determination. He had pared away the things that didn't matter—hair, fears, weaknesses—and worked on building those that did.

He paid for his meal and went outside to the GMC pickup he had bought here. Four-wheel drive, decent stereo system, shitty mileage, but this was where gas came from, right? Thinking about John Ikos made him want to see the trapper, to tell him about the guy he had just met. John was the old-timer here. If Dane meant anything in these parts, he'd know it.

Finding Ikos, of course, was different than looking for him. He lived out in the wilderness and he danced to his own tune, no one else's. Andy headed out the main gate and off the pavement, onto the rutted dirt track that led toward John's cabin. His headlights cut twin tunnels through the blackness. Wind puffed flurries of snow into his path.

The trapper's cabin, built into the side of a low hill and camouflaged by perpetual snowdrifts, was empty. Andy got back in the truck. John wouldn't carry a cell phone, and there was no signal this far from town anyway. Andy wrote a brief note telling John he wanted to see him and tacked it to the cabin door with a staple he ripped from a gun magazine under his seat.

He had gone almost a mile back toward town when his headlights swept across two forms, tiny in the vast wilderness.

The taller of the two was John Ikos.

Andy didn't know who the smaller one was—but whoever, or whatever, it was giving John a hard time, writhing and kicking and swinging tiny fists at the big trapper.

Looks like John's gone hunting again. Caught himself a live one this time.

20

ANDY STOPPED THE TRUCK fifty yards or so away from Ikos and stepped out into his own headlights so the trapper could identify him. "John!" he shouted, waving his arms.

Ikos gave him a partial left-handed wave in return, but whoever he hung onto used that moment to wriggle from his grasp and break into a desperate sprint.

"Ah shit . . . get him!" Ikos shouted.

Andy started running to intercept the smaller person—it looked like a kid—who veered away from him at about a thirty-degree angle. John Ikos raced behind the kid and a little to his right, herding him Andy's way. Andy's feet crunched over hard-packed snow; the cold air he sucked in tore painfully at his lungs. With Ikos running hard behind him, the kid had little choice but to head in Andy's direction. Close enough for Andy to make a last-second shift, anyway.

He leapt and caught the kid's legs. They both crashed to a heap on the hard snow.

As Andy started clawing his way up the kid's body, the kid turned and snarled at him, showing long white teeth and wild eyes. Spittle flew from his gnashing jaws.

"Jesus!" Andy cried. "Vampire!" He almost pissed himself from the instantaneous wave of sheer terror—he would never get used to the sight. His guns were in the truck. The kid, who couldn't have been older than thirteen or taller than five feet, clawed at Andy. Andy didn't want to release him, but he didn't want those fangs to sink into his flesh, either. He kept a tight grip on the kid's foot, holding it at arm's length. The vampire kid kept trying to yank his foot free while bending at the waist, hoping to get his claws into Andy.

Andy scooted backward on his ass, taking little hops to keep the kid at bay, tugging on his ankle all the while and wondering what had become of John. Finally he realized John stood a few butt scoots behind him, laughing out loud.

"John, do something!" he shouted.

John slammed the butt of his shotgun into the vampire kid's skull and the thing's mouth went slack. Its eyes rolled up in its head and it dropped back onto the snow.

"Jesus! Vampire!" John mocked, barely able to catch his breath between roars of laughter. "What do you think I'd catch, just some kid?"

"I know you usually hunt them," Andy said, getting to his feet. "I just wasn't expecting one so small."

"You get bitten, don't matter how big you are, or how old, you can become one, too."

The vampire kid stirred, then bolted upright, spitting and drooling blood.

"We got to get his head off," John said. "Put him

down for good. I'd just shoot him but I'm runnin' low on ammo, need to make a trip into town."

"Well, I don't have anything on me," Andy said. "I didn't think this was a hunting expedition; I was just looking for you."

John clutched at his belt, undid the snap over the scabbard he wore. He drew a hunting knife from the scabbard. Andy guessed the blade was about seven inches long, with a serrated back edge. He handed it to Andy. "Here. Use this."

Andy turned the wicked tool over in his hands. John swatted the kid with the butt of his gun again, and the kid—not nearly as strong as a full-grown vampire, it appeared—keeled back again.

Andy glanced up at the tall, bearded hunter. In his ragged skin coat and shaggy mane, he looked like one of the creatures he might have hunted, before he turned his attentions toward vampires. John gave him a nod. Andy knew what it meant. He wanted Andy to do the beheading, and to do it before the kid woke up again.

Vampire, not kid, vampire, not kid, Andy reminded himself. He couldn't afford to think of this bloodsucker as any different than the rest, just because he was younger. Maybe the kid hadn't been at this long, maybe he had just been turned recently—that might explain the odd behavior—but he'd get the hang of the vampire life, soon enough. Once he did he'd be killing and feeding just like the others.

Andy knelt beside him, feeling the snow seeping

through his jeans. The vampire was out cold, it seemed. Hand trembling, Andy held the knife against the kid's scrawny throat.

The vampire twitched, one leg kicking out. His right eyelid fluttered.

"Better get it done," John warned.

"I know!" Andy screamed, pressing harder on the blade. "Goddammit!" Pale skin gave way under the steel edge. He pushed down harder still and saw droplets of blood form, then run down the vampire's neck in little streams. The vampire gave a tiny cry, like a newborn kitten mewling. Andy bit down on his lower lip and leaned on the blade, sawing with it.

Blood sprayed his hand, his arms. The vampire's eyes snapped open. Andy sawed faster.

Slender-fingered hands clutched at his wrist. Andy put all his weight on the blade, hunching over the vampire. Bone snapped. Clawed fingertips dug into his arm.

"John! . . . for crissakes!"

"You're doin' fine, Andy. Finish it."

"I'm trying!" Andy sliced at the monster's neck like it was a recalcitrant slab of meat and he an angry butcher. He chopped through gristle and muscle and bone shards, finally forcing the blade through to the snow beneath, soaked now with hot blood.

The vampire twitched a couple more times, brown eyes still open and staring up at the stars. Andy shuddered, blew out a sigh, tossed the knife aside, and started scooping up clean snow to wash his hands.

John bent down and picked up his knife. "That wasn't so bad, was it?"

"Fuck you," Andy said. He wanted to vomit. "He's just a little kid."

"He's not a kid, Andy. He's a vampire. It's not the same thing."

"Yeah, I know," Andy said, rubbing snow up and down his arms. "But it still feels wrong. I can't get past it."

John wiped the blade on his coat and returned the knife to its scabbard, snapping the flap over it. "You've come a long way since I first met you, Agent Gray. I hardly recognize you for the punk-ass you were when you came to Barrow. Tell you the truth, I didn't think you'd do it at all."

"Then why'd you give me the knife?"

"Had to find out for sure, right?"

"Christ, John, there might have been a better way."

"I don't know of any."

Andy stood, dusting the snow from his arms and legs. His jeans were soaked through and he was starting to feel the cold. "Yeah, well, you've never struck me as the imaginative type."

"Maybe not, but I'd like to think I'm practical as hell," John said. He started gathering downed wood from nearby trees and piling it near the body. Andy did the same, still fuming about John testing him that way.

"You were looking for me?" John called as he scavenged some good-sized branches.

"Yeah," Andy said. He started stacking the wood they

had found into a kind of pyre, with small kindling at the bottom. Snaking a lighter from his pocket—he didn't smoke anymore, but it never did well to be caught without fire around here—he held its flame to the kindling until tiny flames danced from the twigs, crackling gently and sending up the smell of wood smoke. He placed some of the larger sticks over the burning kindling, then as they caught he stood back to keep the smoke from his eyes and watched it burn.

"Any particular reason?"

"Met a strange guy, down at the Polar Bar. He said he knew Stella Olemaun—and he still does. There was just something about him that struck me as odd. Made me think of Paul . . . same situation, almost."

John started setting some large branches on top of the fire. "This guy have a name?"

"He just called himself Dane."

John froze, one log halfway in place. "You're shitting me."

"That's what he said."

"Black hair? Maybe a thin little goatee, mustache?"

"That's the guy," Andy said, surprised, stopping himself. John Ikos was full of surprises. "You know him?"

"Met him." John put the rest of the wood on the fire, which was burning steadily now, giving off heat that sizzled the snow around it.

"In Barrow?"

"Let's get him on there," John said, nodding toward the headless corpse of the vampire kid. He went around and picked up the kid's shoulders, and Andy took him by the ankles. He wasn't heavy, but they had to straddle the fire with him to get his body on the sturdiest logs. Once they had him in place, his clothes already beginning to smolder, John fetched the head and tossed it in as well. "You remember me tellin' you I went to Los Angeles, looking for that fucker Norris?"

"Yeah. You didn't much care for it, if I recall."

"Hell on earth. Bloodsucking leeches every fuckin' place you look. And that's just the human population. Vampires are worse—only way you can tell 'em apart is the bloodsuckers don't spend hours under sunlamps to get that bogus LA tan."

"You don't have to tell me," Andy said. He'd heard the story before, but once John got rolling on the horrors of Los Angeles you couldn't stop him. "I've spent more than enough time there."

"Right. Anyhow, you know I ran up against this one pale-skinned bastard, Santana Lutz. Had a whole gang of bloodsuckers with him, called themselves the Night Crew. They thought it was pretty cool, you know, like a rock band or a super-villain team in the funny books. I don't like to say it, but all together they might have been too much for me to handle. I had help, though. A vampire named Billy—just a kid, a little older than this one. A teenager, I guess. And another one, who could kick some serious ass."

Andy thought he saw where John was headed, and the idea filled him with dread. "Let me guess. Dane."

"Dane."

"He's one of them?"

"That's right."

"But I just met him in downtown Barrow."

"Dane's got some wild tricks, I know that much. Must've figured out a way to get in."

"But why?"

The big man shrugged. "Can't be good's all I know. Dane once claimed that Lutz and some like him were tryin' to start a war with humanity, to bring vampirism out into the open once and for all. Lutz thought they'd win and could become the dominant species on Earth. Grow humans for food."

"Jesus," Andy said.

"Dane's not like him, though. He thinks the vamps are in the minority because of what they are—that they'll never rule, and they shouldn't. He steals blood from hospitals instead of killing for it, when he can."

"Yeah, but come on—he's still a vampire, John. A fucking monster."

"Maybe." John's gaze rested on the bubbling flesh of the vampire boy. "But he's got bigger stones than ninety-nine percent of the human beings I've met. Maybe a bigger heart, too. Say what you want, Dane is one brave motherfucker. He saved my life. I returned the favor. Well, saved his . . . unlife. Whatever. Thing is, if he's here now there must be a reason for it. And I got a feeling trouble follows him like a dog after a bag of meat.

"And then there's this whole thing about Stella Olemaun."

"Yeah, he told me he knew her. Didn't say how or when."

Andy turned away from the fire. The stench was starting to gag him. "Well, now I'm glad I came to tell you. I think."

"I know what you mean," John said. "I think I'm glad to know. Not sure. Got to sort that out still."

"I think there'll be a lot of sorting out done around here."

"You think there's something new in the works? Maybe they want to declare war for real—startin' with Barrow, 'cause we're the only ones who've kicked their asses in the past?"

"I don't know," Andy replied.

"There's always a few vampires up here, from late summer on, wantin' to take advantage of the long nights. . . . Hey, speaking of takin' advantage, I keep forgettin' to ask you—whatever happened to that DVD you got your hands on, that showed the proof of the first attack?"

"That, my friend," Andy remarked with a small grin, "is information that's strictly on a need-to-know basis."

Ikos stared at Andy in disbelief.

"Are you kidding? Well fuck you then, Mister Andy Gray."

"Oh, stop it. . . . Look, long story short: I burned some copies and got them into the hands of different people. The *right* people, let's say. People who know the truth, who have reasons to spread the word. When I say go—or if anything happens to me—they know what to do."

"Well, of course, if it's war, then everyone will know anyway."

"Yes, I suppose you could say that."

"This is some fucked-up shit, Andy," John said. "This is seriously fucked."

21

"YOU DIDN'T TELL HIM about YouTube?"

"Marcus, my boy . . . there are some things John Ikos is never going to understand," Andy said. "YouTube is one of them. You're not going to find him friending anyone on MySpace, either. If the time ever comes, there's no one I'd rather have at my side in a fight, but he's pretty much of a Luddite if I ever met one."

"Word," Marcus said. He was, what? Thirteen? He talked funny. That was okay. It reminded Andy of his daughters, of the fact that they'd never reach that age, but it also reminded him that other kids did, and that was good. Life went on. People grew up.

And some lived their whole lives without encountering vampires.

Marcus Kitka didn't have the good fortune to be one of them.

In the last attack, back in 2003, he'd been trapped in the house his dad—the town's new sheriff and brother of William Kitka, who had died in the first attack—had rented. As the story went, only the intercession of Stella and Eben Olemaun—in new, vampiric forms—had saved his life.

Since then, the kid had developed a marked interest in fighting vampires. Since his technical skills far surpassed Andy's, he made a valuable ally.

Together, cobbling equipment from all over the state, they had built what Marcus liked to call Andy's Fortress of Techitude. Andy just called it the War Room.

He had a dozen computers—mostly Macs, since service could be hard to come by in Barrow, but a couple of PCs as well. He had two satellite links and a T-1 line. DVD burners and video editing capability and triple failsafe network security with firewalls galore. The whole thing was in an old house that had been abandoned after the first attack, but had survived the fire. The walls were stone, twelve inches thick. The place had two woodburning stoves and a fireplace almost big enough to stand up in. Andy had turned the back bedroom—one of three—into the War Room.

He let Marcus do the tricky hacking stuff. Andy had envisioned the War Room as a way to track who else across the globe knew about vampires—knew the truth, not the nonsense. He had found a surprising number of people who claimed they did, but at least half of them were wack jobs who had wet dreams about Frank Langella's *Dracula* or those vampire romance novels by Anne Rice. When Andy did find people who really did seem to know what they were talking about, though, he wanted to check them out in more depth. His own FBI passwords and access codes had long since been deleted from the Bureau's systems, but it turned out that Marcus could find ways in without them.

Together they ran complete background checks on the people Andy had identified. If they came up clean, then he initiated discreet contact by email. From their responses—and these people almost always replied, some within minutes of his first overture—he determined if they were people he wanted to take into his confidence.

Marcus even came in handy during some of this deliberation. He was just a kid, but he was also surprisingly adept at reading people. Maybe it was because he spent a lot of time on email and instant messaging, but he caught cues online that would have soared right past Andy. Together, they came up with a small network of people they trusted, and it was to these people that Andy had sent copies of the DVD and its damning evidence.

At Marcus's urging, he had also posted the video of the attack on YouTube. Surprisingly, that had not been a terrific success.

His posts had been removed, or spoofed, but never taken seriously. Andy had envisioned a worldwide uproar over this, proof positive of the existence of the undead, and instead people thought it was a gag video, something done with Hollywood blood and latex appliances. He and some of the other supporters in his network had also built websites, displaying the footage in QuickTime, but those sites had either been shut down by their servers or otherwise blown off-line. Wikipedia entries made by his network were almost immediately edited or deleted.

Andy highly suspected the FBI's Operation Red-

Blooded was behind the suppression. From what he had learned about them—precious little, unfortunately—it seemed like just their style. They knew about the threat of vampires, that much was obvious. They also seemed to want to make sure the rest of the world didn't know what they did.

Marcus, on the other hand, blamed the vampire community. It stood to reason, he insisted, that some of the people who had been turned were as tech savvy as he was, if not more so. There was no reason to think they'd lose those skills after they became vampires, and they would have a vested interest in keeping the truth of their existence quiet.

Andy had agreed with this, until tonight's talk with John Ikos.

Maybe it was both. Which was an infinitely scarier prospect.

Marcus had tried backtracking some of the internet attacks, to see who was responsible, but so far without success.

A couple of Feds had visited the town a few months back. Andy didn't recognize them, and they didn't even see him, but he swore they were Operation Red-Blooded types. They tiptoed around the whole question of vampires, but they didn't really ask about anything else. As if questioning people about "events in Barrow in late 2001" could mean anything else. It wasn't like an al Qaeda cell had cropped up here.

"Yo," Marcus said, from a computer station across the

room. "I think I've got your database whipped into shape. You want to take a look?"

"I'll bring it up over here," Andy said. "Thanks, Marcus."

"No big."

He was glad that Brian Kitka didn't mind Marcus staying at his place all hours. After his brief visit with John Ikos, Andy hadn't wanted to get home and go to bed. He had found Marcus in the War Room, working on the database. School would be starting soon—even with Barrow's population decimated by the two attacks, they made every attempt to continue with "normal" life—and his availability would be curtailed.

Andy opened the database across the network. At a glance, it looked good. Thorough. He'd been compiling statistics on violent murders that might have been vampire related, really just amassing data and dumping it onto Marcus. Marcus had come up with a database that could organize it all. Andy could search it by location, by general type of crime, by number of victims, by any arrests made, and even by the specifics of the crime—stabbings, shootings, stranglings, beheadings, assault with blunt objects, and the like.

He ran it through some tests and was pleased to see how functional Marcus had made it. It wouldn't draw conclusions for him, but it would let him see at a glance how many fatal stabbings had occurred in North America in a given three-week period, for instance. A subfield showed how many of those crime scenes were notable for the lack of spilled blood, which might indicate a vampire's attack.

"That's awesome, Marcus," he said after he played with it for a few minutes. "Why don't you go on home and get some sleep?"

Marcus had switched to his Nintendo DS as soon as he'd finished the database. He didn't look up from the screen. "Yeah, cool," he said. A couple minutes later, when he finished whichever crucial task he'd been embroiled in, he took off.

Andy returned to the database, fell into the familiar patterns of investigation, and promptly lost all track of time.

Alone in his hotel room, Dane listened to the daytime sounds of Barrow and thought about Stella . . . as well as what his next move could possibly be in this entire messy affair, one largely of his own making.

A radio in the room softly played KBRW, the *Thistle and Shamrock* show. Outside, trucks ground through their gears, people greeted one another on the street, shouting and laughing, a bird perched on the sill of Dane's window and scolded those below on the street.

He had slept a while, then awakened while the sun still shone against the curtain over his window. After showering, he had poured himself a glass of blood and sat in the room's easy chair, sifting through the previous evening's events, pondering why he had come to Barrow.

But Stella kept intruding in those thoughts.

When the curtain started to go gray, he guessed he didn't have much longer to wait until dark. He wasn't sure what his first move would be tonight, but he didn't want a night to pass without trying to come up with some answers. Before full dark fell, though, he was startled out of his reverie by a sharp rapping at his door.

He opened it a couple of inches, blocking the door with his body in case anyone tried to rush him. Andy Gray, the guy he had met at the Polar Bar, stood there. Once again, intuition seemed to have paid off.

"Hello," Dane said.

"I saw John Ikos last night," Andy said, without preamble. "I understand you two know each other."

Dane stepped away from the door, inviting Andy inside. "Yes. We've met. Come in."

"That's about the way he put it, too. I guess you wouldn't call yourselves friends." Andy stepped into the room, closed the door behind himself.

"Not friends exactly," Dane said. "*Compadres,* maybe. I don't know if we have the right word in English."

"It does have its limitations," Andy admitted. Dane sat on the bed, indicated the easy chair with a nod of his head. Andy peeled off his parka and sat down with the jacket in his lap. "You keep it dark in here, I see."

"If you talked to Ikos, he probably told you why."

Andy nodded his head slowly. "I don't know how you got into Barrow. Or how you got by me."

Dane regarded the man carefully. Andy sat in the chair, but his head thrust forward on his neck and moved slowly, taking in the room in a steady sweep, like a vulture sitting on a telephone pole scanning the landscape for carrion. With his shaved head and the way his muscles bunched when he moved, he looked like someone who had spent time gearing up for a championship cage fight. "Who are you, anyway? You're not just anybody. Not even in this town."

Andy drew in a breath, held it for a minute. His chest, already swollen by weightlifting, expanded his shirt even more. "I used to be with the Bureau," he said. "My partner—you may have heard of him—was an agent named Paul Norris. We were investigating Stella Olemaun, when he . . . became one of you. I tried to bring him in, and he murdered my family. We wound up here in Barrow, where John and I took care of Paul. That's the short and sweet version."

Dane chuckled at that, breathy, exasperated. "I met your ex-partner. He shot me in the head."

"Really."

Both fell suddenly silent, the radio still playing softly in the background.

"So. I presume you didn't come in here trying to put a stake through my heart or anything stupid like that, did you?" Dane finally asked.

"Like I said, I talked to John. I know you helped him out, in LA. I don't think you're here to do these people any damage. If I did, you'd be dead by now."

"Or you would."

"There's always that possibility."

Dane couldn't hold back another grin. "You're just brimming with self-confidence, aren't you?"

"I didn't used to, believe me. But I like me better this way."

"I bet you do."

They glared at each other in gloom.

"So are you going to tell me why you're here?" Andy asked.

"I'm here because I heard that there's something going on. Something big and something very bad. But I don't know where and I don't know who's involved. That help any?"

"Not a hell of a lot." Andy studied him for long enough to make Dane wonder if he'd spilled blood on his chin.

"Well then," Dane said, spreading his hands. "Now what?"

22

"WELCOME TO the War Room," Andy said, reluctantly ushering Dane and John Ikos in. They had stopped by the Polar Bar and picked up John, who had arranged with Andy to meet them there so Dane wouldn't have to go back and forth through the security checkpoints.

He and John had greeted each other warmly enough, but Dane thought he noticed a certain diffidence, as if the vampire hunter still had his doubts about the vampire. Would Andy really be so trusting as to let an envoy of "the enemy" of all people into the alleged inner sanctum?

Considering that he was in the proverbial belly of the beast—maybe even now traveled up to its brain center— he was probably lucky that he was able to find two people willing to work alongside a vampire at all. Dane stopped just inside the door, stunned at how much high-tech equipment Andy had jammed into a relatively small room in an old stone house. "Impressive. By war, you mean war against us. Me."

"Present company excluded," Andy said and looked at Dane. "For now."

Dane nodded, smiling. It had been a long time since

he'd had to contend with male bonding rituals—he almost forgot that insults and threats for some humans were a sign of acceptance. "You do understand that some vampires—maybe more than I first realized—want exactly that: a war with humankind. Aren't you worried that you're playing into their hands?"

Andy dropped into an office chair and started rocking slowly back and forth. John took a second one, spun it around and straddled the back. "The difference," Andy said, "is that I'm talking about war on *our* terms, not on theirs. I wouldn't want to see every city, town, and village on Earth turned into an armed camp, like Barrow. My guess is if we can bring it hard and fast, we can do significant damage to the bloodsuckers before they can organize a defense. But if we sit on our hands until they decide it's time—and only then persuade the world's population that it's a real threat—then we're toast."

"That's probably pretty accurate," Dane had to admit. He hoped that he wouldn't be in the center of it all when it did finally come hard and fast against his kind. It could only get nasty.

He examined the equipment, some of which, on closer inspection, looked like it had been carried around Alaska on the back of a mule. It all seemed functional, though, as far as he could tell. "You wanted to show me something special?"

"I wanted to show you both something," Andy said. "You were pretty vague about why you came here."

"There's not much to say," Dane said. "I had a run-in

with . . . and killed a vampire named Bork Dela, who was murdering residents of Savannah in a horribly public fashion, draining his victims and beheading them and taking others, presumably alive, for reasons yet to be determined." He hadn't told anyone about what happened to Ananu, and while he couldn't actually say why not, he decided to keep quiet about it for a while longer. "Before I finished him off, he told me that there was something going on, up north, that would eventually make the attack on Barrow look tame. I'm guessing that it had something to do with the live victims he had taken, but I have no idea what. In the house he had been using for a sanctuary, I found rooms—almost like meat lockers—where he had been stashing people. I think he was shipping them out someplace, probably still alive. But like I said, this is all speculation. I'm still at an impasse over this."

"It's hard to speculate about what a bloodsucker'll do," John added. "Even, I guess, if you are one."

"That's still more than I knew before," Andy said. "That'll help narrow things down a little."

"Narrow what?" Dane asked.

"My search. We've been building this handy little database. If I put in beheadings plus blood draining plus abductions, that should give us a pretty limited number of events to look at." Andy turned to his keyboard and pecked at it for a minute, then leaned back in the desk chair, folding his arms over his chest. On his monitor, a little rainbow-colored wheel spun around and around.

When it stopped, Andy leaned toward the screen and gave a low whistle. "Not so limited after all," he said. "This shows more than a hundred similar incidents."

"Over how long?" John asked.

"In the last thirty days," Andy said. "I'm a little afraid to search any wider than that. Decapitation, kidnapping, drained bodies. That pretty much sums it up, no?"

"Pretty much," Dane agreed, nodding.

"Are there any other common links?" John asked. "Did they all take place in the same area?"

"No, they're all over the map. U.S., Canada, Sweden, Russia, the Balkans . . . all northern hemisphere, but that's about the only commonality."

"So what does that tell us?" Dane asked. "That Dela wasn't alone in whatever he was doing? That's not much to go on."

"This is where the powers of the amazing Marcus come in," Andy said. "It's not foolproof, but it's a hell of a lot better than I could have done. Now that I've selected these, all I have to do is ask the database and it'll hack into as many of the local police agencies investigating these crimes as it can and snake their official reports. Maybe we'll find something more out that way."

"Can you really do that?" Dane asked. "They just let you in?"

Andy gave a small laugh. "Not exactly. But Marcus has created a program that uses passwords he's already discovered and checks to see if they're still good. If they're not, it takes the old one as a model and tries out more—

as many as a hundred a minute. It won't crack every-thing, and some systems he hasn't been able to hack at all. And some still just keep their files on paper instead of entering them on computers, but that's happening less and less. A lot of smaller police departments don't have very sophisticated network security and we can get right in. Hell, there was a computer consultant in Illinois who used programs he found online to snag the FBI director's secret password and get access to the Bureau's system, where he was able to get the passwords of thirty-eight thousand Bureau employees. Post-9/11 or not, there's still some serious problems with online security. I'd say out of these we can probably get forty or fifty case files, easy. Maybe a lot more."

"That's not bad," John said. "It'll tell us more than we knew before."

"That's the idea." Andy punched some keys. "Here we go."

"Now we wait?" Dane asked.

"Now we wait."

"Got anything to drink in the house?" John asked.

"Not by your standards," Andy said. "No whiskey or beer. Just some fruit juice, some sports beverages. Water." He glanced at Dane. "I guess not by your standards, ei-ther . . . I'm sorry, I'm having somewhat of a hard time with this. With you here."

"Understood. If it makes you feel any better, I'm not going to hurt you. And don't worry about me," Dane said.

Andy nodded, although Dane wasn't entirely certain if he was reassured on that point.

"You're right, though," John said, breaking through the awkwardness of the moment. "Right about now I could use a decent shot."

"Alcohol's hard to come by around here," Andy sighed, speaking to Dane. "A lot of communities in this area have a 'damp' law, which prohibits the sale of alcoholic beverages, but import, possession, and consumption, that's okay. I don't drink anymore—which was not the case before I got here. It's available some places, but the closer it gets to the dark time, the less available it is. Once the sun goes down, you can't get a drop anywhere. No one wants to be responsible for the combination of dark days and booze. Not a good idea around these parts."

"Seems reasonable," Dane said.

The three of them fell silent for a few minutes, all, Dane supposed, dwelling on the things that haunted them in their most private moments.

For Dane, it was one of the rare occasions when he let a human like Andy Gray get under his skin. What he must think of Dane, of vampires in general to have set up . . . all this. A "war room." It was pretty mind-blowing, come to think of it.

It would be ironic for Andy to know that Dane didn't kill the innocent—he would only select from people who weren't contributing anything to society anyway . . . criminals, dealers, pimps, the kind of scumbags the world would be better off without anyway.

Still, Dane did kill to live. A moral gray area, to be sure—playing God, to a certain extent. It did still bother him after all this time, despite the fact that killing was a last resort. Before he got to that point, he preferred getting blood from blood banks or plasma centers. Animal blood wasn't the greatest option—okay in a pinch, but only a temporary one.

Before he decided to break away from Marlow and go his own way, Dane had killed as a regular habit, like Marlow and the rest of the vampires he knew. It wasn't until he was on his own and met vampires like Merrin and poor Yuki and some others, that he realized there were options. Compromises. Since then, he had tried to limit himself. He regretted the earlier murders, but chalked them up to not knowing any better. The people he did kill now, he was convinced, preyed on their fellow humans and deserved what they got.

Dane continued to be haunted by the thought of roads not taken. What might have been if he hadn't been turned, if he had remained human and married Vanessa Steward, for instance? He would be long since dead by now. But he might have had children and grandchildren. A line of decent, law-abiding citizens might have descended from him. Who could say what their contributions might have been?

Just as likely, of course, he might have died on a battlefield at Gettysburg or Manassas or Chickamauga. Scavenger birds would have picked at his flesh, humans would have taken his weapons and buttons and boots and that one gold tooth, and the walking mosquitoes would have sucked the blood from his still warm corpse. He had wondered from time to time if he should have had the courage to destroy himself as soon as he reached the bug-eater stage. He had decided, though, that he didn't truly think that. Vampires and humans could coexist, he believed. But it would take enlightened vampires like himself to make the rest understand that, and to convince humans that it was worth it.

And really, in the end, he had been prone to fits of heightened pride and emotion. After all, hadn't Dane been the one who had sought out Stella back in 2003 . . . Dane mistakenly believing Eben to be responsible for Marlow's death . . . Dane out to teach Stella a lesson she wouldn't soon forget during the short time of her remaining life?

"Andy," John Ikos said after a time. "I don't think Dane and me are going to be that helpful at interpreting police files. How about we take a walk and catch up with you later?"

"Sure," Andy said. "They've just started to come in, so I'll have plenty to keep me busy for a while."

John caught Dane's eye and ticked his gaze toward the door. Dane shrugged, turned the knob. The door led straight outside, down a couple of steps, and to a walkway between the house and a tall plank fence. As with most occupied structures in town, floodlights washed down the sides of the building near every door.

He and John passed through the gate. Andy lived on a quiet residential street with no sidewalks, a few blocks from the commercial district. They headed in that direction, just walking, with no particular destination that Dane knew of.

After they had covered a couple of blocks, John finally spoke. "I just wanted to say, you showed a lot of balls, comin' here. The people around here found out what you were, me and Andy wouldn't be able to help you. Period. They hate your kind, me included, and for a damn good reason."

"I guess we haven't given them much reason to do anything else."

"That's for sure. Anyhow, I just wanted to say that."

"I appreciate it."

They passed a couple in their midforties, walking hand-in-hand and talking softly, puffs of steam issuing from their mouths like visual evidence of the words of love they shared. Dane smiled at them as they passed, and John tossed them a brisk nod. When the people were out of earshot, he continued. "And Andy in there. He's good people, and you can trust him, don't worry about that."

"I didn't get the sense he was a big proponent of letting vampires live."

"None of us are. But ones like you . . . Miss Olemaun, there are exceptions."

"There are more like us than you think."

"I know for sure there are plenty of the other kind."

He and Dane turned a corner and walked past a church, empty at this hour, its tall steeple and white walls washed by floodlights as if to declare its steadfastness to enemies viewing it from a distance.

Dane hadn't been inside a church since his battle with Marlow in the cathedral. He didn't think it was appropriate for him to enter one. That did not, however, preclude him from thinking about faith and God and a higher purpose. With Ferrando Merrin and Alexandra Keeffe, who had been a traditional 50s housewife, literally baking a boysenberry pie when she was turned—she opened a window to set the pie out to cool and two rough hands reached in, grabbed her, drew her out (to this day she preferred Capri pants and sheath dresses to the typical black pants and shirts worn by most *nosferatu*)—and Matthew and Benjamin, a father and son who had been turned together in a Louisiana bayou in the late 1930s, Dane had conversed literally hundreds, if not thousands, of times about subjects that would have sent Marlow into fits of sputtering, violent rage.

Did vampires fit into God's plan?

Most undead would have laughed at the suggestion. Dane and his friends were cautious about with whom they raised such ideas. But among themselves, in private, they were anxious to explore them.

Yes, vampires were murderers, and God hated murder. And yet, hadn't He created sharks and spiders and every other predator on Earth, vampires included? Why would He allow such creatures to exist, if not intentionally?

Wasn't it possible that there was some unknown purpose for them, to be revealed in the fullness of time?

Marlow and his ilk would have regarded such ideas as the height of hypocrisy. Maybe they were, Dane thought, but hypocrisy was in no shortage these days, from a pres-

ident who professed Christianity and yet lied to send soldiers to their deaths all the way down to the grocer who
keeps ground beef for sale a few days past its prime because it's still pink—courtesy of the carbon monoxide
pumped into it—because it wouldn't be his kids eating
the burgers made from it.

After the cathedral incident, Dane didn't see Marlow
again until the summer of 2001. He was back in New
York and it was August, the nights hot and steamy, and
no one had any idea that, in another few weeks, the city
and the world would irrevocably change. He had visited
with some acquaintances, vampires, but not the ones
with whom he had formed a small group of like-minded
individuals. Dane was about to leave to go back to his
safe house—most vampires had them, but he and Merrin
and the others had set up their own network of them, secret even from the rest of the undead—when the front
door opened and Marlow strode in.

They regarded each other for several moments, warily,
like two wolves from different packs encountering one
another on contested ground. History had settled in between them, a mountain range of forbidding peaks and
dangerous canyons. Their first words had been civil but
cautious. Seeing Marlow there, however, had been an
emotional moment, almost like running into a long-
estranged parent or lover, and Dane decided not to leave
right away after all.

Marlow's attire certainly had changed with the times
since their last encounter all those years ago. Still bald, he

now blended in perfectly with the punk scene, complete with beat-up leather jacket, six earrings in his left ear, and he was smoking like a chimney.

Beyond that, though, the son of a bitch hadn't changed one bit.

By the time the night had wound down, he and Marlow had somehow found common ground again. They were, after all, if not father and son then the next best thing. The bond between them could be stretched, endangered, but never truly severed. Marlow's blood ran in Dane, and vice versa.

They had spent most of that week together, as long as Dane's business kept him in the city. Near the end of it, Marlow had invited Dane to Barrow, that autumn, for a feeding frenzy the likes of which no one had ever seen. "Why don't you come with me, for old time's sake?" Marlow had asked. Dane thought about it, briefly considered proving to Marlow that he could keep an open mind. But then again, Dane was his own person—what the hell did he have to prove to anyone anymore?

Not wishing to anger Marlow, however, Dane decided to do the next best thing: tell a little white lie. "I'm sorry, my friend, but I have some important business to attend to on the West Coast. A little real estate investment I've had my eye on for quite some time is closing before year's end. I'd hate to be away during that time. But you go . . . enjoy yourself. I'll be with you in spirit, so to speak."

Marlow laughed, an ugly, guttural sound. "I'll raise a glass to you then, maybe? Is that how it is?"

"Don't make it out to be more than it is. Seriously, I just have some pressing business to attend to. This was good tonight. *Very* good, and I've really enjoyed seeing you again. Let's meet up upon your return . . . for old time's sake, as you say."

They embraced as friends, promising to meet again in New York after the New Year.

Marlow didn't survive the trip, the shock of which might never leave Dane, despite everything since then.

And now ironically Dane had returned to Barrow, working with some of the people who had battled against the vampires last time.

"What do you really think that guy was talking about?" John asked, dragging Dane's thoughts back to the present. "What's going on up north?"

Dane hesitated. "I'm not sure yet . . . I hope it's not what I think it is."

23

"SO HERE'S WHERE we are," announced Andy Gray.

Dane and John had returned to Andy's house after a couple of hours of roaming Barrow's neighborhoods, John giving Dane a thumbnail historical tour of the town. A high point, to John, was the former location of the Ikos Diner, where his brother Sam had once fed the whole town and regaled his diners with stories at the same time.

Dane had a hard time imagining the taciturn John Ikos sprouting from the same tree as an outgoing, gregarious restaurateur, but sometimes siblings could be more different than strangers, he knew.

Andy still sat where they had left him, in front of the computer screen. His eyes were bloodshot and ringed, and Dane realized that, with the exception of coming to fetch him at the hotel, he must have been sitting there for most of the last twenty-four hours or so. He rubbed a hand across his smooth head and gestured toward two empty chairs—he had brought in a folding chair from someplace to supplement the desk chairs. "Sit," he said. "This'll take a while."

"What'd you find out?" John asked.

"Plenty, and the program Marcus wrote is still pulling

down case files now, so I think we'll get more. These crimes—many of them, anyway—are definitely linked, although I don't think the same perpetrator committed them all. There are too many of them, in locations too far-flung, and sometimes practically simultaneously. After you guys left I widened the search parameters a bit, to include abductions without drained bodies, but with no ransom demands or recovered victims, figuring that while vampires might be tempted to feed on most occasions there also could be times when they'd skip that. That put a few hundred more crimes into the mix. Some are certainly not involved, but others looked to be pretty close to our model scenario."

Dane figured Andy must have gotten used to giving lectures during his FBI days. He would have thought an agent would spend more time listening than talking, but the FBI was a huge bureaucracy—even Andy called it "the Bureau"—so probably there were meetings upon meetings, at which agents had to blather on about what they had learned.

In order, it appeared, for other agents and top brass to ignore them.

"So what did you find out?" John asked again.

"Like I said, we've got very similar crimes happening in wildly diverse locations. I tagged the ones in Savannah that you told us about and used those as the baseline. Somebody goes into a residence, kills one victim, drains their blood, and takes one or more others alive. No demand for ransom is ever made, and the victims don't turn up again. This is a pretty specific and unusual scenario."

Andy paused, waiting, as if someone might ask another question. No one did, so he took a deep breath and continued. "The files I've been reading through all share those same basic features. The sheer number of abductions is pretty staggering. So far—and like I said, they're still rolling in—I count almost two hundred people snatched in the past month alone."

"And we have no idea how long this has been going on," Dane said.

"That's right. You can do the math as well as I can— over the course of a year, if it's been happening for that long, we're talking about thousands."

"And no one has put this all together before now?" John asked.

"I don't think anyone has tried," Andy said. "Why would they? Why would they assume that murders in Boston are tied in any way to murders in Belgrade? We're just lucky Dane heard about the Savannah incidents and realized what they had to mean."

Dane scratched his chin. "I don't know about your definition of 'lucky,' but okay."

"Because they haven't connected these incidents," Andy continued, "they haven't caught some interesting aspects of them that I noticed tonight."

"Like what?"

"Like, at some locations—not all of them, but enough to attract my notice—crime scene investigators found sawdust embedded in the perp's footprints."

"Sawdust?" Dane asked. "He's a carpenter?"

"Maybe. I'm not sure yet what it means. It's just a strange anomaly, and the repetition made me think that maybe it was important. The sawdust was only found at scenes in northern Europe—Finland, Poland, Russia, Sweden, and so on. One of the crime scene units, in Copenhagen—you'd be surprised how thorough the Danish cops are—sent the samples they collected to a lab, and that lab came up with something that I found very curious.

"The sawdust comes from a distinctive source. Not the lumber itself, which comes from a variety of trees common to northern climates. But the trees themselves have another common element—they're suffering from a particular type of hypoxia, a form of oxygen deprivation due to pollutants from a coal-fired power plant. The lab was able to identify, through the particular makeup of the pollutants, which plant it is, which is the Alta plant, in the northernmost section of Norway."

"Let me make sure I have this right," Dane said. "This particular sawdust, from this one region of Norway, was found at scenes all across northern Europe?"

"That's right."

"Which indicates a single predator hit all these places?"

"No," Andy said. "That's what's really interesting. Some of these incidents happened on the same night. I don't care who you are, you're not going to be able to hit homes in Krakow and Stockholm within an hour's time."

"No—it's not very likely," said Dane.

"Not at all."

"Which leaves what?" John asked.

"Which leaves the probability," Andy replied, "that we're talking about various perpetrators who had all spent time—very recently—at the same place."

"In Norway. A sawmill, a lumberyard?"

"Could be those, or even a large construction project."

"Could be. An apartment complex, an office building . . . most construction is still framed out with lumber." Andy fixed Ikos with a steady look.

"The more I think about it, the more I'm afraid that might be what all this is about," Dane said. "A kind of stockyard for humans. They're being abducted for breeding, food. So it'd really be more of a combination stockyard and—"

"Slaughterhouse," said a voice from behind the three men.

Dane, Ikos, and Gray turned.

Eben Olemaun stood behind them, having clearly heard most of the conversation. Dane hadn't detected Eben's approach this time, which was rather disturbing. Dane couldn't help but notice his stonelike expression, not that of a vampire, but one of a determined cop, someone who couldn't help but get involved.

Two men and two vampires stood inside a home in Barrow, Alaska, each waiting for the other to make a move. Andy Gray was silent. He had never seen Eben— it was like having a legend in his home. Ikos was looking from man to man, wondering if there'd be a fight, but it was Dane who opened his mouth to speak.

Eben beat him to the punch, again.

"So . . . sounds like we need to check it out, right?" Eben said.

There was another long silence until another familiar shape appeared behind Eben, suprising even him.

It was his wife.

"There'll be three of us, then," Stella announced.

"No," Eben said sharply. "No, Stella. Barrow can't be left completely undefended. It's still a while till the dark comes, but we don't know that whoever'll wait that long if they decide to come back."

The argument had escalated to the point where the three vampires thought it best to go outside the walls of Barrow to continue the conversation. Eben obviously didn't like Dane—and that was putting it mildly—but he seemed to like the entire growing situation even less. In another moment of irony, Eben and Dane found themselves on the same side of the fence on not one, but several points, the most important of which was possibly going in search of the alleged slaughterhouse, the second being Stella had to stay behind.

Convincing her would be another thing altogether.

"He's right, Stella," Dane said. "This has been ground zero too many times to rethink it now."

"Eben . . . you've never even been out of the country before!"

"But I have," Dane shot back. "Trust me, I'll keep an eye on him." *I can't even believe I said that,* he thought.

Stella still fumed but said nothing. No point in arguing with the truth, Dane guessed.

Dane had put off mentioning the other thing, but now he felt he had to. After all his talk about how they could trust him, he couldn't keep his secret under wraps any longer. "Something else happened in Savannah. . . . Before I caught him, Bork Dela sexually assaulted a young woman. She's now pregnant. We couldn't do anything about it, so she's carrying the baby to term."

"Oh my God," Stella said. "Is that even possible?"

"It's so rare as to be essentially legendary," Dane answered. "And in those legends, vampires always destroy the infant at birth."

"What would the child be like?" Eben asked.

"That's what we don't know. Something completely new, I guess."

"But if the vampires have always destroyed them . . ." Stella began.

"I was thinking along the same lines, Stella," Dane said. "I don't know what they expected, or what they saw when those babies were born—if it ever really happened. But if they didn't want them around, maybe there's a good reason for that."

"How does the lady in question feel about it?"

"She's pretty freaked out," Dane admitted. "As might be expected. I've got her in a safe place, with a trusted friend looking after her."

"Are you sure this 'friend' will leave the baby alone when it's born?" Eben asked.

"Yes. I have absolute faith in Ferrando."

"When is she due?" Stella asked.

"That's hard to say. When I left, she seemed to be progressing at hyperspeed. I haven't been in touch since I got here . . . so my hope is that she hasn't had the baby already."

24

ANANU WOKE UP when Ferrando Merrin swept into her room and drew back the curtains.

From her bed she could see stars outside the second-floor window. Somehow she had quickly adjusted to sleeping through the day, but she still missed the sun's warmth, the golden light of morning that should have been allowed to stream in through that east-facing window, the sight of blue skies mottled by clouds.

Her protectors, Dane and Merrin, had insisted that she adopt their ways, avoiding the sunlight, and she had gone along, but she still wasn't convinced it was necessary. How could the sun hurt her? She was still herself, after all.

Merrin insisted, though, and he watched over her like a mother hen. Even though he didn't eat himself—not regular food, and he was polite enough not to *feed* when she was around—he was an incredible cook. Even if he was just whipping up toast and eggs for breakfast, he put something special into it that she never would have thought of, seasoning the toast with a little rosemary and flakes of Parmesan cheese, for instance. During the long nights he made sure she didn't watch too much late-night TV—mostly movies and infomercials at that hour—but tried to keep her entertained with books and games and music (unlike Mitch, his musical tastes had never stalled, but over the vast span of his unlife he had explored music from virtually every era and every culture, and while he could talk about it all with a fierce intelligence, he never left her feeling baffled or stupid).

Sometimes they went out at night, down to the coast so she could see moonlight on the water and great ships passing by out at sea, or into local swamps to watch the alligators and birds and fish engaged in their nightly dance of survival, all accompanied by the incessant trilling of insects.

She found that she actually missed Dane and Mitch and even AJ—their odd "family" had only been together for a couple of weeks, but at this point it was the only one she had. Merrin tried his best but he couldn't replace the sounds of multiple voices in different parts of the house, footsteps here and there indicating someone's presence, and the solicitous way that one or another checked in on her off and on throughout the days and the nights.

She had always felt safer with them around, too. Someone had always been awake, alert, watching out for danger. Merrin could most likely take care of himself—he wouldn't have lasted so many years if he couldn't—but he was still just one person. He had to rest sometimes and he couldn't be everywhere at once.

It never dawned on her that this situation should be an aberration, something so unnatural despite feeling so right.

"Did you sleep well, Ana?" he asked her once he'd tucked the drapes into their tiebacks.

"Okay, I guess. I had some strange dreams."

"Do you remember them?" He looked to be in his seventies, with black hair that had mostly turned white and a long, thin face, cheeks so pink he might have rouged them. His eyes were small and black, just tiny buttons really, dwarfed by a long nose that he'd mastered the art of looking down disapprovingly when he needed to. He stood as straight as a post and almost as thin as one, his arms and legs like a spider's limbs.

"No." She rubbed her eyes with the knuckles of her right hand, then pushed back the blankets and swung her legs off the bed. Fuzzy slippers had been parked next to the bed; she pushed her feet into them, then brought them back up, crossing her legs, Indian-style, on the mattress. "I never do these days. I just dream the weirdest shit, but then when I wake up it's like *poof*! All gone."

"It sounds like a horrible cliché, but sometimes we can discover great truths in our dreams," he said. "Things that we hide from our conscious minds can reveal themselves there."

"Do you dream? I mean, people like you?"

"Oh, heavens yes," Merrin said. "Dreams like you wouldn't believe. I'm not certain, but sometimes I think there's a kind of racial memory that manifests itself only in our dreams—it's as if in my dreams, I can see things that only the first vampire experienced, and moments belonging to all of them since then."

"Do you remember those?" Ananu asked.

"Sometimes," he said. "I write them down, when I do. I have dozens of dream journals, on one of the book-shelves at my home. I'd be pleased to show it to you someday—my home, I mean."

"I'd like that. Thank you."

"It's rather nice. Some would call it a mansion, al-though my neighbors—the ones with real mansions—wouldn't. It's in the hills outside Asheville, North Carolina. God's country, I used to call it there."

"Do you believe in God?"

Merrin hesitated before answering, his cheeks pinking up a little more than they had been. "Let's just say that if he exists, I hope he's awfully damned forgiving." He of-fered a smile. "Breakfast is ready. Would you like it down-stairs, or shall I bring it up?"

"I'll come down," Ana said. An urgent need gripped her. "Just let me pee and I'll be right down."

Before he left the room, the mobile phone he kept with him constantly chirped. He snatched it from his belt before the second ring, glanced at the screen before an-swering. "Dane," he said. "How are things?"

Merrin listened and made mm-hmm noises for a minute, frowned deeply, blew out a sigh, then handed the phone to Ananu. She clamped her thighs together, wig-gling in discomfort. "Hi, Dane?"

"Hello, Ananu," he said. "Even across the miles, his voice sounded like he was right there with her. Just hearing him made her feel more secure. "How's everything going there? You feeling okay?"

"I'm okay," she said. "But—"

"Merrin's treating you well?"

"It's like he thinks he's a butler or something. He won't let me do anything for myself."

"He likes taking care of others," Dane said. "I think it makes him feel needed."

"Well, he's good at it."

"Listen, the main reason I called is that I'm not coming back as soon as I thought. I'm not sure when I'll be able to get in touch again. I didn't want to leave without checking in to make sure everything's going okay there."

"It's copacetic," she said. "Only . . ." She paused, expecting him to interrupt again.

"Only what?"

"Only . . . when a pregnant girl has to pee, she really fuckin' has to pee, okay?"

Dane seemed to get the message. "I won't keep you then, Ana. Take care. If you need me for anything, Merrin can try to get word to me."

"Bye." She punched the END button on Merrin's phone and dropped the unit on the bed. "Sorry," she said. She slid off the bed, past Merrin, and out the door. The bathroom was two doors down the hall.

She barely made it in time.

*   *   *

AJ drove up from Orange Park during the afternoon, cruising into Savannah just after ten. He had been warned against coming back here, but his place in Florida was just a few blocks from the Jacks River, and he could smell the river every day when he left the apartment and again when he came back. Smelling it without being on it would kill him, he knew that much about himself. Kill him as surely as a bullet to the heart. He needed that rocking rhythm under his feet, needed the thrum of the engine working up through his legs, the brilliant shards of light thrown into his eyes off the water. He wasn't due back at work until Monday, so he figured he would have time to pick up the *Midlife Crisis* and pilot her back down to Orange Park.

Dane's friend Merrin had some kind of connections, to pull things together as fast as he had. Overnight AJ Roddy had a new name—Brent John Masters, too sophisticated for him but maybe that was the point. No one who knew AJ would ever look for him under a name like that. He also had a hack license and a car, a bank account with a few grand in it, an apartment, and identification, including a commercial class driver's license and a Visa card. His apartment complex was full of singles, including at least three available, youngish widows living on what appeared to be decent insurance settlements. He had left behind debts and some overdue movie rentals, but Merrin had assured him that those things would be taken care of. He wore new clothes, more suited to Brent John Masters than anything AJ had ever owned—a blue blazer with brass buttons, a Hawaiian print shirt from Tommy Bahama, white linen slacks, and Sperry Topsiders with no socks.

The new life hadn't come with a boat, though. AJ loved the sensation of water under his feet, the tang of salt water or the briny scent of rivers in his nostrils, the wind in what hair he had left for as long as he'd have it. Once he had the Weekender down there he'd repaint her, change the name. Merrin could deal with the registration issues. If that guy was connected to organized crime in some way, AJ didn't want to know about it. It would explain a lot, but the explanations that he had been given—that he and Dane and the shitheel who messed up Ana were all vampires—was more than he wanted to deal with.

The whole world had turned topsy-turvy these last few years, as if the new millennium had been some kind of insanity trigger, and pulling it had changed all the rules. People flew airplanes into buildings and started wars seemingly at random and mailed anthrax and set off bombs in subways and blew themselves up; and skilled politicians self-destructed in new and spectacular ways and everyone worshipped celebrities like gods only to turn on them like jackals at the slightest hint of weakness, and he just did not fucking understand any of it.

Now adding vampires to the mix, and not just the fact that there were people who were dead but wouldn't lie down and drank blood, but the additional fact that they didn't all get along with each other, that there were factions, like the Democrats and Republicans in Congress always at each other's throats, only made everything worse.

Jesus. It was like being told that Jack and Jill really did fall down the hill and some freaky goose really wrote stories down to scare kids and that monster really did live in his closet after all.

He parked among the other cars in the Tubby's lot and walked across to the docks. A few lights shone here and there and he heard a radio playing some kind of salsa music from one of the boats, but other than that and cars passing by all he could hear was the slap of water against the hulls and the creak of the wood and the ropes. The scent of the water reminded him of why he had come. The water was real. He could navigate it and he could dunk his head in it and he could drink it. It had always been there and always would be, and at this point he needed something real in his life.

Sneaking up to his own boat made AJ feel like a common criminal. He walked down the docks toward the *Midlife Crisis,* trying to stand tall but avoid the lights at the same time. By now, he figured, whatever had been going on had blown over, but Dane and Merrin had both told him it wasn't safe to return to Savannah, so he didn't want to take unnecessary chances. No one saw him, so he heaved a sigh of relief when he stepped onto the familiar deck.

He would start the engine, then untie the boat and head out. In five minutes he'd be away from the docks and on his way out to sea.

The boat shifted and swayed as he crossed the deck,

water slapped its sides, and he didn't hear the tread of another foot until something hard and metal slammed down
across the side of his head, catching his upper ear and
blasting points of light through the darkness of the deck.

Stella was in luck—John Ikos was home, and he didn't
shoot at her as she approached his secluded lodge. She
had been around here before but still couldn't quite get
used to the bunkerlike structure built into the side of a
hill—concrete wall with weapons slits and a steel-clad
door disguising what had once been a standard hunting
cabin made of logs like her place. Except even inside that
the cabin obviously belonged to someone a little obsessed
with guns—everywhere she looked in the cabin were
guns and gun racks, ammo boxes, cleaning supplies. She
had almost never seen John without a gun close at hand,
and some of the weapons he had were so high-tech she
wondered if the military had even adopted them yet. The
spicy aroma of bubbling stew from a pot suspended in the
big fireplace filled the cabin.

"Cooking tonight?"

"Some of us have more varied diets than others," John
remarked. For once he was out of his fur-lined parka,
wearing just a sweater, jeans, and boots. He looked oddly
naked. "I got some venison in the pot, along with some
potatoes and vegetables from in town."

"Smells good," Stella said. "In the sense of something I
would have liked, once upon a time." It was heartbreak-
ing to admit.

"No one invited you to stay for supper."

"John, I need to speak with you."

"What's up?"

"Can I sit?"

"Sure, sorry. Be my guest."

Stella pulled a chair out from under the dining table, both rough-hewn wood with some bark remaining on. On the wall above the fireplace a sampler added an unexpected touch of domesticity to the place, until Stella read the stitched-in message: TOUCH MY SHIT AND I'LL KILL YOU. That sounded like the John Ikos she remembered, from another life. She lowered herself onto the chair, then waited for him to do the same across from her. "I understand you know Dane."

"Yeah, I know him. Good enough guy, for one of the—one of you."

"He and Eben are going away soon. They said they wanted to see you before they go. I just wanted to see you first."

"What about?"

She thought about the situation. She, the former vampire hunter turned vampire herself, who lost her husband only to be reunited with him again in the worst way possible. And John Ikos, who kept to himself, who lost his brother—as far as she knew, the only family he had—in the first Barrow attack, who had turned his hunting skills toward a different kind of prey. He now stalked the most dangerous predator of all, the kind she had learned more about than almost any other human on Earth.

They had fought side by side for their town—the town neither chose to live in, but both considered themselves protectors of—and would do so again. This time, however, she would be leaving it in his hands. "I need to go away, too" she said. "The nights are getting longer, and Eben won't be here. It's possible that there may be another attack. I just wanted to make sure you can handle things."

"Every time it happens, folks in Barrow get smarter. Maybe the vamps do, too, I don't know about that. But I know our folks have better fences, UV lights, everybody's armed and knows what to point at. I think they could hold 'em off even without my help, much less yours."

"I hope you're right," she said. "But now there seem to be many things going on in other places, and it all has to be checked out."

She hadn't even told Eben she planned to go to Georgia. He wouldn't take it well. He would, most likely, pitch a fit. Better to go, then let him figure out that she had done so. Maybe even after he got home and wondered where she was.

If he got home.

According to Dane, the incident down in Savannah was too important to be taken lightly. Dane insisted that the mother was safe, and perhaps she was. But if Stella knew her nightcrawlers—and she thought she did—they would learn the mother's whereabouts somehow. They would come for her, for the baby, and they would not be easily dissuaded. Whatever protection Dane had put in place could stand reinforcing.

"If you wanted to tell me where you're off to, I expect you would've already, so I won't ask," John said.

"You're right—I don't intend to tell you," Stella replied.

"That's just fine. Don't tell me where you're going. The less I know, the better. You takin' someone with you?"

"I hadn't planned on it."

"Might not be a bad idea to have some backup that can be out in daylight."

"I know that." She couldn't quite grasp what he was getting at, and he was ordinarily a very direct guy. "If you're thinking you should come along, John, I appreciate it but I think you'll be needed here."

She had never seen John Ikos blush before, hadn't known that it was even possible. His gaunt cheeks turned pink and hot. The smell of his blood filling his capillaries piqued her hunger. "No," he said quickly. "No, that's not . . . not what I meant. I'm not talking about me. But there is someone . . ."

PART THREE

INTO THE UNDERWORLD

25

IT TURNED OUT THAT Tromsø was the largest city above the Arctic Circle, and had its own airport. Dane and Eben still had to get to Oslo, but there they boarded an overnight Norwegian Air flight directly to Tromsø. By the time they landed, the eastern sky was beginning to pale, so they jumped in a cab and asked to be taken to the Quality Hotel Saga, which seemed to have a central location.

From what Dane could see, the city looked modern and scenic, with ships churning up and down a body of water that might have been a river or a fjord. The cabbie pointed out Skarven, a restaurant and pub he recommended, and Dane thanked him politely without mentioning that they probably wouldn't be visiting a lot of restaurants. The trees had shed most of their leaves, but scatters of gold and orange blew along the curbs as the taxi rushed past. Dane might have been more interested in the view if he hadn't been worried about the sun.

Safely ensconced in their room, curtains drawn against the day, Dane and Eben warily regarded each other. Dane still didn't like Eben and he figured the feeling was mutual, and then some. Eben lounged in a chair, leaving Dane no place to sit but on one of the beds.

"Now what?" Eben remarked.

"Now we get some rest," Dane recommended. "And then we get busy trying to find the local vampires. City this size has to have a population. I want to make some calls, but we need to be ready to move by sundown. I don't want to spend any more time here than I have to."

"Makes two of us," Eben said brusquely. He yawned, scraped his sleeve across his open mouth.

Dane wished they had decided on two rooms, instead of one. Eben's trust in him didn't extend that far, unfortunately. He wondered if Eben would sleep with one eye open, just in case Dane tried anything. Or vice versa.

What Eben might try, he had no idea. And Dane really had no interest in putting something over on Eben. All he wanted was to find out what the connection was between sawdust from this region and the Headsman-style murders Andy Gray had turned up.

Well, if Eben doesn't want to be friendly, I can't force him, Dane thought. He stripped and climbed into the bed he had been sitting on. Eben still sat in the chair by the window, a vacant expression on his face, staring toward the ceiling.

What kind of baggage does this man have? What could it have been like to be truly dead for a year and a half?

There are no answers up there on the ceiling, Eben. Pretty sure about that one.

But you just keep right on looking.

*   *   *

After sleeping for six hours, Dane went to work. His mobile phone had service here, which pleasantly surprised him. He had been expecting some Arctic wilderness and instead found the city referred to as the Paris of the North, so civilized that Barrow, by contrast, might have been an Inupiat fishing village. Merrin had promised to do some digging while Dane traveled, while once again imploring him to be careful, so his first call was back to Georgia, which seemed a million miles away. And Merrin had indeed come up with some suggestions.

None of the members of their network dwelled in this area anymore—the more aggressive, warlike vampires had moved into the areas above the Arctic Circle, forcing others into more southerly climes. But Merrin found one who had, for a time, had a safe house in Tavlik, not far away. That vampire recommended a specific part of the city where a number of busy nightclubs—Tromsø, it happened, was famous for its nightlife—provided ample feeding opportunities for vampires, if they didn't mind a little hard liquor in their meals.

He had also located a busy sawmill in the nearby community of Lyggen.

After hanging up, Dane described both options to Eben, who sat up in his bed, his short dark hair mussed from sleep. "I'm for the nightclubs," Eben said. "Nothing like fucking up some vamps to start a trip off right."

"Keeping in mind that you are one," Dane pointed out.

"Not something that slips my mind," Eben said. "It

was my choice . . . but I hate like hell that I was forced into that position in the first place."

"Some people were born for it, and never realize their own potential until it happens. Others—like me—would rather have died when our time came than go on this way."

"I can kill you now, if that's what you want."

A grim smile traced Dane's lips. "At one time I'd have taken you up on that. Not anymore. Things are different now anyway. I mean, here we are, actually trying to be civil, or as much as possible, while attempting to stave off a full-scale war. This could be really nasty. I'm not as sure as some are that any vampires would survive it."

"And that'd be bad how?"

"It's not the destination I'm worried about, so much as the trip. Neither species would come out of it very well, I'm afraid."

"You're probably right." Eben kicked off his blankets. "Kind of unfortunate."

They dressed in cold-weather gear to blend in and headed out into the night. Dane had ordered a rental car earlier in the day, which had been delivered to the hotel, so after collecting the keys they went outside and found a dark green Saab. Dane had a fake international driver's license, while Eben's Alaska one had never been updated for obvious reasons, so Dane got in behind the wheel.

"All these Norwegian words look like somebody typing with their face to me," Eben commented.

"It's not an easy language," Dane said. "But the traffic signs are pretty consistent internationally, so I think we'll be okay." He consulted a map from the hotel's front desk and pulled out into the street.

Although it was dark, it wasn't late and there were plenty of people out, shopping and dining and generally appearing to have a good time. At least half of the women smoked, Dane noted, and many of the men—far more than in most U.S. cities these days. He left his window open a crack, letting in air scented with wood smoke and exhaust and thousands of dinners being cooked in apartments and restaurants, a pungent blend that he found common to European cities but almost unknown in the States.

He also sensed vampires.

Dozens of them, at least, just among the people they passed on the street. The vampires were mixed in with the locals, not attacking them. Like they lived here. Like they had been migrating here in numbers he couldn't have imagined.

With Eben navigating, they made their way up Storgata and eventually found the district Merrin had described. They drove slowly through the area and kept going, driving through the city, looking at residential areas and the business district, swinging past the harbor (which reminded Dane of the dockside warehouse in Savannah, and his belief that Bork Dela had been shipping his captives offshore). Finally they returned to the nightclub area around midnight, made another sweep through it, and parked the car a few blocks away.

The night had grown markedly colder. A stiff wind bit

at Dane's cheeks. Not uncomfortable, but it would have been when he'd been human. They wandered closer to the nightclubs and then took up positions in darkened doorways, almost a block apart but from which they could see each other, and waited.

People came out of the clubs, walked or staggered to parked cars, sometimes talking and laughing loudly, sometimes huddling together against the cold. Others arrived, parked, went into the clubs.

No one was attacked.

Plenty of *nosferatu,* but they mingled with the humans, never taking any for food. Very strange.

After two hours had passed and the traffic thinned, Dane hiked back up to Eben's station. "This was a waste of time," he said. He spread his arms. "Any ideas?"

"We could just nab one off the street, beat the crap out of him until he tells us why he isn't feeding on the locals."

They both knew why. It all pointed to the slaughter-house idea being a reality. "They're all just . . . blending in here. Wherever they really are, I don't think it's in town."

"There's always that sawmill."

"True." Dane didn't know what good it would do to check out a sawmill in the middle of the night—that seemed to be a daytime sort of business to him. But if it was, in fact, a front for some sort of vampiric activity, then it would likely yield some clues after dark.

Back in the car, Eben unfolded the map again and gave Dane directions. As they traveled, they didn't speak except when Eben warned of an upcoming turn. They still hadn't talked much at all. Dane had thought of this excursion as a necessary evil, not a bonding experience. At least, he and Eben weren't at each other's throats . . . for the time being.

Outside the city, they found a pine forest, dark and aromatic but sparse by conventional standards. Snow drifted around the trunks of the trees, clinging to some of their branches. The water kept this area's weather moderate, preventing it from being bare tundra, but it was still no horticulturalist's dream landscape. Beyond the forests, mountains rose like dark, silent behemoths.

After a few more miles, Eben told Dane to watch for a left turn. It came up suddenly after a curve in the road and was unmarked, a graded, wide, dirt and gravel lane leading off into the trees.

"It should be at the end of this road," Eben said. "Doesn't sound like it's very far, maybe a kilometer or two."

Dane cut the lights and took the road slowly, its washboard surface jolting them over and over again. Through the trees, the outline of a large structure started to become clear.

"I would pull off," Eben said. He pointed toward a side track joining the main road. "Go the rest of the way on foot. If they are here, they're probably listening for cars."

Dane pulled onto the narrow lane and killed the engine. He flicked off the dome light and opened his door, and Eben did the same. Together, they made their way back to the dirt road and continued toward the structure up ahead. Here, away from the city, the breeze blew harder and the cold felt more intense. Unforgiving. A human wouldn't want to be lost out here for very long.

There was no sound but the wind through the branches, a lonely sound, like a Norse goddess weeping for fallen Asgard, and no odor but pine.

"Nobody here," Dane said. "The place is dead."

"I'm thinking that, too."

They kept on trudging up the road toward the mill. Its bulk loomed dark against the starry sky. No lights shone from within, no one moved about. A tall fence, topped with barbed wire, surrounded the place, but the gate stood open. On one side of the main building were piles of trees, cut down and shorn of branches. On another, stacks of cut lumber waited to be loaded onto trucks.

"Another waste of time," Dane remarked, regarding the forlorn scene. The realization sent a shock of depression through him. He had halted things temporarily, but not the overall scheme, whatever it was. And there were plenty more like Bork Dela out there, killing wantonly, abducting terrified victims for purposes unknown. The trail had led all the way here, then stopped cold.

Eben shoved his hands into the pockets of his parka, and almost as if he had triggered it, his cell phone started to ring.

*   *   *

Andy Gray's number showed on the screen. "Andy Gray. Hello."

"Uh, Mr. Olemaun? Mr. Gray's not here. It's me. Marcus."

"Marcus Kitka?"

"Yeah. Umm, that's right."

The new sheriff's kid, sounding nervous as hell. And why shouldn't he? "What can I do for you, Marcus?"

"Uhh, Andy, Mr. Gray, I mean, he told me to do some checking. Like on shipping schedules?" He paused, and Eben wondered if he was supposed to know what the kid was talking about. Marcus went on, the words tumbling out of him in a rush. "I guess this all happened in the last day or so, after you left. He said to tell you there was another incident that turned up, like just a few days ago. Five days ago, I guess. For some reason it didn't turn up on the database right away, but when it did, it hit all the markers he was looking for. So then he decided to see if he could tie it to where you were going, in Norway, and that's when he brought me in.

"I tried all kinds of different variations, trying to connect the two. Finally, I found something. The whatever, incident, happened in a place called Cork. In Ireland? And so I checked on ships and found one called the *Caroline G*. It docked in Ireland the night of the incident there and now it's docking in, what do you call it, Tromsø? Tonight. It's supposed to come into Slip 22. Are you anywhere near the docks?"

"Tonight?" Eben asked. "Are you sure?"

"Yeah, I mean, I just looked at a picture of it from a satellite a few minutes ago. Not live, but taken tonight. It wasn't far from shore."

"Fuck." Eben pulled the phone away from his ear. "We aren't near the docks, are we?"

"We were, at the hotel," Dane said.

"Apparently we need to go back there," Eben said. "Now." He held the phone up again. "Is there anything else?"

"No, I think that's pretty much it. Mr. Gray, he just said to tell you if I found anything like that."

"Where is Andy?"

"I don't know. He's not here."

"Okay, Marcus. Thank you. Bye."

"Bye, Mr. Olemaun."

Eben clicked END and stuffed the phone back into his pocket. "The docks," he said. "Apparently there was another incident and abduction in Ireland, few nights ago. A ship docked nearby at the time is coming into Tromsø tonight."

"So you think if they put someone on the ship, that someone will be off-loaded tonight?"

"And maybe taken to wherever the sawdust comes from, right. Andy wouldn't have had Marcus tell us unless he thought the same thing."

"But Andy's not there?"

"No."

"Do you know where he is?"

For about the hundredth time since they began this trip, Eben wanted to tear Dane's head from his shoulders and beat his corpse with it. He recognized that it was mostly because he was, as Stella once said, "a jealous bastard who should have more confidence in himself," but the reason didn't matter as much as the fact that it bothered the hell out of him that Dane still walked the earth. Under other circumstances, he might even have liked the guy. But those circumstances didn't exist, and these did. "Let's not stand here talking about it." He started toward the car. "We've got to get moving."

Dane came up behind him. "So you don't know where Andy is."

"That's right," Eben said. "I don't know where the hell Andy is. Now shut up and let's go."

26

CRUISE SHIPS, white and opulent in the thin moonlight as spectral wedding cakes, clogged Tromsø's port. Dane moved past them, down to the less glamorous, more functional freight docks. Here the roadway was wet, glistening in bright lights from overhead. Men in dirty coveralls moved rapidly here and there, some carrying heavy tools that Dane didn't know the uses of, or dragging hoses. Others blew on their hands to warm them, or walked with them jammed deep into pockets. These docks were all-night affairs, no banker's hours here.

"Slip 22," Eben remarked.

"I know." Dane watched for the numbers, glad that he could at least read those. A ship had indeed docked at Slip 22, a massive freighter sitting low in the water. A crane hoisted off huge steel containers, while another one, with a giant net, seemed to be lifting a dozen wooden crates at a time. Containers, yellow and blue and green and brown and rust orange, were already stacked on the tarmac, and forklifts buzzed about hauling crates into a gigantic nearby warehouse.

Dane parked the equivalent of a couple of city blocks

away, and they slinked as close as they could get without being noticed by the dockhands. From the shadows, they watched the rush of activity.

"Looks like they've been unloading for a while," Eben said. "What if we're too late?"

A dark, windowless van rolled down the tarmac and came to a stop. "I don't think so," Dane said. He inclined his head toward the people getting out of the van. Gaunt, pale skinned, wearing black clothes hardly suited to the weather, they gathered just out of the twin tubes of the van's headlights and waited for something.

Three sailors led a dozen people down a gangway— people of every age, from a girl who couldn't have been more than seven to a fiercely lined man in his eighties or nineties who walked with a cane, his spine curved like a question mark. One of the women was hugely obese, four hundred pounds, Dane estimated. Most were in better physical condition. Most were women. They all walked single file, shuffling their feet, eyes directed straight ahead.

"They look drugged," Dane whispered.

Reaching the dock, the sailors led the people to the ones who had emerged from the van. A small packet changed hands. Money, Dane guessed, paying off the sailors. One of the people in black opened the back of the van, and the people from the ship filed in, one at a time. When the big woman climbed in the shocks groaned and the van sank at that corner, then righted itself.

"Those are the people they've abducted," Eben speculated.

"The latest batch, anyway." Dane started toward the Saab.

"Where are you going?"

"We've got to follow the van."

"Shouldn't we try to help those people?"

"We will. Not here, though. Wherever they're being taken, that's where we'll find everything, I think."

Eben reluctantly shot a last glance toward the van, then joined Dane in a hurried but cautious walk back to the rented car. Reaching it, Dane got in behind the wheel and started the engine. Lights off, he crept forward to a position from which he could see the van. With the last of the passengers loaded on, one of the people in black—vampires, he corrected himself, he was certain of it—closed the back doors and climbed into the front.

The van's taillights glowed, and the vehicle lurched into motion. Dane gave it a few moments to turn up a nearby street, then clicked on his headlights and followed.

The van took a direct route out of town, headed north—the direction from which Dane and Eben had just returned. As traffic thinned, Eben grew increasingly concerned. "Stay way back," he said.

"I am."

"Maybe I should be driving. I'm trained at vehicular surveillance."

"You were a sheriff in Barrow. How much surveillance could there be?"

"Fuck you, my friend. You'd be surprised," Eben snapped.

Dane drifted back a little farther, until the van's tail-lights were mere dots in the distance. He didn't bother to say it—his relationship with Eben was strained enough as it was—but he had learned as much about surveillance techniques from TV shows and crime novels as Eben seemed to know, so screw him. He had been letting other vehicles get between their car and the van whenever possible. He tried to stay far enough back that the vampires in the van couldn't make out any details of the car or its occupants.

The side road they had taken earlier, down to the sawmill, flashed past. They kept going, ever north. Trees grew farther apart, shorter, with branches twisted and gnarled by wind and weather. Dane had to stay farther behind, because there was no other traffic on the road. His main worry would have been getting off the highway before the sun rose, but he knew the vampires in the van would have the same concern. Whenever they got off, he would, too.

Finally, he saw brake lights flash ahead, and he slowed correspondingly. A moment later the van disappeared from sight.

"Shit! How'd they do that?" Eben asked.

Dane didn't answer. He kept the Saab moving forward at a reduced speed, and as he neared the last point where he had seen the van, he cut the lights. No other vehicles were in sight so he didn't worry about being run into.

In another minute they came upon the answer. A dirt road headed off to the right, any view of its entrance blocked from the south by a huge boulder. Natural camouflage. Dane turned onto the road, really not much more than a rutted track carved into the tundra by regular traffic. Mud sucked at the Saab's tires, and Dane feared getting stuck in it. But the van had made it, so he kept on.

It was probably usually an icy road. Another effect of global warming. The mud pulled at the car, wrenching the wheel almost out of his hands, and Dane had to wrestle with it to stay on a steady course. They still hadn't spotted the van again, but the road twisted and turned, angling gradually uphill through a narrow canyon, the sides growing taller as they went. As long as there were no other side roads, Dane figured it was still up ahead of them. The moon ducked behind a ribbon of cloud and Dane wished he could use headlights, but didn't want to risk that—bad enough that the car's engine growled and churned as they traveled.

"They could be watching us right now," Eben said.

"True."

"We could get out and keep going on foot."

"We could, but we have no idea how far. What if we're still out here when the sun comes up? Dammit, I don't like any of this," Dane said. He pointed the car up a steep section of road. At the top of the rise, he braked to a stop.

A shallow valley spread out below them. Near the center of it, ringed by low, scrubby trees, was yet another sawmill. This one was smaller than the first one they had seen, just two stories with a few stacks of wood around its perimeter. If the other had been a big commercial operation, this one looked like a family affair, maybe for a little furniture business or something. Except it was parked out here in the middle of nowhere, without even many trees to speak of nearby.

And something else—attached behind the two-story wooden building was a second structure, flat roofed and low to the ground. Moonlight glinted off sharp edges. The road they had been traveling on came to an end at a parking area next to the building, and the van had just pulled in next to about four dozen other vehicles of every size and description. The vampires who had been inside got out, and others emerged from the mill to meet them. Opening the back of the van, they helped the captives out and led them inside.

"That's it," Eben said, his voice hushed by something resembling awe. "It's got to be."

"Yes, it looks that way," Dane agreed.

"It doesn't look very big. I expected something . . . I don't know. Grand."

"Not very grand from here," Dane agreed. "It looks like a supermarket connected to a mill."

"Pretty much."

"What do you think, a couple of miles from here?

"About that. You want to walk or drive?"

"It's supposedly there for vampires, right? I say we drive up like we own the place."

Dane hoped they were getting close. It appeared so. But getting inside the stockyard/slaughterhouse and shutting it down were two very different things.

It would be well guarded and full of *nosferatu* anxious to protect it.

Two against . . . how many? No way to know from here. But many, based on the number of vehicles outside.

The odds, frankly, were stacked against them.

But then again, living forever had its disadvantages, too.

Since settling in Barrow, Andy Gray had known of Stella and Eben Olemaun and had learned that not every vampire was an unmitigated bastard like Paul Norris. Dane seemed to fit into the same category. So far, of the four bloodsuckers he now knew personally, three turned out to be pretty decent folks.

Except for the bloodsucking part.

That didn't mean, however, that he wanted to hang with them on a regular basis. And traveling across the country with one? That had been completely outside his life's expectations.

Traveling with a woman like Stella would have been a challenge under any circumstances—she was attractive, headstrong, passionate, and she didn't hesitate to point out stupidity when she saw it. Plus she was something of an icon to Andy—her book had forever altered the way he looked at the world.

With those changes, Andy had gained self-confidence along with a new sense of his own physicality. Even with

all that, Stella could, with a few sharp words and a with-
ering glance, make him feel like he was back in high
school. No wonder she was who she was before . . . all this
happened.

Travel with a vampire was its own kind of adventure.
Because Stella had to avoid sunlight, they couldn't just fly
to Anchorage and then to Savannah. They had to make
the trip in stages, holing up during the daytime and
avoiding the sun. Andy had been back and forth across
the country more times than he liked to think about, but
never this way.

The most recent red-eye had taken them as far as Atlanta. They'd be in Savannah soon, and he was just beginning to feel comfortable with her. Somewhat. After having
slept for a while, he had ordered in room service: a salad
and some chicken breasts, no skins, with vegetables on the
side. Stella joined him in his room, bringing with her a six-
teen-ounce Coke bottle full of blood that, unbelieveably,
one of her local fans had delivered to the hotel for her.

The conversation had started awkwardly as usual, although not as awkwardly as they had over the past few
days. It had turned to war stories, though, of which they
both had plenty, and Andy had started to feel looser as
the meal went on. ". . . so there we were," he was saying,
"fourteen of us in our windbreakers with the big FBI emblazoned on the back, assault weapons in our hands, surrounding the house where these known terrorists had
been planning who-knows-what, ordering explosives off
the internet, for God's sake. The Special Agent in Charge

gives the order and we move in on the place, announcing ourselves, pounding on the door and then one of the guys uses a ram on it and we charge inside. Expecting to find, you know, a group of Middle Eastern guys with guns pointed at us, reading translated bomb-making manuals or something."

Stella eyed him over the lip of her bottle. When she drew it away from her mouth, he saw a little blood on her lips. Her tongue darted out, pink and delicate, lashing it away with a surprisingly sexy move.

"But no dice," he went on. "Instead we found a woman who had to be in her fifties, on her bed with two guys who were at least a decade older. They were all white, one of the guys was skinny as a bean, and the other was like Marlon Brando or Orson Welles, you know, the size of a small continent and all gravitas, saying, 'Excuse me, but is there something illegal about this?'"

Stella started to grin. "Oh, no," she said. "They were—"

"She was on her hands and knees, with the little guy behind her and the big one in her mouth. Or at least he had been until we bashed in the door." He laughed, too, remembering the look on the big man's face, stern and serious but confused at the same time, as if he might have broken a law he didn't know about. "What's worse is the agents who came in the back door. They walked right into another room, where twelve other guys were sitting around in their Skivvies, waiting for their turns. One of them tried to run, but he had his boxers down around his ankles and he tripped and landed on his face. It turned out the Special Agent in Charge had transposed two numbers in the address, and the real terrorists—who were really just a pack of idiots with delusions of grandeur—were cowering in their basement across the street the whole time."

"So you caught them eventually?" Stella asked.

"Sure, once the SAIC figured out his mistake. He apologized profusely to the woman, who didn't bother to put any clothes on the whole time we were trooping around inside her house. When he told her we were going to go raid her neighbors' house, all she said was, "I did them once. They weren't very good, young and kind of nervous. I prefer men with a little more maturity under their belts, if you know what I mean."

Stella almost did a spit-take. Wouldn't that have been something special for the maid service to clean up.

"Barrow is provincial compared to the big city," she said when she could control herself. "The biggest sex scandal Eben and I ever had to deal with was when a couple of pipeline roughnecks brought in some mail-order Russian brides and set them up in a brothel. The hookers we already had in town complained because the Russians were undercutting them on price, and we had to shut them down."

Andy polished off the last of his chicken. Stella's bottle was nearly empty, too. She had a few more in her room. If she got hungry, though, she could easily tear off his head and drink him, and there wouldn't be much he could do about it. "Stella, do you ever think about . . . you know . . ." He touched his own neck. "I mean . . ."

"You mean do I think about feeding on you? Or people in general? Absolutely, it crosses my mind. I had the same question, the first time I spent any real time with Dane. The real answer is that some of us can control our hunger. When your wife was alive, you probably saw other women you were attracted to, ones you wanted to be with, right? But you chose not to act on those impulses, on that hunger. Same way you might want a big burger dripping with grease, or deep-fried chicken instead of roasted. But you do what's best for you. We're all bundles of lusts and hungers, but we have free will, too."

She took another drink, swallowed, smacked her lips together.

"But to answer your question, yes, fresh is better."

She then looked at him dead-on with the black eyes of a shark. Andy's stomach clenched as he met her gaze, unable to tear away, completely defenseless.

Fresh is better.

"Maybe we should get going soon," she finally said.

"Yeah . . ." Andy eventually replied, still staring, disturbed. "Let me finish up. Give me a few."

Stella stood, turning her back to Andy.

The thought that was worming its way from the back of his brain since the journey began now came to the forefront—maybe, just maybe, despite all of the trust and assurances of John Ikos, this road trip idea might have been a colossal blunder.

A life-threatening mistake.

27

DANE FELT EYES on them almost as soon as they crested the hill and started the long sweep into the valley.

The sensation unnerved him, although he fully expected it. If the structure below was what they believed, the vampires would have security all over the place. His main worry was that he or Eben might somehow be recognized, in which case their whole reason for coming would be utterly finished before it could begin.

The smell of blood was strong.

"We need to get in, need to figure out what the lay of the land is," said Dane. "To fit in we might need to feed. You understand that, right?"

"Yeah," Eben said, with resignation. "I get it. It's just that it sickens me, the whole idea of the place."

"That's why we came, right?"

"That's why we came."

They parked in the lot and left the car. Before they reached the mill door they had seen the others use, it opened and an old man stepped out. He wore a leather barn coat against the cold and a cap with earflaps and boots that would have been at home in a stable, and his grizzled skeletal face was split in a grin that gave him the look of an elf gone to seed and at least half feeble-minded. He said something in Norwegian, in a voice that sounded like his throat was filled with ground glass.

"Do you speak English?" Eben asked him.

"Oh, English, yes sure," he said. His accent was so thick it was hardly an improvement.

Dane took a deep sniff. The smell of vampires was everywhere, but this guy was not one.

"You are Englishmen?" he asked.

"Canadian," Dane said quickly. Safer that way, and not just because most of Europe had decided to dislike the U.S. these last few years. He and Eben both had their own reputations in the vampire community, but everyone knew they were American.

"Ahh, we have many Canadians who come here," the old man said. He beckoned them closer. "Come in, come in. Your teeth, please, show your teeth."

Dane and Eben opened their mouths, displaying fangs. The old man bent forward and twisted his scrawny neck and looked in their mouths. "Yes, yes, good, yes sure," he said. "Come in. I am Esa. Esa Immonen. This is of myself and Anu, my wife Anu, this mill." He turned and started toward the door, Dane and Eben following.

The door was wooden, easily three times the old man's height, but it swung open at a touch on silent, lubricated hinges.

When it did, the stench smacked Dane in the face.

Bug eaters.

People who had been turned but hadn't yet finished the change. They would become vampires, sometimes in a couple of days, sometimes a little longer. Until then, they lived under the thrall of those who had turned them.

The mill was a false front.

Once they were past the front room, where the saws did their cutting, the old man's wife Anu welcomed them to something that resembled a bar or nightclub more than a sawmill.

They came into a large room filled with rows of rough wooden benches and tables that could have seated a few hundred, illuminated by flickering kerosene lanterns hung on the walls and a few fat candles sputtering on the tables. Forty or fifty bug eaters sat at the benches, some nodding like heroin addicts, others raving, twitching, breaking into pieces the insects Anu shook from pails onto the big tables and greedily shoving the bits into their mouths.

The old woman had a face that could have been carved from a tree root, brown and gnarled, and her back was hunched, but her hands were quick and she showed even, white teeth when she laughed. Dane recognized the irony of her name being so similar to Ananu's—Dela must have as well.

"Not for you, this," Esa said in his broken English, pushing at Dane and Eben. "For you below. Enok's house. Below!"

Did he just say what I thought he said? Dane thought. *Oh no.*

With a hand on each of their shoulders, he guided them between the rows of bug eaters—pathetic creatures, Dane thought, embarrassed at the memory of his own such period—toward a staircase leading down. He put a hand on the heavy wooden banister, just below a newel cap carved in the shape of a demon so realistic that Dane almost expected it to bite the man. Then he realized that the balustrades were carved snakes, not simple poles, alternating between head up and head down.

The walls of the stairway were of the same dark wood, but without carvings that Dane could see from here. A single lantern hung on the landing, halfway down.

The scents of blood and bloodsuckers wafted up from below. "For you it is below!" Esa said, cackling.

"Okay, we get it, we're going down," Eben growled, shaking off the man's clutching hand. He started down into the darkness, with Dane close behind. Vampires didn't need a lot of light, actually found the dark comforting, and it was obvious even from up here that there were far fewer lanterns and candles below. As they descended, Dane glanced up to see Esa and Anu watching them go, both laughing insanely.

"I hope this isn't some elaborate trap," Dane whispered.

"I don't think so," Eben replied. "It smells like an abattoir."

"Well, that's what we're looking for."

"What was he talking about, though, when he said 'Enok's house'?"

"Oh, you don't want to know."

"What do you mean?"

Dane started to answer, but they had reached the next level. The staircase continued to wind down and out of sight. Peering over the side, he thought he could make out another seven or so levels before they blended together in the dark. *Place is huge,* he thought. *Deceptive from above.* It was like a building turned upside down, built down into the earth instead of up from it.

This level looked more like a nightclub than the rustic beer hall layout upstairs. Dimly lit alcoves held curved benches or private booths, some partitioned by heavy drapes. Here and there were bars, with a few vampires leaning on each one, although the bartenders seemed to serve only the one beverage. "Blood on tap," Dane observed quietly.

A tall, slender female separated from the darkness and walked toward them, her gait sinuous, as if all her muscles had liquefied. She had long, black hair cascading over her left shoulder, and a black dress cut low in front revealing shallow cleavage. "Welcome," she said in clear, vaguely European-accented English. "I have not seen you before."

"First time," Dane said. "We've been hearing about it so long, we just had to check it out."

"From America?"

"Canada," Eben answered.

"Not so much unlike Norway, then."

"Not so much, no," Dane said. "This looks like a great place."

"It is. We have dreamed for so long of such a place, but only Enok could build it."

Enok again. Shit. "We're pleased that he did."

"Won't you please have a drink?" she asked. The perfect hostess. She inclined her head toward the nearest bar, that long, thick hair moving like a curtain.

"I'd love to," Dane said.

"Absolutely," Eben added.

The hostess gestured with her hand and let them make their own way to the bar. She had some sort of signal arranged with the bartender, though, because he was already setting two thick cut glass mugs of blood down on the sleek wooden bar top. Dane and Eben sat on leather-covered barstools in front of the mugs.

"Thanks," Dane said, picking one up and downing it hungrily. Never mind pangs of conscience, he was starved. Eben followed suit, although more tentatively. The bartender, a sallow-complexioned vampire with the build and demeanor of a Hell's Angel, put up two more mugs.

"So what's all this Enok business?" Eben asked. "The name sounds vaguely familiar but I'm not sure why."

Dane studied Eben for a moment. "I keep forgetting, no one turned you but you."

"What, did I miss something?"

"In a way, yes. I mean, whoever turns you is supposed to make some effort to teach you what's up, how to get along. But there's also a kind of, I guess, racial memory that vampires have. It seems to get more diluted the more of us there are, and there's also been some speculation that early, consistent contact with whoever turns you can enhance it, or lack of contact can dull it, or both. Kind of like the bonding experience with parents, in the first days of life, can alter the brain chemistry or whatever, making a child more or less susceptible to certain stimuli. Does that sound vague?"

"Yes, it does."

"Good, because it's all theoretical as far as I know, and I'm no biologist. I'm just saying what I've heard and what sort of makes sense, according to my perceptions."

"And it has to do with this Enok . . . how?"

"In the sense that if your own racial memory was working at top capacity, you'd know why you recognize the name. Enok is one of the oldest of us, maybe the *absolute* oldest. And one of the meanest, from what I hear, as well. He turned Vicente, who I believe you've . . . met. Also Lilith, who Stella took care of."

"She told me."

"Well, Enok made both of them—two of the baddest bloodsuckers you ever want to meet. I know, you're tougher than Vicente. But believe it or not, Eben, you are a special case. And just because you beat Vicente doesn't mean it's the same situation here. If he is behind all this, then this place is *serious* bad news. Worse than I thought."

"What's worse than you thought?"

Dane had been speaking in hushed tones, aware that vampire hearing was far better than human. But at least part of his speech had been overheard.

His audience looked like a young woman, maybe in her late twenties or early thirties. She had an open, friendly face, with big brown eyes and a cute little nub of a nose over thin lips. Her light brown hair had been hacked short, as if she had cut it herself, without a mirror. Her plain cotton dress looked a size too large for her, maybe a couple of sizes, and there were tears at the high neckline and the right shoulder. "Sorry," she said, "it's just that I don't hear English very often in here, especially on this level." She stuck out a hand, thin fingers, scraped knuckles. "My name is Sarah Cavalier," she said. "From Columbus. Ohio. In America."

"I'm Bob," Dane said, picking the first name that popped into his head. "This is Charles."

"We're from Toronto. Canada," Eben added.

"Pleased to meet you," Sarah said. "I don't think I've seen you here before."

"Do you come here often?" A pickup line if there ever was one, but Dane couldn't do anything about that.

"What season is it?"

Dane blinked, not understanding the question for a moment.

"Early fall," Eben said.

She tapped her round chin with the tip of her right index finger. Her unpolished nails had been bitten to the quick. "Well, I came in spring. The end of April, beginning of May, around there. I don't remember the date exactly."

"You haven't been out again since?"

Another moment's consideration, then she shook her head vigorously. "No, I guess not. Weird, huh?"

"Kind of."

"But I mean, why would I? What could I want that hasn't been provided here?"

"You have a place to sleep? Shower?"

"There are a few showers around. I sleep wherever, you know. And of course there's plenty to eat."

"Of course."

"And I don't have to, you know, mingle with *them*."

"With who?" Eben asked. Dane feared he already knew the answer.

"You know. People. The humans. I never liked living among them, having an apartment and whatnot. Pretending that I bought groceries and worked nights. Sometimes they brush up against you on the street. Yuck."

"It's rough," Dane said.

"It's *disgusting*." She made a face, then broke into a smile as if she had already forgotten her distaste. "Hey, have you been to the other levels?"

"Just upstairs and here," Eben answered.

"You want to see?"

"Sounds like you're the perfect guide," Dane said.

"Oh, I am. I mean, there are some who've been around longer than me. But I'm right here, right? And it's so nice to speak English again. Norwegian always sounds like somebody about to vomit. Gross, right?"

"Yes. Gross," Dane said. "Show us around."

28

"WHERE IS THE VAMPIRE?"

AJ shook his head, then winced from the blow he knew was coming.

The inside of his mouth was pulp. He had been punched so many times that the linings of his cheeks had been ground raw against his teeth—the ones he hadn't spat out or swallowed. His lips were so swollen it was hard to talk. His right cheek was swollen, too, closing that eye to little more than a slit. He could barely hear with his left ear, and an incessant buzzing sounded in his right one. He breathed through his mouth because his nostrils were clogged with blood and snot.

This time, the guy left his face alone. Instead he jabbed something sharp into the fleshy patch between AJ's left thumb and index finger. AJ screamed and tried to close his hand but leather straps held it open on a table.

The guy looked like someone who would play a government bureaucrat in a movie. Square jaw, small eyes, neatly combed short brown hair, a football player's build. High school ball, maybe college, not pro. Like the kind of guy who had dreamed of going pro until he got into college and learned that the guys on his high school team hadn't really been all that good, so he'd been measuring himself against the wrong yardstick and only then realized that he'd have to have a fallback plan. Better study econ, or engineering, or criminal justice. Then his tor-mentor found himself in a career and he stuck with it, never really getting over the disappointment that walloped him in the gut every time he saw a pro NFL player on TV or in a magazine.

So he took his regrets out on AJ.

"Let's try this again. I know you went somewhere with the vampire. Then you came back for your boat. You can have the boat—you could be out on the water in three hours, if you cooperate. But if you don't . . . let's just say you'll be drydocked for a long time. So . . . where is the vampire?"

The experts, AJ had heard on TV, claimed that torture didn't really work. Or rarely. People being tortured tend to give false information, to tell their torturers whatever they think those professionals want to hear, regardless of truth, just to make the pain stop.

Maybe there's something to that, AJ thought.

Getting the pain to stop would be a good thing. His feet had been cut, some of the flesh peeled off his soles with a little sharp knife, so that standing was excruciating. He had been hit repeatedly in the genitals with a club, so that his genitals felt broken and bruised, like a balloon filled with loose, disconnected objects. The result was that sitting wasn't any better than standing.

He sat anyway. No choice. His hands were strapped to

the table and he was strapped to the chair, feet on the floor, little flames of agony starting there and working up his legs, breaking into a full-on conflagration at his balls, then tapering off a little up the trunk, flaring up again between his shoulders (not tortured there, just in pain from being forced to sit with his hands out for so long) and at the ends of his arms. And of course his head. Everything above the neck was broken. *Show me a mirror,* he thought. *Maybe I'll talk then.*

He didn't say that, though. Instead, he spat—the gob didn't even clear his lap, landing wetly on his pants—and said weakly, "Vampires aren't real."

"That's what your parents told you, right?" his torturer replied. "They lied to you about that, too. They lied about pretty much everything, I guess. They told you they were your parents, but look at you. You were bred in a trailer park. Probably to a brother and sister. Probably to a brother and sister whose parents had also been brother and sister. If you weren't an inbred moron, you'd have told me what I need to know by now and saved yourself a considerable amount of pain.

"And for what? What are you protecting? A monster who kills to live? Who drinks the blood of young girls to keep up his own horrible strength? You're a regular person like me, taking the worst beating of your life to protect a monster. What's up with *that*?"

AJ tried to speak, but launched into a coughing fit. He spat again.

"What?" the guy asked. "What'd you say?"

"I said I'm nothing like you."

"Sure you are. We're both guys. We're both American. We love our country, we respect women. We like a beer now and then. Beer'd taste good right about now, wouldn't it?"

"Sure," AJ managed. "Maybe a football game on TV, too. You like football, right?"

"You sailed that one right over my head, partner," the guy said. "If that was a joke, I didn't get it. Why don't you save your breath for the important stuff? Like . . . where the vampire is."

"Why don't you blow me?"

The guy's hand moved faster than AJ could track, swatting him across the face. AJ blinked, bit down on his ruined lower lip to keep from screaming. But the guy wasn't done. He jabbed his sharp whatever it was, needle or pin or skinny blade, into the tip of AJ's left thumb, just beneath the nail, gave it a little twist, then pulled it out.

AJ did scream then. A long, loud one that made his head throb.

"You might as well let me go," he gasped when he could talk again. His throat felt like he'd been gargling with thumbtacks. "I can't help you. Don't you think I would have . . . already if I could? I don't believe in . . . vampires and I don't know who you're talking . . . about."

He didn't know where the courage to resist had come from. He didn't think of himself as particularly brave. He'd never seen combat, although he'd put in one tour in the army, stationed in Mannheim, Germany. He hadn't been trained at resisting torture. He'd been a grunt, too low on the totem pole to know anything worth torturing for. If someone had asked him a couple of weeks ago if he would endure the worst agony of his life to protect some virtual strangers, he would have laughed at them. *Absolutely not. Hell no.*

Yet here he was. Why? He couldn't begin to guess.

"Look, let's just start over at the beginning. I can see this is hurting you a whole lot. That's not really what I wanted. It's just that you know things that I need to know, and time is of the essence, as they say. If I had more time I'd be your friend, buy you meals and drinks, listen to your problems, and eventually you'd trust me. Just now, I don't have time to win your trust. But we can get past this, make things easier all the way around. My name's Dan, okay? What's yours?"

"Masters."

"Masters what?"

"Brent Masters. Brent John Masters."

The guy who called himself Dan flicked a finger against AJ's puffy cheek. A jolt of pain shot through his head.

"Oh please. What is it really? The boat you were on is registered to Albert Jerome Roddy. Are you Al Roddy?"

He had never gone by Al. "No."

Another finger flick, this time on the ruptured ear.

"You trying to steal a boat, then? Should I turn you over to the cops?"

"Sure."

"Ha-ha, fat chance. Come on, Roddy. Be straight with me. Let's clear this up so we can all go home."

AJ kept his mouth shut.

The damage had been done over the course of many hours. Days, maybe. Every time he fell asleep, someone came in and woke him. Usually this guy, but sometimes others. Men and women, white, dressed in shirtsleeves and ties or conservative business dresses. AJ was inordinately proud that he had bled all over Dan's white shirt.

The room was concrete block walled, tile floored. No windows. Just the one door. A table and two chairs. Pools of his blood stained the black and brown and white linoleum tiles.

"Okay, whatever," Dan said. "You can stew in it for a while longer. If you have to use the toilet or something, too bad. Unless you're ready to talk to us." He pointed toward the ceiling, in the corner. AJ had to twist his neck around, look over his left shoulder. A camera was mounted there. AJ hadn't noticed it before. "If you're ready to talk, then just say so, to that camera. I'll come right in. Otherwise you can sit here and hurt for a while. And think about how much more it's going to hurt when I get serious."

He walked out, slammed the door. Locks clicked.

AJ was left alone with only the persistent buzz in his ear for company.

That and the pain.

"I never even liked killing them," Sarah was saying as she led them down the stairs to the next level. "Because you have to, you know, touch them? Put your mouth on them? I mean, when you were mortal did you want to bite right off a cow's carcass? Or did you want to go to the grocery store and buy steaks all wrapped up in plastic? On that little Styrofoam tray. I liked those."

"And here you don't have to see them," Dane observed.

"You don't *have* to. You *can,* if you want. There are a couple of levels down there—well, you'll see. But up here, on the higher levels, it's all brought up in barrels, or piped up. Except—well, you'll see that too."

They arrived on the second level down. Here there were no kerosene lanterns at all, just a few thick, greasy candles popping as they burned. Dane had wondered upstairs what they were made of, and now it came to him.

Human fat.

More vampires congregated in secluded alcoves, drinking and talking and laughing. Conversations were held in low tones and in various languages. As Sarah had noted, Dane didn't hear much English. Lots of Europeans, he noted, and some Asian and African tongues as well.

"This really was well thought out," she said, almost as if she had read his thoughts. "After that messed-up attack on Barrow, in Alaska—you heard about that, right?"

"We heard," Eben said. He sounded uneasy, but she didn't notice.

"After that, things got different, and someone figured he could do things his own way."

"I'm surprised it took anyone so long," Dane said.

"Yeah, me too. But at least someone finally did it, right? Of course, this is just part of the plan, I hear. A small part, I guess."

"Do you know what the rest of it is?"

"It's not like it's a huge secret. That's why I came here in the first place. Well, that and not having to, you know, act 'normal' anymore. They call this a 'model community.' The United States of the Undead, like. If we're all of a similar mindset, we can finally be in a position to force the humans to accept their proper role."

"Livestock, for our needs," Dane said.

"Yeah, basically. We can build places like this everywhere, keep them, breed them, feed ourselves. Time for us to come out of the shadows and drive them in. I mean, not really out of the shadows, because the sun, you know? But I guess figuratively or something."

"Figuratively," Eben echoed. "We're going to overturn the way things have always been and live like this."

"Awesome, huh?" The idea sparked joy in Sarah's tone. "Genius."

Sarah led them between the booths and bars, across the vast, dark room. Some of the vampires greeted her, and Dane and Eben. Others ignored them. A few trailed along behind, as if some spectacle were about to take place and they didn't want to miss out. Dane could make out a doorway at the far end of the room, and beyond it a space with a warm, reddish glow that spilled out into the main room. "That's where we're going," Sarah said, pointing to it. "In there."

"What's in there?"

"The Lilith Room," she said. Her bright eyes sparkled as if with life, which was unlikely, or madness, which was less so. "It's kind of an initiation ritual for newbies, I guess. And it's kind of fun, too. I think you'll love it."

The Lilith Room.

Dane tried to comprehend what that could possibly mean, but he couldn't. He only knew the one Lilith, and Stella had destroyed her in Los Angeles. Was it some kind of shrine to her memory? Lit by candles, so the vampires could come in and worship her?

Sarah Cavalier hurried ahead of them, almost skipping toward the lighted entryway. She reached the doorway and clung to the jamb like a drowning person, one foot raised off the floor, peering back over her shoulder toward them.

"She's excited," Eben observed.

"I'm not sure it takes a lot."

"You know what this Lilith Room is?"

"Not a clue."

The vampires who had been following started to crowd in around them when they got to the Lilith Room's door. Whatever was in there, apparently everybody wanted to see the reaction of the newbies when they saw it. Dane tried to brace for anything.

The sight that met them couldn't be prepared for.

It was Lilith. Lilith herself. Not destroyed at Stella's hands, after all.

Undead, she writhed on a kind of altar, in obvious pain. Her arms and legs had been torn off, violently, spurs of bone still showing in the sockets. Those wounds and dozens more—chunks had been ripped out all over her naked torso—oozed blood. Her skin ran with it, and Dane couldn't tell if it was all hers or if blood had been poured over her to salve the wounds. Probably both. Fat white maggots writhed in some of the older wounds. Lilith's dark hair was matted, her eyes wild with emotion. With terror.

A vampire rose from a squat in the corner as they entered. This one, a male, was twisted like a pretzel and at least half mad, but he spoke English, perhaps out of deference to Sarah. "Two more new ones for you, Lilith," he said in a singsong tone. "Two more to feast on your flesh. Aren't you happy? Aren't you glad to serve your fellows?" He lifted a metal pitcher and poured some blood on her, splashing it over her breasts and privates, then emptying the last on her face. She smacked at it greedily, licking it off her lips, her cheeks.

Burning on the wall above her, written in little flickering tongues of mystic flame—the source of the reddish light Dane had noticed—were the words: THE OLD WAYS HAVE PROVEN WEAK. NOW IS THE TIME OF THE VAMPIRE.

Sarah noticed Dane staring at the legend. "The words of Enok," she said. "Is there any other way to live?"

29

EBEN WAS ALMOST through the door when someone grabbed his arm. He spun, startled, to see a group of vampires speaking what he guessed was Norwegian, laughing hysterically, like drunks in a bar. There were six of them, all male, and it was obvious that five were leading the sixth into the place that Sarah Cavalier called the Lilith Room. The one who had snagged his arm drew him aside in order to push their friend past, and Eben was glad to let them go.

Maybe this kind of scene was commonplace to Dane, but it wasn't to Eben. He hadn't thought he would ever see anything more horrific than the bodies of the dead in Barrow, vampires slavering over them like starving rats. Images from that long winter, a winter of blood and death and terror (drained bodies stacked like cordwood against a corrugated steel wall, a headless child in the snow, still clutching her mother's severed hand, a vampire licking an icicle that had been sprayed with blood, like a kid with a popsicle) had been seared into his brain, surviving even his death, his destruction by sunlight, and his resurrection—back to a state of undeath, if not life itself—at the hands of his wife.

This might have been worse, though. And it was just getting started.

"He's new, too," Sarah said. "Do you mind if he goes first?"

Eben didn't know what was expected of him here, so he was happy for the chance to find out before he had to take part. "That's fine," he said, standing back to let the other group go.

Dane touched his shoulder. "I'm going to keep going down," he whispered. "See what else there is to see. I'll meet up with you in a little while. Stay sharp."

Eben nodded his agreement. Splitting up was the best course of action, would allow them to cover more ground, even though at the moment he wished he'd been the one to think of leaving first.

Dane stepped quietly away. Sarah, her gaze fixed on Lilith's writhing form (Sarah held her pink tongue between her teeth, its tip resting on her lower lip, an expression at once childish and frightening), didn't even notice that he had gone.

The guys who had barged in quieted, their laughter gone, their mood shifting to something like reverence. They had pushed and cajoled the one they had brought in to a spot just in front of Lilith. Her eyes were wide, her head quaking. She tried to speak, but when her mouth opened he saw that her tongue was gone. Her meaning was clear nonetheless; she begged for mercy.

The newbie who had taken Eben's place apparently

knew what he had come for. He stepped up to Lilith. She tried to wriggle away, but the altar didn't give her much room to move. Bending closer to her, he opened his mouth. Eben realized what he was about to do just before he did it, wanted to look away, but couldn't.

The vampire put his mouth on Lilith's bloody body, finding a fleshy part at the top of her hip, and clamped his sharp teeth together. He shook his head like a dog with a bone, then yanked it away from her. Turning back to his friends, he showed a chunk of meat clenched in his teeth, blood dripping from it onto the floor.

Lilith screamed wordlessly, a guttural, inhuman sound, blood leaking out where the vampire had bitten her.

Eben watched in disgust as the vampire loudly chewed the piece of flesh, swallowing it down. When it was gone his friends clapped him on the back, laughing again, as if he had passed some important rite of initiation.

Which, Eben supposed, he had.

Now it was Eben's turn.

"Well, go on," Sarah Cavalier prodded. She blinked, her gaze darting about the room. "Where's Bob gone?"

"He wanted to look around some more," Eben said, wishing more than ever that he had gone too.

The whole vampire thing filled him with less revulsion than it once had—you did what you had to do to get by—especially after what he did to Stella, but he didn't kill for blood, didn't drink it, still warm, pulsing with the fading beats of a dying heart, like most vampires did.

And this . . . eating flesh, even if it was the flesh of the worst of the worst . . . this was beyond anything he had imagined.

Sarah pulled on his forearm, her eyes insistent. "Everybody gets to, when they're new," she said. "Bob will, too, whenever we find him again." Her tongue flicked across her lips again. "It's fun."

Eben glanced back toward the door. The vampires who had followed them in, and the ones who had accompanied the guy who went before him, were all waiting to watch him do it. If he refused, what might happen? An alarm could be raised. He and Dane might find themselves battling for their lives—their unlives—against impossible odds, before they even knew the whole background about how this place was set up.

No, he had to go through with it, if only to keep up appearances.

He took a step toward Lilith. Her eyes locked on his.

I know you.

He stopped short. It was a woman's voice. Lilith's voice. But inside his head. No words had been spoken out loud, but he heard her just the same.

I can smell you on her. The human who started all this.

You mean Stella, he thought.

Yessssss. Yes. Stella Olemaun.

So she could hear his thoughts as well. *She's my wife.*

I know that. More, I know that you are both nosferatu *now. And one further thing I know—you do not want to do this. . . .*

It hurts. They know it hurts, and they do not care. It is my pun-

ishment, you see, for merely standing in Enok's way. They want it to hurt, and it does. I try not to show them, but I cannot always help it.

I'm sure it hurts like hell, and I have no interest in hurting you. But I'm worried that if I don't . . . He tried to control his thoughts, not knowing how much she could read, or if anyone else listened in.

You are afraid they will know that you are here under false pretenses. Hiding who you really are, and not here to partake of their games. Your mind is open to me, Eben Olemaun. And mine, to you.

He hadn't realized until just then that she was right, hadn't wanted to probe, to know her pain and fear and humiliation on such a basic and personal level. But when she said the words, her consciousness lapped over his defensive walls and flooded in.

And he saw and knew

—Lilith taunting Stella even as she handed over Eben's ashes, and Stella's response—a jacket full of explosive devices left behind, almost finishing Stella on the spot—

—Enok, his face lined and cruel, approaching Lilith, young and beautiful, on a cobblestone road, centuries ago, then clutching her arms, drawing her into a foul embrace, his breath hot and rank on her, and then the tearing, gnashing of his teeth—

—just a moment ago, the vampire's teeth on her side, the sensation as teeth sank in and ripped the flesh from her body—

—six small girls, carrying her weak and wounded form into a cool, dark room—

—feeding, hundreds of years, thousands of victims, enough blood to drown cities—

—Vicente's touch, his hands rough, calloused, intimate at times and casually violent at others—

—Enok again, tall and thin, with broad shoulders and a sunken chest, his cheeks hollow, his eyes bulging, ears rising to points on top, surrounded by a miasma of death and decay, possessing strength beyond reckoning—

—vampires bowing before her, Mother Blood—

—Enok laughing at that appellation, angry that she would seek power and influence for herself that rightfully belonged to him—

—the world as Enok envisioned it, vampires overrunning humans, emerging in the night to slaughter and burn, and more places like this one, where humans were kept like cattle, a food supply. Earth awash in blood and fire, smoke graying the sky, hiding the stars—

Do it.

"What?" He said it out loud, then caught himself.

Bite. You must. Or they will know.

Know what?

Why you are here.

I can't.

Little Eben Olemaun, it is nothing I have not felt a thousand times over.

"Go on, Charles." Sarah's voice surprised him. She regarded him strangely. He didn't know how long he had stood there, communing mentally with Lilith. He must have looked crazy.

Like that's anything different around here, Eben thought.

Do it, Eben. While there is still time.

Don't overthink it, Stella had said to him on more than one occasion. The truth was, throughout their marriage and in their professional life, and now in their new state of being, he'd been the one likely to walk impulsively into a situation and then hesitate, playing out options in his mind and trying to choose the best course of action. Stella worked those questions out ahead of time, but in the thick of it she acted fast and decisively.

Well, he was in this now. He swallowed back bile. He tried to imagine the sensation.

Don't overthink it.

He took a quick, deep bite.

Her flesh was rubbery, unyielding. It tasted vaguely salty but mostly he tasted the sharp tang of the blood that had been poured on her, and her own as well. As his teeth tore through it, it filled his mouth. Underneath, the muscle gave more easily. Blood ran down his throat and out the corners of his mouth, dripping down his chin. He swallowed some down as he tugged on the chunk of meat, trying to break the last elastic strips of skin.

Finally he bit through the last one and a piece of Lilith came off in his mouth. He held it there for a moment, unsure of what to do next.

Swallow it, Eben.

But . . .

You must.

It was too big. He chewed it, his stomach roiling and objecting all the way. Yet he couldn't help feeling a strange sense of satisfaction at the same time, as if his body really wanted it or needed it, like a pregnant woman's cravings for dirt or pickles or other things she would never have eaten before.

As his teeth broke it down, rendering little pieces from the large one, he swallowed them down.

Sarah's hands on his back startled him. "See? Pretty cool, right?"

He tried to smile. "Delicious."

"I told you. Now we have to get Bob back here."

"He'll be thrilled."

One more thing, little Eben Olemaun . . . before you leave my presence.

He stopped where he was, hoping it didn't seem too odd to Sarah. Then again, Sarah was pretty odd herself, so how likely was she to notice? *What?*

He knows.

Who . . . Enok?

Yessssss.

What does he know?

Everything. *How you and Stella defended your little village. He has watched you, or had you watched. He knows about the traitor vampire, too, the one who came here with you. He knows about the humans you have allied with—nuisances, but nothing more. He knows about many things, and some disturb him more than others. He has a plan to deal with them all. Enok, you will find, is careful to amass information and execute the option that best suits him.*

Does he know we're here?

I would not make the mistake of believing he does not, were I you.

"Charles? Are you coming? Is something wrong?"

Sarah stared at him now, her expression curious, wondering. He had been standing still for some time, he supposed. "Wrong? No . . . should anything be wrong?" he replied.

"I don't know, you just looked sort of . . . sort of frozen, I guess."

"I'm fine." He wasn't sure he had ever told a bigger whopper in his life.

"Let's find Bob, then. That poor man needs a taste."

"Okay." Eben let himself be led from the Lilith Room, back into the shadowy main hall.

He had his own reasons for wanting to find Dane—the sooner, the better.

30

THE HOUSE BY the banks of the Ogeechee River looked much like the other houses around it, which Andy figured was exactly the point. No one looking at it from outside would see anything strange about it. Trees pressed in on all sides, branches weighted down with Spanish moss, and Andy had noticed a pathway down to a wooden dock on the river side as he drove up. Its clapboard siding, painted white, showed signs of age—stains, discoloration, mildew around the base. Its shingled roof had seen better days, too, and had as many gaps as a third-grader's teeth. A front porch sagged like it was depressed about something, but the glass was intact in all the windows, the screens taut, and the doors looked sturdy. Lights burned outside and in as he and Stella emerged from their rented car.

They had called before arriving, and Ferrando Merrin expected them. The neighboring houses weren't very close—each house on the river seemed to have a half-acre lot—but he didn't know who was in them and didn't want to raise any eyebrows.

The front door—inside the screened porch—opened before they even reached the plank steps. A man came out—elderly, but spry, his spine straight, hair combed, a welcoming smile on his lean face. "Come in, we've been waiting for you," he said. He stepped quickly to the screen door and held it open.

"How is she?" Stella asked.

"Coming along rather rapidly, I should say," Merrin answered. He shook Stella's hand, then Andy's. His grip was firm and dry. "Delighted to make your acquaintance."

"Strange circumstances," Andy said. "But likewise."

"Strange indeed." He brought them inside the house's front room, a small, badly lit living room stuffed with two yard sales' worth of furniture and accessories. Someone had hung wallpaper with velvet trim, maybe fifty years ago, and every day of that fifty years showed. "Can I fetch you anything?"

"I'm good," Andy said.

"No thank you," Stella replied.

Interesting. Andy was determined to keep a closer eye on Stella. She hadn't had any blood for a while, and now not accepting any from a supposedly trusted host?

She could have torn Andy's head off and downed his at any time, but she hadn't. The dread that had cast a pall over him for the remainder of the trip, since the motel room, refused to clear up.

Plus, traveling with one bloodsucker had been bad enough, but now Andy was here in a house with two of them, and a woman carrying a third. Or if not a vampire then something else. If they turned on him, could he defend himself?

Merrin waved Stella and Andy to chairs—the room contained a wide variety of them, from midcentury modern to a Barcalounger with great gashes in the leatherlike fabric—and they parked themselves. A spring jabbed Andy in the back.

"I'm certainly relieved that you've both come," Merrin said. His voice, like his manner, was as prim as a British governess's, circa 1950. At least according to the movies Andy had seen, since he hadn't been alive then, much less in England, much less in the care of a governess. Merrin gave him that impression, at any rate. "I'm not afraid to say, this entire escapade is entirely out of my usual bailiwick. I've never been a nursemaid to a pregnant girl, much less a midwife, which if you hadn't come soon is a role I'm afraid I would have been forced into."

"We can stay until she delivers," Stella assured him. "At least if she's progressing as fast as she says."

Andy wasn't sure what exactly his role here was. Stella had asked him to accompany her, and he had agreed, albeit reluctantly. They had made the trip, with Andy fearing for his life, and he still didn't know if he was meant to be a bodyguard—unlikely, he knew—or comic relief, or what. So he had decided to let her do the talking, right up until the moment he opened his mouth and words tumbled out. "Maybe faster than any of us are ready for."

"That's certainly seems to be the case," Merrin said.

"Tell you the truth, I don't have a whole lot more experience at it than anybody," Stella said. "Eben and I delivered a baby one winter—couple of kids got stuck in the snow on their way to town in a little Toyota, when they needed four-wheel drive, and by the time we got out to them, it was too late to do anything except stand by to catch."

"I had two daughters," Andy said, wincing inwardly at the necessary use of the past tense. "I was in the delivery room for both of them. If that helps."

"Oh, it'll definitely come to that," Stella said. "Unless we've got a blizzard going I don't know what to do."

"I can virtually guarantee that there will be no blizzard this time," Merrin said. "Beyond that I make no promises whatsoever."

"Maybe we should see the patient," Stella suggested. "Is she awake?"

"I believe so," Merrin finally said. "She was watching television earlier. She can't get enough of it."

"She's upstairs?"

"I told her I thought she should stay in bed as much as possible. She's got so big. And then . . . there are other factors. You'll see."

Andy rose from the Barcalounger. His kidney appreciated the motion, freeing it from the pressure of the broken spring.

"This way," Merrin said.

Merrin led them through a door and up a straight, narrow staircase that seemed to rise at a seventy-degree angle. At the top was a hallway with several bedrooms, including one from which Andy could hear the sounds of spoiled young people arguing bitterly. *Guess a reality show's on,* he thought.

Merrin stopped short, just inside the doorway. Stella almost ran into him, and Andy had to put his hands on her back to slow himself. "Oh, my," Merrin said.

"What?" Stella pushed past the tall vampire. "God!"

Andy joined them inside, heart racing. Anything that could freak out two vampires had to be bad.

It *was* bad.

The young woman sat up in bed, gaze fixed on a 13-inch television set that stood on top of a dresser across the room from her. The TV was on but she didn't see it. Her eyes were glassy, her mouth slack. A thin line of drool ran from the corner of her mouth to the sheets tucked under her arms. Her belly was huge and round, like a beach ball under the blankets.

Dane had told Andy she was African-American, but her skin looked pinkish at first. Then Andy realized it was semitransparent, and the color came from the blood vessels and musculature beneath it. "Merrin?"

"I was up here not twenty minutes before your arrival," the vampire said. He sounded shaken. "She was fine, laughing. Her color was good."

"Well, something's happened," Stella said. She touched Ana's shoulder, gave her a little shake. "Ana?"

No response.

"Is she dead?" Andy asked.

"No, she's breathing." Stella touched her neck. "Her heartbeat feels strong."

"The baby?"

Stella peeled back the covers. Ana wore a thin cotton

nightgown, plain white with pink ribbons around the neck and sleeves. With her health a greater concern than her privacy, Stella pushed up the nightgown to expose her stomach.

Here the skin was even more transparent, stretched thin. It reminded Andy of looking through a domed window somewhere, maybe on a submarine ride. Only this was not a fish or eel looking back at him, it was a fetus. It appeared fully developed, and it revolved slowly inside Ana's womb, slowly spreading the fingers of its right hand. Watching it gave Andy an eerie sensation of voyeurism; he was seeing something he clearly was never meant to. Not in this way.

"My Lord," Ferrando Merrin said. That was not a phrase vampires used often, or lightly, in Andy's limited experience. He couldn't argue with the sentiment, though.

"Yeah. That's . . ." He didn't know how to finish the sentence, so just let it trail off. No one noticed.

"Baby looks healthy enough," Stella said.

"Shouldn't we call nine-one-one?" Andy asked. "For Ana?"

"Yeah." Stella's tone was bitingly sarcastic. "And tell them what? Save the baby, but make sure it doesn't bite you?"

"I see your point." He took another look. From here, he could see no indication that the baby wasn't perfectly normal. Its setting, however—that was about as far from normal as one could get. "I guess it's just us, huh?"

"I guess it is," Stella said. "Hope you remember those Lamaze classes."

31

THE GUY KNEW something about the vampires Dan Bradstreet's team had let slip out of their hands on Savannah's waterfront, and by extension, about the vampire Dan believed was behind the Headsman murders. Dan was as sure of it as he was that official Washington was a cesspool—including the people to whom he ultimately reported. It was to those people, however, that he would have to admit failure if he couldn't break his suspect.

They wouldn't accept failure, and neither would he.

He had known this about himself since high school, when he had pushed himself to not only reach a 4.0 average in every class, but to outdo every classmate in every class. When someone built a working volcano for the science fair, Dan built a scale model Vesuvius that actually wiped out an accurate, miniature Pompeii. When a classmate did a ten-page paper for extra credit, Dan did fifteen. Parents (his mother and a stepfather who tolerated him without liking him—his birth father having died in a car crash that his mom's sisters both claimed was suicide, steering a tiny Datsun into the path of a barreling semi truck) and teachers thought his overachieving ways would take him far in business, but ever since he'd read *So You Want to Be an FBI Agent* in the seventh grade, Dan Bradstreet had considered no other career. The Bureau was for him. Once he made his bones there and eventually found out he could run the *vampire* unit of all vocations, he knew it had been the right decision.

He would not let this . . . this *taxi driver* thwart him. The man knew things, and Dan would find out what those things were. If he had more time he could be more subtle about it. A few months at Gitmo, maybe. To really learn from a suspect, the best way was to befriend him, to establish a human connection, make him want to help you out by telling you what he knew. But Dan had never been good at human connections, only work related ones, which every party knew were nothing like real friendships.

Operation Red-Blooded waited for no man. Something major was under way in the vampire world, and he needed to press every advantage he had until he figured out what it was.

He had left Brent Masters—a phony name if ever he had encountered one—alone for a couple of hours to stew in his own paranoia. Now it was time to get in there and seal the deal. The locals wanted their interrogation room back, and he needed to get his people out of town anyway.

He pushed open the heavy steel door. Brent, or Albert Roddy, his head down on the table with a little puddle of drool beside it, snored softly. Dan walked quietly on his rubber-soled shoes, then slammed his hand down hard on the tabletop. The bang startled Brent, who sat up fast, eyes comically wide. "What the fuck?"

"Time to get down, Brent," Dan said. "Time to get this show on the road. Time to quit screwing around and shoot straight."

Brent wiped his mouth with the back of the hand that wasn't shackled to the table. "You mean you're going to let me out of here?"

"Is that what I said?"

"If we're not screwing around anymore. Because that's all we've been doing since you brought me here."

"You're the one who told me your name was Brent Masters. You're also the one I caught sneaking around on a boat belonging to Albert Roddy, which you claimed was yours. So which is it? Roddy or Masters?"

"Masters. I won the boat in a poker game."

"And Roddy gave you the title, right?"

"He was going to give it to me when I got the boat down to Florida."

"But you know him well enough to know that he wasn't bullshitting you? You didn't see the title, but you believe it's really his boat."

"I don't know him that well, but he knows some friends of mine. Anyway, I didn't say I didn't see the title, so stop trying to put words in my mouth. Look . . . are you charging me with something? I—"

"I'm the one asking the questions, Masters or Roddy or whoever you are. You're the one chained to that table, remember? Do you forget we're in the middle of a war? I don't have to let you see a lawyer, I don't have to charge you with anything. You think I'm going to let you see a lawyer, after what I've done to you? At least until you heal up? All I have to do is keep you here until you answer the questions I've been asking about your bloodsucker friends."

Masters or Roddy shook his head sadly. His eyelids were heavy, hooding his eyes, and for the first time Dan thought he looked like a guy who was telling the truth, someone genuinely sad and disturbed that he had been swept accidentally into a net he hadn't known anything about.

Didn't mean he believed the guy. But he was closer than he had been to thinking maybe this idiot was just a stooge, someone who had been used but who wasn't really involved with the vampires.

In that case, though, why didn't he give them up? What was he protecting?

"I don't know anything about *vampires*!" the man said for about the hundredth time. "If I did, *I'd tell you!* If you want me to write down a complete description of what I've been doing for the last three months, just give me some paper and a pencil. If you want to connect me to a lie detector, go ahead! *I don't know how else to convince you!*"

Dan studied him for a long few moments. The guy still struck him as sincere. He knew the guy was pulling something, but he couldn't figure out what. It bugged the hell out of Dan.

"Sure, why don't you write out a statement?" Dan said. If nothing else, forcing Masters to go over his last couple of weeks in detail would give Dan some openings to poke around in. Since he knew the guy was lying about some things, it might let him know about what. "I'll get you some paper."

He left Masters/Roddy at the table and went into the station house, where he asked a local cop for a legal pad and a pen. He had no intention of handing his own silver Cross pen over to the suspect. The cop dug in his desk and came up with a steno notebook and a new, unsharpened pencil. "What am I supposed to do with this?" Dan asked.

The cop gave a shrug that indicated that he couldn't care less. The locals had been less and less cooperative, and now only the appearance of their captain got any action out of them. Dan knew he was just another Fed to them, maybe more impenetrable than most because he wouldn't tell them the first thing about what he and his group had come for.

"Pencil sharpener on the wall," the cop said before shuffling from the room.

Dan carried the pencil to the ancient hand-crank sharpener, stuck it in, and listened to it grind. He had sent his group out to waste a couple of vampires, just because they could, while he stayed here to interrogate the suspect. He desperately wished he had gone along. Maybe the change of scenery would have given him a new perspective on the current problem, show him what he was missing. Instead he was stuck inside a small town, late-night police station, with the AC blowing on high and the bugs clattering against the lights outside and the hostile cops wishing he would go away so they could resume their ordinary lives.

Back through the steel door, he placed the pad on the table and spun it around, sliding it toward Brent Masters or Albert Roddy or whoever. He dropped the pencil on top of it. "Write," he said. "And don't leave anything out, especially the parts about your vampire friends."

"I don't believe in vampires," the suspect said. "If you do, I think you need to be talking to a shrink instead of to me."

"Just write." Dan left him alone again. In an hour he'd check back in, maybe take him a glass of water. Maybe even take him out for a bathroom trip, if he hadn't pissed in his pants by then.

Dan spent the hour reading emails and reports on his laptop. The station didn't have wireless so he'd had to plug into their T-1 line. When it was over, wishing these bumpkins had had the sense to put some two-way glass in their one and only interrogation room (and a room deodorizer—the place still smelled like puke from the generations of drunks they'd had in there), he went back in to see what masterpiece Masters/Roddy had composed.

The suspect was out again, but this time his head tilted back, not forward. A sharp, metallic stink filled the room.

Blood had pooled on the floor beneath his chair.

Fuck. Dan dashed forward, dodging the table. His foot found some sprayed blood, and he almost slipped on the linoleum. He caught himself on Masters/Roddy's leg, which moved beneath his hand, but lifelessly. *Fuck!*

The notepad was empty except for a thick glop of bright red blood soaking through the layers.

The pencil was jammed deep into the guy's left eye socket, all the yellow buried, only the pink nub of eraser showing. He had done his right eye first; the eyeball, exploded, was all over his shirt and the table. That had to hurt, but it hadn't killed him. Maybe the left one hadn't, either, at first. Losing massive amounts of blood from both wounds had done the job, though.

And he had pissed in his pants, after all.

What a waste.

Dan mentally sighed. Maybe it was just as well. After all, this guy just saved Dan the trouble of having to take him out anyway.

32

ON THE SURFACE, the sun no doubt blazed through Norway's vivid blue sky. Down here, where Dane kept descending through what felt like Dante's circles of Hell, one would never know it. The deeper he went, the more he felt like he had stumbled into one of Enok's nightmares—which, to Enok, would be more akin to paradise on earth.

On these lower levels, the darkness—figurative as well as literal—was almost complete. A few candles spat and smoked, the thin scents they gave off overpowered by the stinks of blood and filth. Even vampires, eyes adjusted to the dark over long centuries, needed some light to see by. But almost as if they were ashamed by what went on (an emotion Dane believed beyond the capacity of most *nosferatu*), they preferred to move about in the near blackness of the deep underground on these levels.

He had passed one almost entirely filled with tanks and pipes—copper, brass, stainless steel, reflecting with their various tints the few candles and handful of kerosene lanterns here. A passing worker had explained that this was where blood was processed to prevent spoilage and bottled for later consumption. This, too, was where the pipes to the bars on the upper levels came, the place from which they took their never-ending supply to serve those who visited this place.

He was surprised not to find security in spots like this. One person could cause havoc by destroying these tanks, knocking the blood delivery system off-line. Enok must have been confident that no one would find out about the place who might consider such an act, and that no non-vampire could make it past the front door except as a captive.

Dane wasn't ready to make trouble. That would mean revealing himself. Just now he didn't even know where Eben was, and he didn't want to take a chance on stirring things up until they had agreed on it, and were both in positions where they could do the most damage.

If, indeed, they decided they could do anything at all.

So far, Dane had seen what he guessed were many hundreds of vampires here. Maybe as many as a thousand. Not nearly that many vehicles in the lot, so many probably came to stay, like Sarah Cavalier.

On the way down, the banister felt rougher under his palm than the ones higher up, as if fewer hands had worn it smooth. This was an unexpected bit of slapdash workmanship—Dane would have expected a banister to be sanded smooth before installation. Maybe the place had been thrown together in a hurry.

This floor had a closed door made of heavy, carved wood like most of the building thus far. It all made Dane wonder just how long Enok had been planning and building the place. That sawmill upstairs must have been busy for years on the project, and since sawdust had led him here, they presumably still used it.

The door swung open when he pushed on it. Inside, the smell of humans was stronger than it had been anywhere else. Sweat, fear, blood, urine, salt—all the odors that wafted from a human body under stress—tore at his nostrils like little barbed hooks, demanding his attention. He rushed through the doorway, pressing the big door closed behind him, and found himself in yet another large room, with columns supporting the floors above interspersed here and there and a few walls delineating specific areas. In one spot, a group of humans stood huddled together. They were naked and looked drugged. Heads drooped down to chests, jaws slack, eyes glazed over. No one conversed, or even looked with any curiosity at Dane, although he was sure a couple saw him enter.

He heard movement from behind a wall and stepped quickly into shadows. A couple of vampires emerged, took one of the humans—a man, obese and hairy—and led him back behind the wall. A moment later Dane heard a sharp report, almost like a gunshot but with less reverberation. Accompanying it was a hushed grunt, presumably from the big man. Then another noise, familiar but awful: a sharp blade slicing flesh. A liquid patter followed, like rain on a tin roof. Finally, the clatter of steel wheels on the floor.

Dane thought he recognized the sounds, and it turned his stomach. The two vampires had taken the man to a gurney or some similar contraption, used a pressure hammer to kill him, slit his throat, and bled him into a metal bucket or trough, then whisked him away for further "work."

He could be wrong, of course. He needed a closer look.

The front section of the big room had been used for storage—big wooden cases on wheels were rolled into what looked like miniature freight yards. Given what he had just heard, he supposed that they were used for body removal. He worked his way between them, trying not to smell the inescapable aroma of death all around him. Some of the humans watched him come, but still remained unconcerned about his approach. He might have been an ant crossing the room toward them, for all they cared. Either they were drugged or they had been thoroughly broken of everything that had made them human.

He paused when the vampires returned for their next victim. They had developed a pretty efficient system, it seemed. They took away a woman in her late forties or early fifties, brown hair starting to go gray, a body she had obviously tried hard to fight gravity's effects on finally giving in. When they had ducked back behind the wall, Dane continued.

When he got close enough to the pack of humans, he saw that he had been more or less right. They put the woman on her knees in front of a long metal trough, bent her forward over it, and put the gun to the back of her head. One tug on the trigger finished her. Then one of them held her in place while the other drew a blade across her throat. Blood fountained from the cut, joining the pinkish mix of brain and blood that splattered into the trough.

After giving her a couple of minutes there, they hoisted her onto a conveyor belt, hundreds of small steel wheels mounted over the trough, and gave her a shove. Another vampire caught the body a few feet away and dragged it out of Dane's field of view. Blood continued to splash down into the trough as she went, and Dane had no doubt that farther down the line her body was sliced up so that not a drop of the precious fluid would be missed.

He had seen enough of this floor. It really was nothing but a slaughterhouse—slow moving, but if it operated all day every day, it would account for the deaths of more than enough humans to feed all the vampires in this place.

Heading for the door, he ran into one of the wheeled cases and smashed it into some others, making a racket. One of the vampires stopped, the next victim's arm in his hands, and shouted something at him in Norwegian. Dane didn't know what he said, but he didn't sound pleased to see a trespasser.

"Sorry!" Dane answered, waving an arm at him. He went through the door and out, once again noting the lack of any serious security measures. As efficient as the assembly line system was, a little modernization would speed it up tremendously—not that he had any interest in helping improve the operations.

Returning to the stairs, he made his way down another level. This one was pitch black, silent, and smelled musty, vacant. He kept going, passing another, similar one. He began to hear screams—people, not drugged, he guessed, before they were taken upstairs (and it occurred to him here that there must be some sort of service elevator system in addition to these winding stairs). On what seemed to be the lowest level, the screams were louder than ever. Again, he was faced with a wooden door. Again, the door swung open at a touch, and no one challenged his presence there. He passed through.

On the other side, he found pens stretching as far as he could see, possibly a hundred of them or more, each with what looked like eight to a dozen people inside. The pens were screened in with chicken wire fence and short stock panels, like one might see in a pig barn.

Like the ones upstairs, they had been stripped of their clothing, their dignity.

In one pen, egged on by a couple of bug eaters wearing malicious grins, two of them fought each other, bare-handed, drawing blood with teeth and nails and punishing fists.

In another, some of the people sat watching the fight in the first one, while others observed a man and woman rutting on the dirt floor—an act devoid of passion, romance, or sensuality, an animal act. Bug eaters supervised this, as well. From the over-the-shoulder glances the man shot them from time to time, he speculated that the whole thing was their idea, and not the humans'. The purpose was no doubt breeding, not pleasure. Most of the stock came from abductions, but if that could be augmented—possibly replaced, some day—by a breeding program, that would serve the vampires' needs just as well.

Dane supposed that bug eaters, not vampires, served as the overseers on this level, to prevent vampires selfserving from the breeding stock. The bug eaters weren't that far removed from human themselves, but watching them move about the people, casually inflicting pain and humiliation, one might think they didn't remember their former lives. Maybe it was like reformed smokers or drinkers—disapproving more intensely of their old vices than people who had never shared them did.

A vampire, clad in traditional black, with a cloak of all things, like some second-rate Bram Stoker vision, stormed toward him with one hand thrust forward, pointing a finger as if it were loaded and ready to fire. He said something Dane didn't understand, except in the abstract. He wasn't happy at Dane's presence here, that much Dane could follow.

"English?" Dane asked.

"Why do you here?"

"I'm just looking around," Dane said. "Trying to see what's what. Maybe I'm a little lost."

"I think you are. Upstairs, is better for you."

If he needed to, Dane could snap him in half without making an effort. Was he supposed to be the security guard for this level? The bug eaters' supervisor? Enok's master plan had some big holes in it, if that was the case. Not only could the humans, if they wanted to, climb or jump over the low fences that separated them, but they outnumbered the bug eaters and could rise up against them, successfully, Dane believed. One vampire wouldn't be enough to turn the tide against them.

Enok certainly wouldn't be the first leader, of a company or a country, better at ideas than execution. The flaws Dane had begun to perceive in this operation were unexpected, but he took some pleasure in finding them.

Enok was the baddest of them all, they said. But he was not perfect. He took short cuts. Therefore, he was not invincible.

At least, that's how Dane saw the situation. He sincerely hoped he was right.

33

HE KNOWS. EVERYTHING.

When that registered, moments after leaving the Lilith Room, Eben stopped dead in his tracks. Stella was notorious among the vampire community. Her book, *30 Days of Night,* had threatened to expose them—on her terms, not theirs. She had gone up against them and survived, and she had shown others how to do the same. Websites devoted to her had sprung up all over the internet. She had fans, adherents, in cities across the country, if not the globe.

To people who believed in the vampire threat, she was an inspiration. To vampires, she was a menace.

While Eben and Dane were here, she was vulnerable. Sure, she had proven that she could take care of herself. But now? From what Dane had said, and what Lilith had implied, Enok was a threat of a different magnitude than any she had yet faced.

Why had he left her home? Someone needed to watch over Barrow, but surely the townspeople could have handled it for a week or so—the population was vampire-savvy these days; they knew what had to be done and how to do it. Any bloodsuckers attacking Barrow now would be in for a hell of a fight.

Stella, however, was alone. Unprepared. If Enok decided to take advantage of this opportunity . . .

Sarah Cavalier said something, but Eben didn't hear. He turned in a slow circle, mind racing, ignoring his present circumstances. Then he felt pressure on his arm, and he snapped his focus to Sarah, before him, leaning in with a look of concern on her face. "Charles," she said, with some urgency. "What's going on?"

He blinked as if he had just rolled out of bed. She wasn't kidding. Vampires stared at him as if he had just performed a stunt in the middle of the main hall. "Sorry," he said.

"That's twice in a couple of minutes. You've sort of got everybody riled up, wondering what gives."

"I'm fine," Eben declared, pasting a smile to his face.

"They aren't so good with English, most of them."

"Well, fuck them, as I don't know how to say it in anything else," Eben snarled. Why was he even having this conversation? He needed to get home to Stella.

But his weak show of well-being hadn't made as much impression on the gathered vampires as his earlier behavior—almost trancelike, he guessed—had. They had closed ranks, forming a circle around him, still informal at this point, but he got the idea that it would only take a word to set them off. A hundred of them, probably. He wouldn't have a chance.

He wouldn't be able to get to Stella, either.

He had to get out of this, somehow, without raising any more undead eyebrows.

One of them said something to Sarah that Eben didn't understand. She shot Eben an appraising glance and then replied in whatever the original language had been. "He said there's something strange about you. 'The stink of daylight,' he said. I told him you were cool."

"Thanks."

"You are, right?"

"Of course. I can't remember the last time I felt daylight." He did, of course. It had been the day he and Stella sat together waiting for the first sunrise after the long darkness that had almost claimed Barrow. The sun's rays had felt like a thousand slender blades, piercing him everywhere at once. He had well and truly died, to be revived only after Lilith traded his ashes to Stella for a DVD of the Barrow attack that Stella claimed—falsely—was the only copy.

Judging from some of the suspicious glares directed Eben's way, the one who had spoken up wasn't the only one who smelled daylight. Was it maybe because of how Eben had been turned, injecting himself with vampire blood in order to save his town?

Whatever it was, if he had to fight, he would do so. He wouldn't win, not against these odds. But he'd take a few of them out with him, at least.

A tall, dark figure pushed through the gathered crowd, headed right toward Eben. Was this it?

Eben braced for the coming attack.

It took him a moment to realize that the figure was Dane, and his right arm was raised more as a shield than an attack. He swept up to Eben, lowered his arm over Eben's shoulders, and spoke softly. "What's going on?"

"I'll tell you, but not here."

"Fine. I have plenty to show you as well." Dane gave the crowd a confident, relaxed wave and led Eben away, pressing between vampires who, moments ago, looked like they'd as soon tear Eben's head off as let him pass. Dane had chosen the least-defended direction, back toward the Lilith Room, but his entrance seemed to have defused the tension that had filled the hall like smoke from a fire, just moments ago. Eben could hear casual conversations, the scuff of feet as the crowd thinned, vampires wandering back to their feeding or other activities.

"Enok knows where Stella is," Eben whispered, drawing Dane into the Lilith Room, which had emptied out. Except for Lilith, of course. "I have to warn her in case he goes after her while we're here."

Dane showed him a concerned face. "Okay, Eben. You're going to be angry, but . . . she's not there."

"What are you talking about?"

"She went to Georgia. To deal with the pregnant girl. She asked me not to say anything to you. So you wouldn't worry."

"She did what?"

"She went with Andy Gray. They were leaving right after us."

"Oh my God. I could kill you all. I would have told her not to go. Not till I came back, anyway."

"Which might have been too late. The pregnancy was progressing way too fast for that."

"I don't care," Eben snapped. "Why's it even important?"

"Because it's our first chance to really learn what happens when a human and a vampire reproduce," Dane said. His tone made it clear that he considered that a foregone conclusion. Even if it was, Eben didn't consider it more important than Stella's safety. Not even in the same league.

He hadn't liked Dane from the get-go. Not one bit. If Dane imagined that his precious crossbreed baby took precedence over Stella, then their tentative companionship would degenerate into a serious problem, in a hurry. He took Dane's lapel in his hand and was about to tell him that, when Lilith's voice sounded in his head again.

And here is the traitor. Dane.

"Who?" Dane asked aloud.

As an experiment, Eben tried thinking his response. *You heard it, too? It's Lilith.*

*But you—*Dane thought at him.

Apparently I have some skills you didn't know about. Neither did I, to tell you the truth.

I cannot say I am happy that you have come here, Dane, Lilith's voice said. Eben knew from Dane's puzzled expression that both could hear her. *I had hoped never to encounter you again. Unless, of course, I was in a position to do you some terrible harm.*

Dane glanced at her tortured body, prone on the altar. She didn't look their way. *I take it you're not, at present,* he thought.

Did I somehow give you that impression?

You don't look very threatening from here.

After all these years, I am astonished that you still put stock in appearances.

A failing on my part, no doubt.

I have other concerns, little traitor, larger concerns than you, and—

Such as? Speak to me, dear Lilith, of such grievances.

A third voice in his head, this one deep, undeniably masculine, and with a reverberation that made the hairs on Eben's neck stand straight up.

Enok. Lilith's voice. She sounded frightened, which unsettled Eben all the more.

Of course, my dear Lilith. You did not think I had forgotten about you?

One hopes . . .

One must be sadly deluded. My thoughts are with you, Lilith, more often than you suspect. At times I peer into your mind just so I can enjoy your delicious suffering on the most visceral level, from the inside.

Pleasant, Dane's voice said.

Don't—Eben thought, then stopped himself, knowing anything he thought would be picked up by the others, including Enok.

You are correct, Eben Olemaun. While I am, for lack of a better phrase, inside your head, there is nothing you can think that I do not know at the same time you do. No matter how hard you try to suppress it—in fact, the harder you try the more apparent it becomes. Your beloved Stella Olemaun, for instance. You do not want to see her mangled corpse outside your cabin, with her head jammed onto the end of a fir branch and her blood painting the snow red. Your imagination is particularly vivid, too—see the way her left leg is twisted and cocked at such a strange angle, the knee snapped, a shard of bone thrusting out through flesh and clothing alike? See how her fingers are hooked into the snow, as if the pain of her last moments set her to digging. Does she, in your mind, think she can escape it by burrowing beneath the drifts?

Eben didn't know what Enok or the others would think of his thoughts now, coming as they did not in linear word streams but in red and purple bursts of rage, images of Stella (as Enok had so vividly described), blue spikes of terror, outrage at being invaded in this fashion.

Be done with him, Enok, Lilith offered. *He is of little importance.*

Lilith, Lilith. I take great pleasure in your excruciating agony, but you are not the end-all of my existence, or my only interest, by any means. Just now, these two insects, in fact, are far more intriguing than you. In fact, I think I would like to see them. In person.

I don't think that's necessary, Dane thought.

But Eben already heard the shuffling of many feet outside the room. He cast a worried glance toward the doorway, which had been empty a minute before.

No longer. Now vampires filled it and streamed inside, deliberate, their gazes locked on Dane and himself.

34

ENOK RULED FROM a space that might have been a throne room from a Scandinavian folk tale, built for a woodland king.

Dane had expected genuine luxury, but that seemed to have escaped Enok's capabilities here. The touches he had attempted, like the gold paint on his throne, he didn't quite pull off. The paint had bubbled and chipped here and there, showing rough wood beneath, and Dane knew at a glance that the throne wasn't real gold. The cushions on which Enok rested his scrawny rear weren't hand sewn for him, but probably came from a discount department store down in Tromsø. Tapestries on the walls were copies, not originals—Dane had seen the original of one of them in an Austrian castle, fifty years before, and was pretty sure it remained there. Even the strip of red carpet that ran from the doorway to the throne, covering the plank floor, was worn, matted, and stained, more suited to a dormitory hallway than a ruler's inner sanctum.

He didn't feel Enok's presence in his head anymore and wondered what the vampire would think if he knew Dane was reflecting on his failure to impress.

Beyond that, Dane was also rather terrified as to what would happen next.

Dane and Eben had gone along peacefully with the bloodsuckers Enok sent to bring them. They had been vastly outnumbered, making resistance quite possibly suicidal. Besides, he had known—as soon as he discovered Enok's hand in this operation—that they would have to come face-to-face at some point. Easier to let Enok summon them than to try to fight their way to him. The room turned out to be on the level with the processing equipment, a level Dane hadn't bothered to explore very thoroughly.

Enok leaned forward on his "throne"—really an oversized chair mounted up on a dais, four steps off the floor—as if he might spring from it at any time, his right hand clutching the armrest like it was a launching pad. He was thin, almost emaciated looking, making prominent cheekbones into cliffs with deep vertical furrows beneath, running all the way to his sharp-edged chin. Above the cheeks were the deep hollows of his eyes, the eyeballs themselves recessed in hooded slits. A huge mole on his left eyelid added to the impression that he could barely see through that one. His hair was dark and long, hanging in greasy strands around his face. The knuckles of his right hand, the one holding onto the edge of his chair's armrest, were swollen and pale.

"My apologies for the rude way in which I greeted you both," Enok said when they were brought in and released on the red carpet. His opening statement took Dane by surprise. "Honored guests, and the first thing I do is dip inside you like you are just two more of my playthings. I imagine that is what happens when one is essentially unchallenged in day-to-day living. Arrogance becomes habitual. Not pretty, is it?"

"It rarely is," Dane managed to answer.

"And you, Eben Olemaun, I especially grieve for."

"Me? Why?"

"Because I owe you so much gratitude."

Dane glanced at Eben, who clearly didn't understand the comment. "Gratitude?" Eben repeated.

"Of course. You dispatched Vicente. And your wife—while she did not succeed in destroying her—undid Lilith to the point that I was able to best her easily. Two of my children, yes? But also two of my most powerful competitors. Now, no more challenges for me. With them gone, my power over the nightwalkers is essentially absolute. You, Dane. Your handful of followers are no more troublesome to me than maggots."

"I don't have followers," Dane said.

"Exactly my point."

"I don't think you understand. I don't have followers because I'm not some crazed demagogue, imagining that people consider me their leader just because I buy them off with easy food. I have allies, though. And they're no maggots."

Dane had intended this to be a reconnoitering trip, to find out what was taking place in this part of the world, who was behind it, then to possibly return with those allies, in force, to put an end to it. He had learned the answers to the questions, but had been found out too soon, too easily.

Now he had to face Enok, one-on-one—well, two, with Eben, but he didn't really think Eben shared his particular philosophy. Dane and his friends hoped to achieve a balance with the human world, peaceful coexistence, a patch of dirt they could call their own. Eben was a walking contradiction—he seemed to want all vampires destroyed, and if the accomplishment of that goal was to include himself and Stella in that destruction, then so be it.

It had all gone so horribly wrong.

Enok's likely response to his statement would be to kill them both immediately—if not with his own bare hands, then by ordering the hundred or so vampires who had escorted him and Eben here, and who now stood back against the walls of the vast room, to do it for him.

Instead, the self-styled leader of the *nosferatu* laughed, loud and long. "Well spoken," he said. "But . . . how do the Americans say? Bullshit? But convincingly stated bullshit nonetheless."

"I'd hate to think I did you any favors," Eben said. Taking Enok's attention onto himself and off Dane. Dane appreciated the effort. If they were going to beat Enok, they'd have to keep him off guard.

"That is only because you do not know me, Eben Olemaun. I am the sort who does favors in return. Even when I am vexed. Vicente, for instance—I kept his remains, after you vanquished him there in your little village. He performed some good turns for me over the years——centuries, really——and I just might decide to bring him back one of these days so I can do the same for him."

"When it serves your own purposes," Dane said.

"I said I am grateful, not stupid." Enok——rather pointedly, Dane believed——looked away from him, focusing his attention on Eben. "Whether you accept this or not, you and your woman both did me favors. Favors of an enormous scope. And they are greatly appreciated. I could certainly do the same for you."

"I don't have anyone I want killed," Eben said.

That's a lie, Dane thought. Then again, Enok was lying too.

"Not the sort of favor I had in mind," Enok said. "You did me a good turn. And by dispatching of Vicente——a powerful adversary, even for me——you proved that you would be a good addition to my . . . team? As the captains of industry say? What I am offering you is a future. Not a cabin in the snow, outside a pathetic little town that only desires your services when they are in dire need, and would rather pretend you do not exist the rest of the time. Think about it, Eben. Like it or not, you are *vampire*. Those you would protect despise your very nature. There are those who would consider you necessary, perhaps, but hardly popular. If they could do without you, they would do so and breathe a sigh of relief."

"Those people know me!" Eben shot back. "They're my friends, my neighbors. We've been through hell together. They wouldn't turn on me."

"Of course," Enok said, not at all convinced. He settled back in his chair, no longer seeming on the verge of leaping out of it. Even so, he looked tense, restless. His long, thin fingers clicked against the armrests. "And whenever a human goes berserk and decides to murder a group of defenseless children, what is it they say? 'He seemed like such a nice person.' That does not mean they would trust him if he resided next door again after his incarceration, no? When you go into Barrow now, do they invite you into their houses for a drink, to share in good times?"

Eben didn't answer. He chewed on his lower lip. "Don't let him get to you, Eben," Dane whispered, afraid that if Eben exploded, Enok would wipe him out on the spot. Then he would be left completely without allies here.

"Shut up," Eben snapped.

"He's working you."

"I know. Just be quiet."

"At my side, Eben, you would be treated the way you deserve to be treated. As a hero, a champion. Your beloved could join you, if you still want her. But if you would rather not, you could have your pick, some wonderful sport . . . what do you think, 'Sheriff' Olemaun? Power beyond your wildest imaginings? Respect? The next phase in the evolution of planet Earth? Or would you rather remain the nuisance outside of town, the man no one really wants to see coming?"

"Fuck you," Eben said. He sucked in a breath, swelling his chest. His fists were clenched so tight the knuckles had gone pale. "Fuck you and your next phase and your power. Do you honestly believe the shit you sling around, or are you just like one of those monkeys in the zoo, throwing it because you aren't imaginative enough to think of anything better to do?"

Enok looked like he'd been physically struck. Dane felt a stirring of pride at Eben's defiance. Enok's reaction was different. "Take this pig away," he said. "Get him out of my sight."

The vampires who had been standing back swarmed around them again, dozens of hands clutching at Dane and Eben. "Not the other one!" Enok shouted over the sudden din, pointing at Dane. "Just Olemaun!"

Dane struggled to reach Eben, but the weight of the hands on him pulled him back. He caught Eben's gaze, held it, but then Eben was dragged out of sight. Dane remained where he was, on the shabby carpet, surrounded by at least fifty vampires. "What about me?" he asked, bracing for the answer.

"You, insect, have done me no favors at all. Bork Dela was one of my best suppliers. His destruction has left a large void in my operation, and it will take some time to fill it properly. I owed Eben Olemaun a chance. You, I owe nothing. You are a special treat for those down below. Every now and then, I let them have a solid meal. They have to cut it into rather small pieces, but they find sport in that as well."

To a vampire, being eaten by bug eaters was the ultimate humiliation. He must have really pissed Enok off.

Despite the fear roiling in his guts, he couldn't help smiling a little.

"I amuse you? Really?" Enok went on. "You are a disgrace. Not even worthy of the name *nosferatu*. You bring dishonor to the species. Even Lilith deserves a better fate than you." He waved a hand, dismissing Dane from his presence. The hands closed on Dane again, fingers digging in tight. "May these last few moments of your pathetic existence be as unpleasant as possible."

35

EBEN OLEMAUN had known times of extreme terror before. Hiding in a basement watching, and worse, listening, when he couldn't see through the dark and the driving snow, to his town being torn apart, life by life, soul by soul.

The most frightening moment might have been when he realized what he needed to do to save Barrow. In the first instance, he had always had Stella to lean on, had been able to draw strength from her seemingly bottomless reservoir of courage. In the second, however, he had been entirely alone. She would never have gone along with the idea, and he had to keep it hidden even from her—the hardest thing he had ever done, keeping that secret, harder even than plunging the needle into his vein.

Now he was alone again. Alone in terms of allies, anyway, much less friends. Or Stella, who he would probably never again see, never hold her, never smell the dry, slightly fruity aroma of her hair.

On Enok's orders, the vampires had dragged him up to the second level, the one on which the majority of visitors seemed to spend their time, drinking blood from the taps of the floor's many bars. They held him by the arms, the neck, the ears, the hair. Sharp-clawed fingers tore holes through his clothes. All the while, they called out to their fellows, in words he didn't understand.

He could get the sense of it, though, from the looks that the others shot his way. Looks of pure hatred. They were calling him a traitor, or worse.

Bloodsuckers turned away from the bars, leaving behind glasses of rich, fresh blood, and came to join the ones who had brought him here. They emerged from shadowed alcoves and hidden nooks, growling and cursing him. They spat at him; gobs of hot, thick, pink-tinted spittle slapped his face, his chest, his neck. He couldn't block it or fight back. He tried to wrench his arms free, but his captors snarled and tugged back, almost dislocating his left shoulder.

He heard a meaningless snarl, then someone tore at his neck, ripping away a chunk of flesh. Eben remembered what Lilith looked like, bleeding from a hundred wounds, just through the doorway that he could see but not reach.

He didn't want the same to happen to him.

He planted his feet, twisting at the waist, bending a little, putting all his strength into swiveling his shoulders. The motion threw the vampires holding his right side off balance. He could now move his right arm and leg.

He slashed out with his right fist, trying to press his momentary advantage. It slammed into a couple of bloodsuckers, knocking them into their fellows. The vampires gripping him on the left held on all the harder, but with one side free, he twisted again, bringing his fist around and driving it into the ugly face of the nearest. Fangs ripped his knuckles but the blow loosened some, and the vampire released him, spitting blood and teeth on the floor.

Eben lashed out with his right foot next, the boot splintering bone and opening a slightly wider space around him.

Now he had room to move, room to fight.

He widened his stance, ready to take on whoever came at him, tasting the sweet flavor of freedom. "Ha!" he shouted in challenge.

But they didn't come one at a time. They swarmed him, like a tide swamping a sand castle. One second he had space to draw a breath, and the next, powerful arms crushed his ribs, hands clamped onto his shoulders and arms, drawing him down, his legs were immobilized.

That didn't last long, he thought. The promise of release had turned, seconds later, into bondage even more hopeless than before. Eben struggled, mouth open, raging against his enemies. But they weighted him down as surely as if they had cast chains over his shoulders and anchored them to the ground. Again, they tore at him—a piece of flesh from his ribs, another from his cheek.

They were trying to take him apart, bit by bit.

As another hand ripped a chunk out of his back, he was afraid they would succeed.

Prepare yourself, Eben Olemaun.

Lilith's voice, in his head again. Maybe thinking about her had signaled her in some way. Maybe he had come near enough to her room. *For what?* he tried to project toward her.

If she answered, he didn't receive it.

But *they* did.

The vampires around him cried out, staggered back, as if he had suddenly become white-hot to the touch. Fierce eyes glowered at Eben, but they couldn't put their hands on him. He didn't know how Lilith had done it, but no other explanation made any sense.

He also didn't know how long it would last, or if it would be any more useful than the momentary break he had made for himself before. Standing here wouldn't help, though. He lunged toward a couple of the bloodsuckers, both cringing in fear, and when they dodged—as he had hoped—he snatched up the wooden chair standing behind them.

Holding it by two legs, he swung it against the skulls of the two nearest him. Wood splintered, vampires cried out in pain. Eben was left with a sharp-ended chair leg in each fist. He waded into the thickest of them, stabbing with the legs, using them as wooden stakes. He drove them into hearts and heads, pushed them through unyielding flesh and brittle bone and fibrous muscle. Vampires howled, fell to the ground clutching their wounds, trampled one another trying to back away.

Spurred on by the fury pulsing inside him, Eben pursued.

Whatever Lilith had done had given him another chance to survive, and he meant to take it. But he didn't plan to leave here without Dane. He needed to get through the swarming vampires and find his only ally. If that meant spilling enough blood to coat the floor layers deep, then so be it.

Lilith's spell was wearing off. Eben knew it because without warning, the vampires started coming at him again, grabbing and tearing. He fought back with the chair legs, bloodied now, bits of pinkish gray brain matter clinging to the sides. One caught him from behind and Eben spun, driving the leg in his right hand through the monster's throat. Gore spewed onto his already drenched arms. He sensed another closing in on his left, whirled, swinging a chair leg in an arc that smashed it into the bloodsucker's temples. Ducking slashing claws, he stabbed up into his attacker's groin.

One by one, he took the bloodsuckers down.

They were gathering again, though, aware that whatever had protected him briefly had faded. He had weapons now, but they wouldn't let him hold off the masses indefinitely. Too many had swarmed in, the bulk of them between Eben and the staircase. Somewhere down below, Dane waited, quite probably fighting for his own survival.

Eben looked at the throng of vampires between him and his goal. Calibrated his chances. Approximately zero. He could take a few out with him, but he couldn't beat them all.

There might, however, be another way down.

Eben already knew he was stronger than most vampires,

when the rage lived inside him as it did at this moment. How strong had not been tested.

Maybe it was time.

He whirled in a circle, his twin weapons clearing a swath around him. For the moment—brief, he had no doubt—his way was open.

Not *through* the bloodsuckers.

Down.

Eben raised his right leg, knee high, and stamped down on the floorboards. They creaked and groaned. He repeated the action. The third time he jumped into the air, bending his knees, then straightened them as he landed. This time he heard cracking noises.

The vampires gaped at him as if he had completely lost his mind. Maybe they were right.

He dropped to his knees, hammering on the floorboards with his fists. Splinters drove into his flesh. He pounded again. The boards gave a satisfying moan and sagged beneath his pummeling. He picked what seemed to be a weak spot and focused his efforts there.

Vampires made tentative moves toward him. Each time, he snatched up his weapons, snarled and glared and they edged back, not wanting to get too close to the crazy man. Finally the boards gave way. He thrust his hand through the opening he had made, grasping for purchase on the underside, then yanked up on them, enlarging the hole.

The bloodsuckers seemed to understand that they didn't want him to get away with whatever he was doing.

They surged forward. Eben hurled chunks of floorboard at them and dug for more, making the hole bigger each time. Now he could see below, where a network of pipes snaked between this floor and the ceiling of the next level. Vampires screeched out what sounded like warnings or commands. He ignored them. In another few seconds the hole was large enough to pass through.

The gathered, realizing that he was leaving, scrambled to catch him.

Eben dropped down the hole, dodging the pipes and conduits, finding his footing on one of the heavy support beams. Stepping off that, he stomped down on the ceiling panel, just a single layer of pinewood. It cracked under his weight. With vampires clawing at him from above, Eben fell through, bouncing off a steel pipe, gripping it to slow him down, breaking it (blood gushing out, into the narrow crawl space between ceiling and floor) but landing on hands and feet on the floor below.

Above, he could see them gathered around the hole, staring down. Blood from the broken pipe waterfalled toward him. He sidestepped it, allowing himself a quick grin at his escape.

Partial escape, anyway. He still didn't know where Dane was, and this was a big place.

He had started toward the staircase when Enok suddenly came from that direction, sweeping toward him as if his feet barely touched the floor.

"Well done!" He clapped his slender hands together. "Bravo."

"You didn't come here just to congratulate me," Eben said.

"Of course not. Since apparently my followers cannot destroy you, I came to do it myself."

"You can try," Eben said, still confident of his strength.

Enok chuckled dryly. "That's right, the rage makes you stronger. Do you imagine that you'll become strong enough to threaten me?" He tapped his own chest. "Remember who I am, Eben. Remember how little experience you have with all of this. If I were you—" Enok smiled now, friendly, encouraging. "—if I were you, I would drop to my knees right now and beg forgiveness."

Forgiveness. Eben figured Enok only knew about that through rumors he had heard, but had little or no personal experience with the concept. "I guess we'll just have to find out."

36

THEY SLUGGED DANE over the head with something heavy and he sank like a boulder in a fishpond.

A couple of vampires grabbed him by the wrists and dragged him from the throne room. He woke up before they even reached the door, but he feigned unconsciousness. They took him to an elevator, the existence of which he had theorized but which he had not seen (and still barely saw, only risking opening his eyes to narrow slits), and then they were moving down, down, then doors slid open and he was half carried, half dragged, arms gripping under his arms, smashing his ribs, and then (for this part he opened his eyes) he was hurled over a low fence. Still pretending, he managed to throw his hands down but couldn't completely break his fall, not without giving away his wakeful state. Whoever had thrown him, or someone near that one, shouted something in Norwegian when he landed.

Judging from the reaction, the shouted phrase had been something like "Eat him up!" Dane heard a rapid scuffling noise and opened his eyes again just in time to see dozens of bug eaters rushing toward him across the bare wood floor.

Watching them come, Dane felt a vague sense of comfort slip over him like an old familiar sweater. The unease he had been living with for weeks vanished, all at once, and without analyzing it he knew it was because he was no detective, no Sherlock Holmes, no James Bond. He was a fighter. He hadn't always been, not in life—then he had been a pacifist but that was a luxury a vampire could ill afford, and in undeath the one trait he had that set him apart from the others was that he was good in a brawl.

And this—*this,* goddammit—would be one for the ages.

He made it to his feet just before they reached him.

Compared to vampires, bug eaters were weak. They were creatures in transition, not completely comfortable in their own skins. Within a few days, maybe a week, two in extreme cases, they would be *nosferatu,* their strength magnified, senses sharpened.

Until then, they were nothing. Individually, anyway. But there were a *lot* of them here.

The first one in range got Dane's fist against his mouth with enough force—from his own momentum and the power of Dane's punch—to knock his head from his shoulders, sending it spiraling back into the bug-eater ranks.

Then they were on him, swarming like maggots on a days-old corpse. Dane threw kicks and punches, then yanked one female's arm off at the shoulder and used it as a club on the others until it disintegrated in his hand, flesh and muscle peeling off the bone. Teeth snapped at him, some tearing his clothes and nipping his skin. He didn't hold anything back, though, and dozens of bug eaters fell before his crushing blows.

The stink was horrendous: unwashed dead bodies whose diet consisted solely of insects and the few rodents that had managed to tunnel into Enok's base, spilled blood, all the other attendant smells that came from hundreds of recently deceased individuals living together in a confined space. Being on this level with them was bad enough—having them teeming around him with bits of flesh and blood and brain landing on him as he tore through them made it that much worse.

Their bodies piled up thick and high around him. Dane started to have trouble moving his legs, trying to force his way through them. His feet slipped on the viscous muck beneath. They'd need a crane to clear the room, he figured—not that anyone could get a crane all these floors down beneath the sawmill. Anyway, from what he had seen of Enok's management, they'd be more likely to just leave the corpses here to rot.

Still they came, seemingly summoned from other rooms he couldn't see.

And now he realized that the bug eaters were being joined by some vampires. Whether they were the ones he had spotted here before, keeping an eye on the bug eaters, or others sent by Enok, he couldn't tell.

He dispatched two bug eaters with quick blows to the head. The moment gave the first of the vampires time to reach him, and she came in fast and hard, smashing into Dane's ribs. His feet lost purchase on the slippery planks. He went down on the stack of bodies surrounding him (some still moving in their near death, clawing weakly at him), with the vampire on top.

She stabbed toward him with a dagger, its blade nine inches long and sharp. He twisted to avoid it; the blade buried in the face of the bug eater beneath him. He shot the butt of his palm up and into the vampire's chin, snapping her head backward. At the same time he caught the wrist that held the knife and broke it. She let out a scream, glared at him, her eyes fiery with hatred. Her other hand grabbed his ear, tugged on it, trying to rip it from his head. Dane still had a grip on her broken arm, though. Turning it toward her, he closed his fist around her hand and slit her throat with her own weapon. Hot blood showered him, but she went slack and he shoved her off.

Two more vampires closed on him, accompanied by another dozen or so bug eaters. Snatching the knife from the dead vampire's ruined hand, Dane waited until one charged and caught his head in his left hand, driving the dagger through the vampire's right temple and into his brain. Still holding the bloodsucker by the head and the knife's handle, he spun the body around, blocking the next one's attack with it.

Bug eaters came at him around the body, so he threw it toward the vampire, preserving the knife, and turned to them. These he could destroy with a few blows from his left hand (the one attached by Dr. Levin so long ago—guy did good work) and some slashes with the knife. When they were down, this new vampire had a clear shot at him, and took it. Dane threw his legs apart for stability and tried to knife the vamp as he approached, but his foe dodged it, catching Dane's wrist to immobilize it. At the same time, he crashed into Dane, teeth snapping at his throat.

The two grappled, Dane having a harder time beating this one than he had his earlier opponents. This vampire was huge and strong and fought with a deadly ferocity Dane had not encountered in here before. His right fist slammed into Dane's ribs; Dane, already weary from the long struggle and the events of the day, absorbed the punishment only with difficulty.

The bloodsucker kept pummeling him. Dane decided to try a feint, and he relaxed all his muscles at once, slumping forward and releasing the dagger. The vampire yanked him forward, letting Dane's right wrist go and wrapping his hands around Dane's throat. Dane leaned against his opponent for an instant, gathering his strength, and then jabbed a thumb into the vampire's eye. The vampire shrieked and tried to back away but Dane held on, hooking his thumb in his skull, behind the eye socket. The vampire twitched and cried out, fists flailing uselessly against Dane.

In another minute it was over.

The bug eaters had backed off, perhaps preferring to limit their violence to insects who couldn't fight back. No more vampires presented themselves, either, which Dane took as an indication that the ones he had fought were the ones who guarded this floor. The others must have remained on the upper floors.

Where Eben was.

He'd wasted more than enough time here. If Eben had survived this long, they needed to reunite and get the hell out of here, while they still could.

Or was that *if* they still could?

Eben swallowed his fear, like trying to choke down a softball, and braced himself for Enok's attack.

He wished he had brought his old service weapon—a .45 slug in the brainpan would put a quick end to Enok. He wouldn't have been able to get it through airport security, though, and acquiring a firearm in Tromsø, without speaking the language, would have been tough.

Which meant that when he clashed with Enok, he would be armed only with his own wild strength. It took about a microsecond to know that would not be enough.

Enok approached him almost casually, literally strolling across the floor. When they were within striking distance, he stopped. Eben wasn't sure if his intention was conversation or combat, but then, faster than Eben's eye could follow, he lashed out. One of his fists plowed into Eben's gut, doubling him over. A second smashed into Eben's jaw with the force of a screaming 747. Before Eben knew the fight had been joined, he was on the floor, blood streaming from his nose and mouth, and Enok gloated over him, arms folded loosely over his chest, a rakish smile on his face.

"Was that what you had in mind?" Enok asked. "Or since you are already down there, perhaps you'd like to reconsider begging on your knees."

"Eat shit and bark at the moon, motherfucker," Eben replied.

Enok's reaction was to aim a kick toward Eben's head. This time Eben was ready for it. He grabbed Enok's boot in both hands and threw his weight backward, jerking and twisting at the same time. Enok hopped on his other foot but couldn't maintain his balance. He toppled back, catching himself on his hands and tugging his foot free.

"Clever," he said, scooting back out of Eben's reach. "I suppose you are entitled to one last clever move before you cease to exist."

"You're on your ass on the floor, same as me," Eben said. "Maybe you're not as tough as you think."

"Oh, have no worries on that count, Sheriff Olemaun," Enok said. He pushed himself to his feet. Eben did the same. Enok rushed him.

And Eben dodged, as he had back in his high school quarterback days, sliding past Enok's outthrust hands and breaking for the distant staircase. By the time Enok reversed course and gave chase, Eben had hit the stairs, slowing himself by grabbing the banister. His speed snapped the balustrades off their moorings. Eben yanked them off and hurled them at Enok one by one as he descended, heading into the depths of the structure with Enok close behind.

So far, he wasn't at all impressed with the construction job done here. It looked sturdy but it didn't hold up.

He hoped the same went for the vampire who had built it.

37

EBEN AND ENOK battled furiously, raging on for what seemed like an hour, but probably wasn't more than fifteen or twenty minutes.

The longer it went on, the more destructive they both were.

Eben ripped planks from the walls and used them to batter Enok. In turn, Enok threw Eben through the floor, down to the level below, and jumped through after him. Eben rolled away just in time and Enok, landing hard, crashed into the floor and opened another hole. While jagged floorboards pinned Enok's ankles, Eben tore down a support column and used it as a battering ram.

Again and again, he smashed it into Enok. The ancient vampire reeled under the steady pounding. After a few minutes of it, he was able to free his legs and snatch the post from Eben. He hurled it away, as if it was a stray tree branch that had inconvenienced him, and it slammed through a wall. Eben noted that where the wall sagged, the ceiling was starting to fall through.

Then he didn't pay attention to building construction anymore. Enok lunged at him. Eben dodged, but Enok's hand dealt him a glancing blow that sent Eben spinning into a steel tank from which pipes spread like spider legs. Liquid sloshed inside the tank. Eben caught a vague whiff of blood.

As Enok charged him again, he grabbed hold of one of the pipes in both hands, pressed one foot against the tank for leverage, and pulled for all he was worth. Just before Enok reached him, the pipe gave way and a jet of blood blasted out. Eben directed the spray at Enok, who slipped in the sticky fluid. Eben darted behind the big tank and kicked it over, rupturing its steel skin. An ocean of blood washed toward Enok as he tried to regain his footing.

Since keeping out of Enok's reach seemed like the best path to survival, Eben raced through a doorway into another room, this one full of tanks and pipes and huge copper vats. A section of loose pipe lay on the floor; he picked it up and speared one of the vats with it. Blood gushed out, flowing toward the room Eben had just left. He kicked over two more tanks. Pipes released and blood ran everywhere. *Such a waste,* Eben thought. He didn't want to drink it—he couldn't help regretting the humans who had lost their lives for the pleasure and convenience of Enok's followers.

He had almost cleared another doorway when Enok burst into the room—through the wall, not a door—snarling, furious. Debris rained down from the ceiling. Enok charged straight for Eben, who snatched up a piece of sheet metal he had torn from one of the tanks and held it up as a shield. Enok's hands bashed against the metal and he pawed at it, trying to tear it from Eben's' grip. Instead of letting go, Eben turned it sideways and slashed at Enok as if with a big, unwieldy sword. The sharp-edged steel sliced Enok's face, chin to cheekbone.

Enok froze, startled.

Eben realized for the first time that they weren't alone here—an audience of vampires watched, rapt, from the shadows of the dimly lit floor.

"I meant to do a lot more than that," Eben said, wishing he had cut the vampire's head off.

Enok broke his paralysis, lifting a hand to his cheek and pulling it away, seeing his own blood on his fingers to go along with the blood that had drenched nearly every inch of his body. He fixed Eben with a glare of perfect hatred.

"The pig. Is mine." Enok stalked toward Eben, and something had changed in his posture. He walked with the tension of a coiled spring. Eben got the idea—a distressing one, really—that Enok had been playing with him before, maybe happy to have a sparring partner with some skills but otherwise simply amusing himself before the kill.

That part had arrived, Eben believed. If Enok got his hands on Eben again, the kill would follow.

The other vampires cut off his escape route. He could go through them, but not fast enough to keep Enok from catching him. Enok came steadily, not fast, but with a grim determination that Eben didn't like. The older vampire was definitely stronger than him, by a wide margin.

Stella, he thought. *I'm sorry about everything. And I'm sorry I don't get to see you again. I love you. I have always loved you.*

Enok took another step toward him. Eben braced himself for what would certainly be the end. But before Enok could close the space between them, the floor—soaked through with blood from the vats and tanks Eben had ruptured—gave a huge creaking groan, then wood snapped, the sound like fireworks at ground level, and the whole thing collapsed, floor and tanks and vats and pipes and vampires alike dropping through.

The huge vats punched through the floor of the next level, and kept going, floor by floor. Blood and debris plummeted like a cloudburst. Eben twisted and spun in the air. Things slammed into him—pipes and bloodsuckers and planks—and he hit the floor and kept falling as each successive floor was taken out by the massive amounts of rubble.

Eben wound up on the bottom floor, his left leg under a fallen beam, like an insect pinned to a display board in some eighth-grade science project.

Through veils of dust and debris, he saw Enok—hurt, shaken, but not immobilized—scouring the room, presumably looking for him. Enok's gaze landed on Eben, locked there. He started toward the trapped sheriff.

Eben tried to shove the beam off. Flat on his back, he couldn't get any leverage on the thing, couldn't lift it. Something else had landed on top of the beam and held it in place. As strong as he was, Eben couldn't move it an inch.

Enok found a length of iron pipe in the rubble, about two feet long, or a few inches over that. Testing it against his palm, he shot Eben a wicked grin, apparently satisfied with its capability. Trapped here, Eben knew, he would only be able to defend himself for so long. Enok could shatter the bones in his arms and then go to work on his skull, pounding his brain into the floor. From the mad glint in Enok's eyes, it seemed apparent the same thought had occurred to him. Or, of course, he could have simply lifted it from Eben's mind.

Eben strained against the beam, splinters pressing into his hands, to no avail. Then Enok stood over him, slapping the pipe against his palm as if to savor the sound it made. "Are you ready for this?" he asked.

Eben dropped back against the floor, muscles aching from the effort. "Do your worst, bloodsucker," he said. With a loud rumble, the entire structure seemed to shudder. "Maybe you can beat me, but you'll never defeat the human world. At least I can die knowing that."

"Whatever gives you comfort," Enok said with a casually dismissive shrug.

Another rumble sounded from overhead, like nearby thunder—or an earthquake, but coming from above instead of below. A new wave of debris rained down amid blood and dust. Eben saw an arm flop onto the ground not far away, and a chair hit and bounced right behind Enok. "You're pretty easygoing for a guy whose whole world is crumbling around him," Eben said.

"I know that in the end, it will not be my world that

will fall." Standing just out of reach, Enok raised the pipe over his head, holding it in both hands. Eben wondered if his arms would even withstand the first blow. A regular human could crush him with it, trapped as he was. Enok, with his unnatural strength, could do much worse. He tried to hold a picture of Stella (in her hooded parka, furry hood surrounding her face, mouth issuing steam in the Arctic cold) in his head as he waited for the end.

And then the pipe was whistling through the air and the rumbling got worse, louder, the whole inverted building beginning to implode, falling in toward where he and Enok had weakened it, and he meant to raise his arms to block it but why, really, it would just hurt a hell of a lot while it delayed the inevitable, and he didn't want that pain in his head, clouding his judgment, he wanted that image of Stella to be his last thought, so he left his arms at his sides.

A shape, dark, blurred, swooped in, knocking the vampire off-balance, the length of pipe meant for Eben gouging the floor near him. Enok whirled on the intruder, instinctively defending himself from this sudden attack. Brutally connecting the pipe with the lightning-fast shape.

A cry of pain. Eben thought he recognized the voice.

The shape collapsed against Eben's chest. Rose, with difficulty. Dane gave him a stunned, weak grin, but the pipe had caught the back of his head. Blood flowed from his scalp like water from a tap.

Startled, Enok took a couple of steps back, raising the pipe as if Dane might charge him.

Dane was beyond charging. His arms almost gave out again, then, shaking, Dane pushed himself off Eben.

Dane whirled on Enok—blood flying from the gaping wound at the base of his skull—and snatched the pipe from the elder's hands before Enok knew he was coming. He swung it once, one-handed, nailing Enok in the temple and sending him staggering to the floor. Then he hurled the pipe into the dust-shrouded distance and dropped next to Eben.

"Dane! You . . ."

"I'm okay," Dane said. His voice was weaker than it had been, just moments before. The blood flow had slowed, which Eben didn't take as a good sign.

"You're not."

"Okay, you're right." Dane crawled to the beam, rose to his knees, and hooked his hands around it. "Get ready to pull your leg out."

"I'm ready," Eben said. "But do you think you should—"

"*This* is what I should do." Dane hoisted—an inch or so, and his back and shoulders were knotted with trembling muscle, the blood at the back of his head red and glistening, and Eben pulled his leg free, ecstatic to find it only bruised, hurt but not broken.

"Dane!" he cried. "I'm out!"

Dane dropped the beam and collapsed over it. Eben rushed to him, put his arms around Dane's shoulders. "Dane, come on. Let's get the fuck out of here."

"Hold on. One . . . more thing," Dane said. He could barely speak now. His skin looked ashen, even for a vampire. Before he turned to face him, Eben saw brain matter leaking out the wound along with the blood. "Come . . . closer," Dane whispered.

Eben put his ear close to Dane's mouth, so he could hear.

Dane sank his teeth into Eben's neck. Drinking. Exchanging.

Images filled Eben's head as he screamed in pain.

"It'll help," Dane said when he finally released Eben. "You . . . you go. Go and take care of Stella."

Dane dropped to the floor again. The ceiling swayed overhead, and the rumble was almost constant now, like a long, passing train. Eben knew a few things he hadn't known, moments before, and he attributed this knowledge—like his newfound strength—to Dane's bite.

The first thing was that Dane was right. It was too late for him.

But what had Dane done by biting him? *What* would help?

The entire compound was about to come down on their heads, once and for all. Without a glance back, a hand pressed against his bleeding neck, Eben ran for the stairs, reaching them just as the building gave a long, loud screech and began its ultimate collapse. Walls fell in, support posts snapping like twigs. The staircase swayed and buckled. Eben took the steps four and five at a time, shoving his way past panicked vampires, hurling them over the side or down behind him as he climbed.

The dust was so thick that he couldn't tell how high he

had gone, how many levels he'd cleared. All around him were dust and screams and vampires falling—people, too, who had escaped their captors but were too weak to keep up—and body parts severed by the destruction that surrounded him.

He heard—*felt,* like a nagging half memory that won't come clear—Lilith's voice in his head. There one second, then gone again. He couldn't tell what she said. But she didn't sound unhappy.

The staircase gave a huge lurch, pulling away from the wall and spinning dizzily out over what was now a gaping chasm. It creaked and popped like gunshots and Eben knew it was the end, those stairs were going no place but down, and he leapt for . . . for what, he didn't know, couldn't see it through the haze . . . and his hands caught something solid and he pulled himself up, shoulders and chest clearing a surface of some kind, where he could breathe and where the gray light of dawn almost burned his eyes, so adapted were they to the darkness below, in Enok's underground paradise.

Through the overwhelming pain, Dane could feel himself quickly slipping away. Far worse than the last time, four years ago, when Paul Norris put a round into Dane's head at point-blank range. Somehow, Dane had managed to survive that incident. He wasn't too confident it would turn out the same this time around.

As the blackness in his head grew, Dane took comfort in reliving the memory of the first time he ever saw Stella

Olemaun, the most fascinating and terrifying woman he had ever met, at a UCLA book tour reading (despite that the event quickly degenerated into a nightmare).

It wouldn't be long now.

Eben was outside.

Others ran around him, fearfully calling Enok's name or crying for help. Eben knew why. They were among the few who would survive the collapse of the structure, but any minute now the sun would climb over the surrounding hills and they were in a bare valley, their only shelter the death trap they had just escaped. Some ran for the parking lot, but it had caved in as well, the upside-down building having tunneled beneath it.

Eben ran too, but not in panic. He just wanted some distance between himself and Enok's failed utopia. His legs felt powerful, as if he had been training for months and was just beginning a marathon.

When the sky began to lighten from gray to a pale blue, with the first hints of yellow showing at the crests of the eastern hills, Eben found a particularly deep snowdrift, up against a massive rock outcropping. Casting one glance back toward Enok's, he saw a black cloud erupt from inside, and then the sun's rays swept across the valley, and vampires, screaming in agony, began to burst into flames.

He tunneled into the drift, going as deep as he could. He would be wet and uncomfortable, but he could stay until the sun went down again.

Then he could work on getting home. Hah. For all he knew, anyone or anything could be waiting for him back at the hotel.

He had to find a way to get back to Stella, tell her and the others about everything, the coming war on humanity—Enok may have been a general in that war, but it would be foolish to think he was the only one.

And what of Dane? Who gave up everything? Apparently presenting Eben with a frightening gift barely understood, imparted over the years of his undeath. Ironically, he now knew the other recipients had been human beings, the tribe that cast him out, that would never have accepted what he had become.

Eben's mind reeled as he picked over the events of the past several hours.

Right now, he wanted nothing more than to be home again, comforted by Stella, safe and sound once more. God only knew when that would happen.

He sighed in frustration, momentarily overcome by the sudden certainty of darker days ahead.

38

ANANU HAD AWAKENED, during the birth process, as if she had never been gone.

"Hi," Stella said from between Ananu's legs. "Glad you're with us. You can push now."

"It's really coming?" Ananu said, her tone full of expectant hope.

"Looks that way."

Merrin wiped the girl's forehead with a towel, as he had been doing even while she was unconscious. "It's all fine, Ana," he cooed at her. "You're doing wonderfully."

"Thanks, Ferrando." Ananu held up her hands, with their transparent skin, muscle, and veins and bones showing through them. "God, I . . . I look like hell. How long has this been . . . ?"

Andy stood to one side, and Ananu grabbed his hand in a death grip as a contraction washed over her. "I'm . . . I'm Andy," he said, a little dumbfounded, when it had passed and she could focus again.

"Thank you. Thank you for being here," Ananu

said, gasping as another wave of pain overcame her.

"Push, Ana!" Stella shouted.

Ananu gripped Andy and Merrin's hands like oars and bore down.

"Keep pushing!"

Ananu pushed.

And a minute later Stella made noises of encouragement and Andy went around her and the vampire cradled a newborn in her arms, all pink and blue and covered in slime. A fleshy tube connected the infant to its mother.

Stella nodded toward a pair of sharp scissors Merrin had brought in. "Cut it, Andy," Stella said. "Cut the cord."

"Jesus. Are you sure?"

"It's not going to cut itself, and my hands are a little full."

Andy snatched up the scissors before he could think about it too much and reached in and snipped through the tube, from which a little fluid leaked out, right where Stella indicated, about an inch from the baby's belly.

"Ana, you have a baby boy," Stella announced. She held the newborn up so his mother could see him, but Ananu's head lolled on her left shoulder, mouth open, a thin stream of bloody bile running from it.

"Ana . . . ?"

"We . . . lost her," Merrin said. "Just now. When you

cut the umbilical, I believe. She just . . . shut down. Like a machine that's no longer needed."

Merrin's face filled with a sudden and crushing sadness. "The poor thing . . ." he murmured, more to himself.

After they cleaned the infant and fed him some formula—mixed with a few drops of Merrin's bottled blood for good measure—Stella had been rocking him, swathed in blankets that Andy had gathered (and she was staring at the baby rather strangely, Andy had to tensely admit) when the telephone rang. Merrin answered it, listened for a moment, then hung up.

"Mitch says we should turn on the television," he said, doing exactly that as he spoke the words.

A cable news anchor Andy didn't know came on the screen, and superimposed in the upper left corner, in a box, was a picture of a man in his sixties, solid, with white hair and a tanned face, with a name at the bottom of the box. Albert J. Roddy, the screen said. ". . . *have identified the tortured body found yesterday as Pooler, Georgia, resident Albert Roddy, a taxi*—" the anchor said, until Merrin interrupted her.

"I never knew his last name," he said. "And I didn't even realize it."

"Who is it?" Andy asked. The name rang a bell but he couldn't place it.

"AJ. The man who let them use his car and house and boat," Merrin said.

"And was he here?" Andy asked. "In this house?"

"Yes, of course."

"And he was tortured," Andy said, nodding. "Okay. We have to get out of here. Right now. *Now.*"

"We don't know that he said anything," Merrin said. "And the baby . . ."

"We don't know that he didn't. If the cops were able to identify the body and they put him together with known associates, they might have found Mitch, who just called us, and if they had a tap on Mitch's phone, then—"

"Yes, I see. Well then. There's not a moment to waste, I suppose," Merrin said.

"Babies are pretty resilient little creatures, I've heard," Stella said. "Especially this one, I imagine."

"But where will we—?"

"Not you, Ferrando," Stella said. "I mean, you have been a huge help, and we appreciate everything. But the fewer who know where we're going, the better. You rented this place through a friend or something, right? They might be able to trace it to you eventually, so I don't want you to know too much."

"Who is it that we're all hiding from?" Merrin asked.

Stella was already on her feet, putting the slumbering baby down in a padded carrier. "I think it's Operation Red-Blooded," Andy said. "They're FBI, or maybe an interagency task force, I never could find that out for sure. I do know we've got to get out, get far away from here before they do."

They ran about, taking precious few minutes to grab the things they would need, and rushed toward the car. Andy had installed a car seat that Merrin had bought in the rental. They would make their way back to Barrow, he knew—and what happened next was anyone's guess. They were making this up as they went along.

On the way out the door, Stella stopped to kiss Merrin's cheek.

"Take good care of—bother, I expect he'll need a name, right?"

"He will indeed," Stella said.

"Any ideas?" Andy asked.

"I have one," Stella said.

"As do I," Merrin said. "There seems to be only one reasonable option, to me."

Stella attempted to again maintain her composure, even as she gave the baby in the carrier a small smile. The infant's head waggling slightly in his sleep, mouth puckering as if ready to nurse. "Well," Andy said. "Can somebody fill me in?"

"I'm surprised you even have to ask." Stella said.

She raised the carrier to her lips, planting a gentle kiss on the infant's forehead. She already looked like a mother, like motherhood had been in her all along, just dormant.

"He has to be Dane," Stella announced. "Andy Gray, Ferrando Merrin . . . meet little Dane."

As if responding to the name, the infant tilted his head

and opened his blue eyes wide, looking up at his new mother. Perhaps it was a trick of the light, Andy thought. It probably was.

But just maybe, he could have sworn he saw little Dane smile.

ABOUT THE AUTHORS

STEVE NILES is one of the writers responsible for bringing horror comics back to prominence, and was recently named by *Fangoria* magazine as one of one of its "13 rising talents who promise to keep us terrified for the next 25 years." Among his works are *30 Days of Night: Dark Days; 30 Days of Night: Return to Barrow; 30 Days of Night: Bloodsucker Tales; Criminal Macabre; Wake the Dead; Freaks of the Heartland; Hyde; Alistair Arcane;* and *Fused. 30 Days of Night, Criminal Macabre, Wake the Dead, Hyde,* and *Alistair Arcane* are currently in development as major motion pictures. Niles got his start in the industry when he formed his own publishing company called Arcane Comix, where he published, edited, and adapted several comics and anthologies for Eclipse Comics. His adaptations include works by Clive Barker, Richard Matheson, and Harlan Ellison. He also recently formed Creep Entertainment with Rob Zombie, as well as the film production company Raw Entertainment with Tom Jane. Niles resides in Los Angeles with the love of his life, one black cat, a tortoise, and a turtle.

JEFF MARIOTTE is the author of more than thirty novels, including several set in the universes of *Buffy the Vampire Slayer* and *Angel, Charmed, Las Vegas, Conan, Star Trek,* and *Andromeda;* the original novels *Missing White Girl* and *The Slab;* and Stoker Award–nominated teen horror series *Witch Season,* as well as more comic books than he has time to count, some of which have been nominated for Bram Stoker and International Horror Guild awards. With his wife, Maryelizabeth Hart, and partner Terry Gilman, he co-owns Mysterious Galaxy, a bookstore specializing in science fiction, fantasy, mystery, and horror. He lives on the Flying M Ranch in southeastern Arizona with his family and pets, in a home filled with books, music, toys, and other examples of American pop culture. More information than you would ever want to know about him is at www.jeffmariotte.com.

30 DAYS OF NIGHT
GRAPHIC NOVELS BY IDW PUBLISHING!

30 DAYS OF NIGHT

Dive deep into the nightmare world of Barrow, Alaska, where month-long winter darkness provides a siren call to a band of bloodthirsy vampires. The townspeople's only hope of survival lies in the hands of Eben and Stella, the local husband-and-wife sheriff team. Can they save the town they love, or will darkness descend forever?

ISBN: 978-0-9719775-5-6
$17.99

30 DAYS OF NIGHT: DARK DAYS

In *Dark Days*, the action shifts from Barrow, Alaska to Los Angeles, as Stella Olemaun, her life forever altered by the vampires' assault, rededicates herself to wiping out the vampires and alerting the world to their shadowed existence. Along the way she meets new allies and new foes—lots and lots of foes. Intense action and gripping suspense make this a must-have for all fans of *30 Days of Night*!

ISBN: 978-1-932382-16-7
$19.99

Not sure what to read next?

Visit Pocket Books online at
www.simonsays.com

Reading suggestions for
you and your reading group
New release news
Author appearances
Online chats with your favorite writers
Special offers
Order books online
And much, much more!

13456